The
BLESSED
PASSIONARIES

A Catalogue record for this book is available from the British Library

ISBN 978 1 444 90476 5

Typeset in Berkeley Book by Avon DataSet Ltd,
Bidford-on-Avon, Warwickshire

Printed and bound in Great Britain by Clays Ltd, St Ives plc

The paper and board used in this paperback by Hodder Children's Books
are natural recyclable products made from wood grown in
sustainable forests. The manufacturing processes conform to the
environmental regulations of the country of origin.

Hodder Children's Books
a division of Hachette Children's Books
338 Euston Road, London NW1 3BH
An Hachette UK company
www.hachette.co.uk

The
BLESSED
PASSIONARIES

Hodder
Children's
Books

A division of Hachette Children's Books

For Michael and Isabelle

'You will hear thunder
and remember me,
And think: she wanted storms.
The rim
Of the sky will be
The colour of hard crimson,
And your heart,
As it was then,
Will be on fire.'

Anna Akhmatova

Cecilia's Hymn

Your words
Catch in my throat
Stick in my skin
Like sharp grains of shattered glass
Exploded Remnants
Letting Blood
Falling Silently
Down
I don't have to sell my soul
He's already in me
Can't seem to fill the hole
He's digging within thee.
Sing my shredded song
Letting Blood
As I wait
For you

Nunc et in hora mortis nostrae

1

The Black Parade

Cecilia lay motionless in the window chair under a shelf of spray-painted Catholic kitsch, a few of her ever-present apostles gathering patiently across the street. A funeral march could be heard in the distance. The sombre drone of the trumpets drew near in time with the needle about to pierce her flawless skin.

'Can you feel that?' Oyo asked, muscles flexing under the coolest tattoo sleeves she'd ever seen.

Cecilia laughed. She was practically oblivious to the sharp object in her arm.

'If you can't feel this, then I ain't doing my job.' Oyo scowled, holding the tattoo wand above her wrist. The music outside grew louder. 'Here they come.'

Cecilia glanced out of the window and felt a mix of pride and alarm. Her apostles mingled with the marchers and spectators, looking for a glimpse both of her and the statue. But the boisterous crowd could just as easily give cover to would-be vandals with murderous intentions. Followed or stalked, she was never quite sure – which was a big reason she preferred to get inked before the shop even opened, in the early morning light, both for privacy and safety.

But try as she might, Cecilia's instinct for self-preservation was unable to overcome her rebellious streak, which demanded that she park herself right in the storefront window. On display. Part tease for the faithful and part middle finger to the wicked. Mostly, however, as advertisement for Oyo, payback for their accommodation.

Cecilia sightings were rare these days and each of her public appearances was growing larger and more intense as a result, like a sold-out festival audience waiting impatiently for the headliner to take the stage. Followers shared her movements, her location via tweets, texts and status updates, creating a digital trail for anyone, well meaning or not. The larger the groups became, the harder it was to tell the difference between apostle and assassin.

But for the most part, her followers never approached her, they just watched or took pictures, some prayed, others threw roses and offerings they'd made for her, a 'What Would Cecilia

Do?' tee, bone guitar picks, but mostly edgy pieces of jewellery – spiked rosaries, vintage reliquary necklaces, studded cuffs.

Another person, Cecilia considered as she reclined there watching the scene, might turn these devotees and their merchandise into a profit centre. A crowd-funded sainthood. How very modern. But then again, maybe not so novel after all. What were church collection plates for but exchanging a small donation for a piece of spiritual equity? The thought made her think of Lucy and how they hadn't been in touch for a while. Not since the investigation wrapped up.

'Our Lady of Sorrows,' Oyo murmured. The melancholy blare of the procession was a sombre soundtrack to Cecilia's pain and her suspicion. Appropriate for a grey, rainy Good Friday morning.

'What?' Cecilia snapped, still distracted by the events outside.

'The Our Lady of Sorrows procession.'

Cecilia smiled. 'A good friend of mine calls me that. Our Lady of Sorrow.'

'Is that right? Then maybe this parade is in your honour,' Oyo said, glancing down at her clothes.

Cecilia looked down at her outfit – vintage black mini dress, caplet encrusted in tiny gold spikes around her shoulders, fishnets and black ankle boots with gold pyramid studs – before looking out the window again.

'Well, we do match,' she said, the statue of Mary draped in

black and gold coming into sight. She'd seen the march for the first time a few years earlier when she was looking for sublets in what she called 'Death Valley', the industrial stretch of road between Cobble Hill and Park Slope, filled with casket factories and penetrated by the milky green waters and noxious stench of the Gowanus Canal. The only canal on record to have tested positive for a sexually transmitted disease. The reason most people called it Gowanorrhea.

At the time, she'd thought the ritual march was strange and morbid. But now, she couldn't help but find it oddly romantic. Straight out of a Fellini movie. A glass coffin carrying Jesus was trailed by a statue of Mary dressed in medieval garb and hoisted on a pedestal by what looked to be pallbearers. Women dressed in black cloaks sang mournfully in Italian as the procession snaked through Brooklyn. They weren't singing for attention, or for money, but out of sorrow. Wailing for the woman who lost her son. Singing for all who had lost a child. Calling everyone who had lost someone. Women came out of their homes to pay tribute, some in aprons and ratty slippers, and others in their Sunday best – black veils and dresses, and others in housecoats drinking glasses of wine. All bowing their heads and making the sign of the cross as the procession passed.

It was a celebration of sadness, but it wasn't sad. In fact, it was a collective, if not joyful, release. Couldn't get more oppositional, more punk, than that. An annual Good Friday

funeral for everyone to cry and let go. To hold one another. It was all so heart wrenching. And so beautiful. After everything that had happened, Cecilia understood it. Deep within.

A single black tear, tainted with mascara and flecks of gold liner, fell from her eye and traced her jawline. Mourning Sebastian. Mourning her future. She knew what was coming, accepted her fate just like Sebastian had, but how and when it would come, she had no idea.

'Are you OK?' Oyo asked, handing her a black hankie.

'It doesn't really matter, Oyo,' she said. 'Whatever will be, will be.'

'It matters to me, chica,' he said.

'My life is like a game of Russian Roulette. I have to wonder every morning when I wake up if this is the day I'll die.' She paused, allowing herself a moment of vulnerability as she wiped away her tear. 'Wonder if I'll read in the paper or online somewhere that Lucy or Agnes have been killed.'

'Can I do anything?' Oyo asked. 'I know a lot of people on the street who owe me favours.'

'No, this is my thing to deal with,' she confided. 'I'm ready for it, whatever and whenever.'

'Just know you aren't alone,' Oyo reminded, bringing his fingers to her chaplet and then to his lips.

'Thanks, Oyo,' Cecilia smiled. 'Let's finish this.'

'You sure?'

She nodded, preparing herself.

'Kick it up to third,' she demanded as the statue moved into position by the faithful in front of the window. She fixated on the dagger in Mary's chest. 'Bring the pain.'

Oyo revved up the wand.

Cecilia bit down on a purple towel to stifle any screams from escaping her pale lips. She peered out of the storefront, digging her heels into the deep red vinyl-upholstered cushion until it ripped. Images of the statue intercut with flashes in her mind's eye of Sebastian's death, of that night, as the parade passed and her pain intensified.

Mary's black lace veil covering her despair.

The three of them – Lucy, Cecilia, Agnes – a human shield, protecting Sebastian.

The dagger piercing Mary's heart.

Sebastian's body sprayed with bullets.

Mary's black lace cloak covering her.

Their hands covering his open wounds.

Mary's face; bursting with sorrow as she watched her only son's lifeless body get carried away. Always behind him. Always watching him. Adoring him. The procession stopped. A few women in the march took notice of Cecilia and began to point her out in the shop window. Some, mockers she called them, spat on the ground in her direction. Others kneeled right there on the street, repeatedly blessing themselves at the sight of her. She was used to it. Some believed the neighbourhood gossip, the stories in the papers. That Cecilia was a saint. One of three

that were chosen to prepare the way for the Second Coming. The only hope left. The last chance at redemption. Some did not. Those that did believed wholeheartedly and without doubt. The others didn't believe at all. There was no in between. Like her music. Accepted by a few and rejected by most. The story of her life.

'Are you sure you want to fill in this heart and all the arrows? It's right on the bone. It's gonna hurt like hell,' Oyo said.

'Good,' she said, staring at the women. 'Do it.'

Cecilia eyed the outline of the tattoo as Oyo made his way around her wrist. She reached into her gold studded bag and pulled out a glassine envelope. The kind that usually held one injectable, illegal narcotic or another.

'Fill it with this,' she ordered.

Oyo shook the grey powdery contents of the bag and let them settle at the bottom.

'Ashes?' he asked. 'Why do you pull this shit on me when I'm in the middle of something for you?'

'So you can't say no.'

'Would it matter if I did?'

They both knew the answer. Oyo, holding the bag in his palm, suddenly realized that these were not just ashes, but remains.

'Have you worked with human ashes before?' she asked. 'Have you done a memorial tat?'

'No, but I'm guessing that's about to change.'

Cecilia nodded.

He took hold of her wrist and turned it from back to front, planning his work, when the bandage on her hand caught his eye. Fresh blood trickled through a clean but poorly prepared dressing on the palm side. Her warning that something was about to happen.

'Cheating on me?' He offered a sympathetic smile.

'Nah,' she smiled back. 'Self-inflicted.'

'You know there are doctors in this city right?' he half-joked.

'There's no cure for what I got.'

'So this is what it looks like?' he asked, referring to her stigmata. He'd heard about it, read about it, everyone had, but to see it in the flesh was something on a whole other level. 'Look, I know this is a lot to handle – me here, his ashes, the blood . . .' she began. 'But this is why I came to you.'

'Can I ask you something?' he began. 'And tell me if this is too personal?'

'Shoot,' she said.

'Don't you have to be, you know, pure, to be a saint?'

'Well, my attitude is still a virgin because I never gave a fuck.'

'You know what I'm saying, though, right?'

'Yes, I do,' she acknowledged. 'It's complicated.'

He nodded. Oyo sprinkled a pinch of the remains on to his palate and mixed it with the inks he intended to use.

'Board of Health ain't gonna like this, CeCe,' Oyo smirked.

'It's regulation that you got to heat human cremains to a certain temp before injecting them. I could lose my license. Or worse.'

'Then don't tell them,' she replied.

The ink master loaded up his pen with ink and ash and began to fill the elaborate piece.

Cecilia winced.

'Hold on,' he recommended.

'Pop the clutch, Oyo,' she ordered through gritted teeth, grabbing tightly on to the armrests.

The needle pierced Cecilia's forearm over and over. Inserting him into her as she bled. She embraced the pain. It connected her to Sebastian even more. It was what was left between them. His death had changed everything, changed her, and she was ready to keep her promises.

'Looks killer if I do say so myself,' Oyo observed proudly. 'Might be my best work, yet.'

Cecilia looked at the fresh ink, a gorgeous black sacred heart pierced with seven arrows. The detail was extraordinary, and the fact that it was all black made the artistry stand out even more.

'Thank you,' CeCe said softly. 'It's a masterpiece.'

It was one of a kind, fitting. And painful. She felt it; felt him, inside her. Sebastian had definitely left his mark. Not only on her flesh, her soul, her heart, but everyone on the street seemed to be mythologizing him or demonizing him. One thing was clear; he was on the tongues of many.

Oyo bandaged her wrist and as he did, he leaned into her chair and whispered in her ear. 'Pyro and his crew got what the hell was coming to them,' he said. 'The world is a better place.'

Cecilia carefully put on her leather coat.

'People say that they see him – Sebastian – in Brooklyn,' he continued. 'Hell, they see him all over the world. He's a legend now. Chicks buildin' shrines to him and shit.'

'From maniac to miracle worker. I read the papers. The blogs.' CeCe acknowledged somewhat resentfully.

'People hold vigils. Pray to him for intercession. They wonder where he'll appear next,' Oyo said, the superstitious believer in him coming through. 'I'm surprised you're not more curious.'

Cecilia looked Oyo directly in the eye. 'I don't need to wonder. I know where he is.'

Oyo could see that he touched a nerve. He didn't ask her to clarify if she meant that Sebastian was in heaven, or in her heart, or even if he had appeared to her as others had claimed. It seemed to him as if she was jealous of his apparition appearing to so many. Spiritual cheating. He nodded and covered the new tattoo with a cellophane bandage. He helped her off the chair. 'Have you seen the other girls?'

She wanted to reach out to Agnes and Lucy, but hadn't. She missed them terribly in the weeks and months since Sebastian's death, but she felt they all had to mourn in their own way before they could come together and face what had happened

– and what was happening – to them, and to the world since he left it. It was clear that time was coming.

'No,' Cecilia said. 'Not since everything went down. I see Lucy on TV sometimes, but that's about it.'

'I'm surprised,' Oyo said.

'I've been pretty hard to reach,' Cecilia explained, fingering the cell phone in her pocket. 'Just this trusty pay-as-you-go flip. No laptop. No internet unless I creep someone else's.'

'No location functions to worry about,' Oyo deadpanned. 'Off the grid.'

'Exactly,' she smiled.

'It's all pretty fresh I guess,' Oyo commiserated. 'Just a few months since . . .'

Cecilia interrupted.

'We just need some time. We'll hook up when the time is right.'

She noticed her hands bleeding even more and tried to staunch it with Oyo's hankie.

Oyo reached toward her for a hug. 'Your fans miss you, Prophetista. When you gonna get your ass back on stage?'

Cecilia held up her bandaged wrist, pumped full of his ashes; her stigmata bleeding from her palms all the way down her forearm.

'Feels like the time is now.'

2

Blessed Be the Bones

'Agnes, wait up!'

Agnes slowed and turned her head. Her copper hair, highlighted by the sun, fell over her shoulders and draped down her hand-knitted cardigan. She wore a white tank underneath with an anatomical heart outlined in black surrounded by pale cutout flowers. Her long tiered skirt gently brushed the sidewalk as she walked.

'It's so nice out, isn't it?' Hazel caught up to her.

'Springtime, finally,' Agnes observed.

'Makes you want to crank up some music and look for guys. Shit, I wish we had a car.'

Agnes smiled indifferently at the suggestion and stopped to

notice some crocuses breaking through the cold ground – bright yellow and deep purple outside the bakery. She looked up and saw an impressive display of vibrantly coloured eggs baked into the braided Easter bread, topped off with rainbow sprinkles, in the window.

'Come on, Agnes, we can't be late again,' Hazel said, knowing full well that Agnes would stand there all day, admiring the flowers and holiday treats and obsessing about him, if Hazel would let her. Hazel called her Saint Zombie now.

Agnes appreciated Hazel keeping her moving. She was never in a rush to get to class these days. In fact, she often wondered if her overbearing mother had put Hazel up to it. It would be just like Martha to do something like that. For Agnes, the days felt like some kind of waking dream, except for school, which was mostly a nightmare. For the most part, she'd trained herself to ignore the haters – the jokes, the stares, the rumours, the pettiness and the lies. Some girls had reputations for being virgins, but none for being saints. It was a whole other level in terms of gossip and guts.

Hazel grabbed her arm and dragged her away from the flowers.

'You can't sit on a mushroom all day!'

'Bet you I can,' Agnes said smiling, steeling herself.

The two girls continued, walking up the steps and into the old parochial school building, shoes and voices echoing,

bouncing off the high ceilings and tiled floors. Agnes was only a few feet down the hallway when a group of boys and girls fell to their knees in mock devotion.

'Hail Agnes,' they chanted snidely.

'Really?' Hazel complained.

'I confess to almighty Agnes,' one guy said. 'I've been thinking of you in dirty ways. On my face.'

'Well, we know that's a lie,' Hazel said. 'The thinking part gave you away.'

'And you like it,' he added. 'You can't get enough of it.'

'Don't listen,' Agnes said, taking Hazel's hand and pulling her toward her locker.

'I don't know how you can take their shit every day,' Hazel whispered.

'I'm not taking it,' Agnes protested, placing her bohemian book bag inside the metal cabinet.

'I guess it's not all bad right? With the fan mail and everything?'

'Fan mail?' Agnes asked dubiously. 'You mean guys asking for pictures of my feet. Or wanting to know if they can be my first, or worse, boil me in a pot?'

Hazel looked sympathetically at her friend. 'Don't take this the wrong way, but you kinda did ask for it. All this saint stuff.'

'Like rape victims ask to be raped because of what they wear?' Agnes was incredulous. 'I didn't ask for this, Hazel.'

'But you accepted it,' Hazel said. 'You can't just expect

people to pretend that nothing happened. It was everywhere. And you can't expect people to understand it. You can't just go back to a normal life.'

'My life was never normal.' Agnes thought about trying to explain herself, her feelings. She did accept her fate, Sebastian, wholeheartedly, but to ask brainless highschoolers to comprehend any of it would be asking too much. She didn't expect them to. Maybe a little curiosity, but she had been blindsided by the mockery and condemnation. It was hard enough to figure everything out without all the cruelty she had to bear on top of it. 'You know what? You're right. Why should I expect anyone to believe me, to believe this, when my own mother won't?'

'I thought that was getting better,' Hazel said, pulling a ChapStick from her bag and swiping the waxy ointment across her lips.

'It did for a minute, but now I think she's in total denial about the whole thing.'

'What do you mean?'

'She looks at me like one of those kids that was brainwashed by a cult and returned ten years later.'

'I know the face.'

'It's the one she gives the terminal patients in the cancer ward where she volunteers,' Agnes elaborated. 'Sympathetic. Patronizing.'

'You know how she is,' Hazel said, hoping to ease some of

Agnes's tension. 'She's probably just angry at the people hanging around your house and everything. '

'Bullshit.'

'OK, she's angry about the people hanging around. And jealous.'

'So much to be jealous about, as you just saw,' Agnes sniped. 'I don't know if people want to kiss me or kill me.' Agnes caught herself. 'I hate bitching like this.'

'You've been through a lot,' Hazel said, hugging her. 'I guess it comes with the territory. You should really talk to someone.'

'Who? Who should I talk to about this? Who could possibly understand?'

For Agnes it was more than just a rhetorical question. Much more. There were so many things happening, none of which she could talk about with Hazel or anyone except for Cecilia and Lucy. It was a strange, terrifying feeling. She longed to see them, wanted to know if they had similar things happening, mourn with them, talk about what they needed to do, and more importantly, commiserate about him. But, what if they didn't feel the same things? Didn't hear the voices calling? Didn't feel out of body on occasion – in two places at once. It was all so crazy, and one thing she didn't want to appear was crazy. She'd been there. She told them she'd be strong, and she was trying her best. Besides, things were happening now that hadn't happened before, and she felt in her heart that the time for them to be together was nearing.

'There's a plan for you, girl,' Hazel said sincerely. 'Work it.' Hazel wasn't especially deep or insightful, but these were comforting words, maybe even wise ones. Hazel was trying and that's all Agnes could hope for. That was the mark of a true friend. Whatever it was that Sebastian had gifted or cursed her with was hers to bear, hers to figure out.

The bell rang announcing the start of the school day.

'I don't want to be late, gotta bounce,' Hazel said, heading down another hallway to her class. 'You know where to find me.'

Agnes waved to Hazel and waited for the hallways to empty. She walked slowly down the main corridor, turning her head toward the row of windows facing the street. The buses had pulled away, but a small crowd still lingered, buzzing in anticipation. She hoped they weren't waiting for her. She had her own set of followers, but not in the same way Cecilia and Lucy did. Cecilia's followers hung on her every word like a prophet, agreed with everything she said. Lucy's followers wanted a piece of her fame, wanted to take pictures with her, be her. It was only now that Cecilia has something to actually say and Lucy had something to actually give. However, Agnes was new to all of this. It was quite innocent and yet, so terrifying to have people wait for you, stare at you, adore you. Thankfully, her followers were a peaceful lot. They didn't trail her to school or anything, they just waited peacefully outside her house at a safe distance, hoping for a glimpse or the opportunity to offer

her little gifts like handmade candles, oils, soaps, jewelled rosaries, mala beads, baked goods like sacred heart cookies and ask politely for favours, prayers.

Agnes strained to see through the raindrops on the windowpane as a low-pitched brassy dirge and the roll of snare drums bled in from outdoors. She stood, transfixed, as the figure of Our Lady passed by. The same way it had just passed Cecilia. The face of the impaled statue was pained, anguished. That much was obvious to Agnes even from a distance, even through the condensation that obstructed her view.

'Mater Dolorosa.'

Agnes turned, startled by the voice behind her.

'I'm sorry?'

'Mother of Sorrows,' the woman said.

'I'm ashamed to say that I don't . . .'

'Our Lady of Sorrow is an example of the pain and suffering we feel when we lose someone we love. She shows us that it is appropriate to mourn while never losing our faith. Our hope.'

Agnes turned back to the procession outside. She thought about Sebastian. Her loss. The loss that no one seemed to acknowledge. No sympathy, only ridicule. A tear fell from her eye as she watched the statue being carried by a group of distinguished men. Holding her up. Supporting her. Carrying her.

'Excuse me,' Agnes said, wiping the tears from her eyes.

'Is there something wrong, dear?'

'I just don't want to be here,' Agnes said, gesturing toward the parade and the wider world outside. 'The answers I'm looking for aren't in textbooks or job fairs. They are out there.'

'No,' the sister replied. 'They are in here.' She pointed to Agnes's chest. Agnes smiled slightly.

'There is a difference between education and vocation,' the woman noted. 'Some of us do what we are trained to do, others what we are compelled to do, called to do.'

Agnes placed her hand on the damp windowpane, palm side down. The woman noticed the extravagant mourning ring on Agnes's hand – black onyx with elaborate gold detailing. It was beautiful on the outside, but contained something even more precious within. A single strand of Sebastian's hair, one she found the day he was killed, matted in blood on her lambswool cowl. She put it inside the ring for safekeeping and told no one. She was astonished to see it mysteriously lengthen and grow each time she checked on it. A private relic of her own. A living piece of him. Until now. She'd noticed recently that it had stopped growing. Agnes caught the woman looking at it, then noticing her bone chaplet with her sacred heart milagro. She jerked her hand down, defensively, covering both items.

'Those are beautiful pieces,' the woman said.

'I got the ring from my grandmother.'

'I've never seen anything like it before.'

'I only started wearing it recently,' Agnes said, uncomfortable about revealing its contents. 'And, the bracelet . . .' Agnes paused, not knowing exactly how to explain to a stranger.

The woman waited as the girl struggled to find the words.

Agnes looked up at her with surprise. 'Wait, I know you.'

'Yes.'

'You're the nun that was taking care of Jude on the playground last fall.'

'Sister Dorothea,' she said, offering her hand.

'How is he?' Agnes asked, grasping it gently.

'The boy is fine,' the nun advised. 'I see him often.'

'What are you doing here?'

'I'm a counsellor,' Sister Dorothea said.

Agnes paused. 'Well, I'm sure this place keeps you pretty busy.'

The nun smiled.

'I'm here if you need me.'

3

Heartless

'I hate people,' Lucy bitched, leaving her Vinegar Hill apartment building. She dropped her shades down over her eyes as the usual suspects – gawkers, stalkers, tourists and doomsday types – called out to her for autographs, photographs, and secrets of salvation from across the street.

Details had got out about the Church of the Precious Blood 'incident', spreading like hellfire, quick as the click of a mouse. Producers and bookers who'd rejected Lucy before now sought The Word from her, not for the sake of their souls, but for the sake of their ratings. It was all she ever wanted, or thought she wanted. She didn't do parties, premieres, openings or endorsements any longer, but she was a lifer on the invite lists. The more she refused the more she was pursued.

Lucy was more famous than she ever could have imagined. But this was not how she pictured it.

She was struggling. Conflicted. What happened at the church was beyond imagination, but try as she did, she was not beyond bitterness. The loss of Sebastian was so senseless, the crowds that gathered to honour or even just ogle her, an unpleasant reminder. And yet her impatience with it all made her feel guilty. Survivor's guilt. Even though deep down she knew this was all part of his plan, to die, she couldn't help but wish he hadn't. Selfishly. She missed him. She was committed to honouring him by fulfilling her mission. Their mission.

It was times like these that she felt him the most. In her moments of doubt and uncertainty, the very thought of him fortified her; filled her with peace and with patience. Just like in the church, he knew how to get to her. She believed in him, in his plan, and knew she would see him again. Of that she had no doubt.

She stopped to look at herself in the baroque floor-to-ceiling mirror that stood in the lobby. As usual, she was dressed to the nines. She was always a stickler for fashion and now that spring had come, the off-the-shoulder dress, blazer and ribbon sandals laced up her legs were just the thing to make her presence known. Like Cecilia and Agnes, Lucy felt different on the inside, but to her, the outside still mattered. Even more because now there was meaning to it. A reason. That was who she was, why she was chosen. Sebastian didn't want her to change.

'Why are these people so close to the building?' she asked Jimmy the doorman. 'I need a cab.'

'No chance this morning. There's a . . .'

Just then, an explosion of brass and woodwinds, prayers and lamentation thundered down the cobblestone street, overwhelming Jimmy's reply.

Lucy reached for her ears, cutting him off. 'What is that racket?'

Jimmy pointed.

She looked down the street and got her answer. 'That's what I was trying to tell you,' Jimmy yelled. 'The procession is coming this way.'

'What procession?'

Before he could answer, the marchers, musicians, mourners and statues were upon them. The instruments were closer, louder now but somehow less abrasive. She looked up at the veiled statue of Mary, stabbed through its plaster chest, which seemed to pass by her in slow motion. Creeping.

It has just passed Cecilia and Agnes, and now it was her turn. Threading her in.

Lucy was getting dizzy, something that had been happening more and more frequently. She tried to remember if she'd had anything to eat for breakfast and couldn't, even though she'd only just left her apartment. She felt a sudden shift in perception. Now she was not seeing the parade, not hearing

the music and prayers. Now she was experiencing it. Becoming part of it, swept up in the energy of the moment. She could see the march's progress, all the way to its end point, even though the procession had barely moved from beyond her building.

A hand reached out and touched her. She wasn't sure if it was real or imagined. Ordinarily, she'd pull away, especially in the middle of such chaos, but it was a familiar touch. Lucy didn't feel threatened.

'Come,' the woman said, as she walked. 'For Sebastian.'

'Perpetua?' Lucy shouted.

The woman turned her head and returned to her song.

Lucy walked toward her, drawn to the procession, but Jimmy pulled her back. Smart phone cameras caught her every move.

'I can't let you get caught up in that mess.'

'I'm already caught up in it,' Lucy admitted, struggling desperately to break free of his grasp like an addict jonesing for a fix.

He let go.

Lucy was handed a candle and given a veil to put over her flawless face. She no longer stood out. They were all women in mourning, something she could finally do openly. She began to walk. With them.

'Miss Ambrose?' She heard a voice call out but kept walking, gripping her candle in desperation. 'Lucy?'

She turned toward the sound and found herself staring directly at the starched and stiffened white collar of a priest. Lucy shut her eyes tightly and leaned into him to make sure he was real. He led her away from the tumult and after a moment, her head cleared, candle still in hand.

'Thank you, Father,' she said sincerely. 'I don't know what came over me.'

'Do any of us?' he asked. 'These are strange days.'

They walked together for a while, not talking, as onlooker after onlooker faded back. The further they walked, the more she felt his anxiety. He finally broke the swollen silence.

'Sebastian, the boy who died in the church that night . . .'

Lucy's mood darkened.

'I'm not talking about this,' she said, unlinking her arm from his.

'Please,' he responded.

'Who are you?' she asked. 'Who are you, really?'

'I am a priest,' he said. 'You can trust me.'

'That's a joke, right?'

'I am from the cult of Saint Lucy,' he said. 'Part of the lineage. A devoted follower. Please, believe that.'

Lucy nodded her head for him to continue.

'I understand that it must still be painful.'

'Don't dare pity me,' she said through clenched teeth, stopping. 'Dr Frey was cleared following the police investigation. Big surprise. He's back upstairs at Perpetual Help running the

loony bin, back to indoctrinating the next generation of psychotic assassins. Probably got a rise, a bogus title and a dedication at some made-up award dinner. Painful, yes.'

'He has fooled so many.'

'You make it sound like some kind of illusion. It isn't. I can't even walk down the street without fearing for my life and a beautiful guy is gone.'

'Such a shame about Sebastian.'

'Spare me, Father. He doesn't need your pity. Not now. Neither do I.'

Lucy turned away.

'Listen . . .'

'Are you some kind of reporter in disguise? Because I've said all I'm ever going to say about it to the police, and a lot of good it did.'

'At least the construction has been halted. There are people outside the church every day, demanding it be re-established . . .'

'I was inside.'

The priest took a step back, giving her a little room. He was just close enough to see tears welling in the reddened lids of her otherworldly blue eyes.

'Faith is coming alive again. The three of you have given us a chance against them. Hope.'

Lucy stopped and looked deep into his eyes, probing him. 'Against who?'

'The ones who hide in plain sight. 'Vandals.' He whispered. 'Ciphers.'

'What about them?'

'They are worried now. You three have put shame on them. You are their biggest threat. Their only obstacle. You are in their way.'

'You know most people think I'm crazy, right?'

'I know you see things,' he said. 'I don't care what sceptics say, nor should you.'

Lucy went silent. It was true. She was seeing things. Visions. Things she couldn't explain or understand. Then she erupted.

'That's easy for you to say, Padre,' Lucy said, frustrated. 'You aren't out here on the front lines taking shit like I do.'

'I read the accounts, I know you are not crazy,' he persisted.

'Accounts? That sounds so respectable,' Lucy rasped. 'You mean the tabloids don't you?'

'I just want you to know that I believe you and so do many others. People you don't even know around the world are starting to believe you. You can trust me, Lucia.'

'I'm not looking to trust anyone. I don't need your understanding, or approval,' she said. 'Sebastian is dead. Cremated. It doesn't matter what anyone thinks.'

'Are you sure?'

'That's he's dead? I saw him die. We have his ashes. He was cremated.'

'He wasn't.'

'Wasn't what?'

'Cremated,' the priest said. 'Not *all* of him.'

'What are you talking about?' she asked.

'I've heard things.'

'What things?'

'Before he was cremated, his body was—'

Lucy's confusion turned to outright rage. She dropped her burning candle and backhanded the priest across the face. Cameras flashed, capturing her every move.

'You sick sonofabitch,' she railed as the bottom of her skirt started to catch fire. Cloaked women ran to her to put it out, but she remained oblivious to everything but the priest. 'What about his body?'

'His heart,' he gasped, wiping the blood from his lip, trying to stay incognito before slipping away into the crowd. 'It's been taken.'

4

The One You Feed

The lights in the penthouse boardroom at Perpetual Help Hospital burned brightly long after midnight. An assembly had been called. A Senator, an international bank chairman, hedge fund CEO, university president, Silicon Valley entrepreneur, telecom magnate, ad agency founder. Barometers of public markets, consumption and perception with the means and mechanisms at their disposal to shape them. Men and women with global influence and reach. Big shots. Their names and reputations widely recognized and acclaimed but their agenda known only to each other. All the chairs around the conference table were filled. All but one. The one reserved for the media mogul, Daniel Less. Frey noted the absence and rose to speak.

'Ladies and gentlemen, thank you for coming. Good Friday . . . night.' Dr Frey circled the table, pouring glass after glass of fine Bordeaux into each of his seven distinguished guests' goblets.

He raised his drink and offered a toast. 'To the future.'

The others joined, but their lack of enthusiasm was obvious to him.

'Your invitation sounded urgent, Doctor,' the billionaire investor began. 'I didn't come here for a cocktail.'

'I've asked you here to quiet rumblings I've been hearing. Concerns about the rise of the three Brooklyn girls, Lucy Ambrose, Cecilia Trent and Agnes Fremont.

Frey's tone was somewhat casual. It did not land well on the ears of his colleagues. Sebastian's escape, the events at Precious Blood and the investigation and trial that followed had caused a fracturing in their normally united front. He had not expected the meeting to become so contentious so quickly.

'Don't soothe us like one of your patients, Doctor,' the Ivy League chancellor groused. 'You have brought much unwanted attention to yourself and notoriety to the girls. Exactly the sort of thing we hoped to avoid.'

'Don't worry, no one's anonymity has been compromised.'

'We are expecting that you have some news to report.'

Frey returned to the head of the table and took his seat. 'I do have some news.'

'About those girls, I trust. And why they are still alive?' the Senator asked. 'Is your strategy to lull them into a false sense of security before you act?'

Frey considered his next statement before speaking. 'The girls are alive because I need them to be alive.'

'Need them?

'Yes.'

The sour faces in the room hardened further.

'Surely I don't have to remind you of the legends?' the banker nearly shouted.

'It has taken our kind nearly two thousand years to undo the events in Bethlehem,' the tech wizard insisted.

Frey inhaled deeply. 'Sebastian identified them. Empowered them. They imagine themselves the incarnation of ancient Christian saints. Martyrs.'

'Be that as it may; we are the ancestors of the brave and the powerful. Of Herod, of Pilate, of Maximus Thrax,' the ad agency executive shot back. 'Of those who sent their kind to the lions, the chopping block and to the cross.'

'And they must be sent again, before things spiral out of our control,' the telecom tycoon added. 'Unleash those worthless addicts, those vandals, on them as you must and let's be done with this.'

'There is time,' Frey advised calmly.

'Time for what?' another challenged. 'Once the spark is ignited, the fire spreads quickly. Remember, the so-called

martyrs whose legacies they claim were born into a pagan world. It didn't take them long to change it.'

'Yes,' the mogul concurred. 'These girls herald the parousia, the Second Coming, and we cannot afford to let that happen.'

'We will not fail again.'

'I have my reasons,' Frey said, doing little to calm the angst of those assembled.

'And I have my doubts, Doctor,' the fund manager interrupted. 'They made quick work of your assassins in the bone chapel. They will be even harder to defeat the longer this goes on.'

'They are like heat-seeking missiles, launched from the distant past into the present,' the Senator analogized. 'They must be extinguished before they hit their target and complete their mission.'

'Thank you for the history lesson,' Frey replied arrogantly. 'It is most unnecessary.'

The room grew thick with tension. The banker rose and slammed his fist on the boardroom table. Frey remained calm, his eyes closed.

'They are disruptors,' the tech wiz croaked. 'Each day that passes their reputation grows.'

'While our job becomes more difficult.'

'Billboards. Websites. Headlines. Rumours of miracles. People following them to corner bodegas, camping out in front of their homes, turning stoops to shrines, roadside altars,

genuflecting to them in the streets.'

'I would think such chaos would provide perfect cover for some sort of accident?' the banker opined. 'Surely our friends in law enforcement and the media would help us manage such an occurrence.'

Frey rose and pointed at the billboard of Lucy, eyes aglow, suspended above the distant Brooklyn Queens Expressway, visible from the penthouse window. It read simply:

SEE FOR YOURSELF

'Yes, but why? Why do people follow them?' Frey questioned the group like a professor goading his students.

The gathering fell silent, unwilling to believe that Frey would ask such an obvious question. Frey answered it himself.

'Because they believe them. They believe in them.'

'How long before they realize their full power and become impossible to defeat?'

'To kill them is not to defeat them.' Frey insisted. 'People die. In colosseums. On crosses. Not ideas. History is proof of that.'

'You've framed the problem,' the Wall Street titan advised. 'What is your solution, Doctor?'

'They must be rejected first. It was the mistake made at the very beginning and we've paid for it through history.'

'And how do you propose to do that?'

'This brings me to the second reason I need them alive.'

'Are we in a classroom, Doctor?'

Frey once again took his seat, looking each of his colleagues in the eye as he began his discourse.

'When the subway workers brought the chaplets of Saint Lucy, Saint Agnes and Saint Cecilia from Europe, they brought not only antiquities, but their cults of devotion from the old world to the new. They brought their faith. An entire legacy of it.'

'And they paid a heavy price,' the advertising bigwig noted.

'Yes, but so did we. Precious Blood rose above their graves. The chapel was dedicated to their memory, the pews filled for generations, their bones revered, the chaplets enshrined. Waiting for this moment.'

'But no longer,' the ad agency bigwig noted. 'We chipped away at the culture, the so-called morality, at the congregation until it was but a shell, like so many others here and around the world. Marginalized. Brought low.'

The meeting was interrupted when the conference room door opened unexpectedly.

'But it has *not* been brought low,' the newcomer exclaimed abrasively, taking his seat opposite Dr Frey's. 'Sebastian changed all of that.'

'Mr Less, so good of you to come,' Frey welcomed through pursed lips. 'And congratulations on the quarterly earnings for the teen fashion magazine group you publish.'

'It's my pleasure to improve the value of your stock portfolio, Alan, but don't expect the same for next quarter.'

'The economic downturn,' Frey suggested snidely.

'No, not the economy. The climate. The cultural climate. Truckloads of subscriptions have been cancelled in the New York area alone. Tired of their insecurities being preyed upon is the feedback we're getting.'

'Teens can be fickle,' Frey replied defensively.

'Yes, they tend to gravitate to what's happening and those girls are happening,' Less informed. 'It is no longer just the old, the desperate and the old-fashioned that gravitate to them.'

'Say your piece. We are listening.'

'The empowerment message they are peddling is resonating across the board and it doesn't need to be merchandised and therefore cannot be co-opted.'

'Are you saying we are powerless?' the tech guru laughed. 'With the assets at our disposal?'

'No, I'm saying we are losing.'

Less's sobering analysis threw a pall of silence over the meeting. The media mogul took his seat and continued.

'The symbolism of replacing Precious Blood with a gleaming high-rise of multi-million dollar condos was perfect. The triumph of money and modernism over a bankrupt morality and outdated superstition,' Less enthused. 'But now, the church has been replaced not by soaring steel and glass but by these three girls. It is revived in them.'

The Constellation Entertainment chairman was known

among the group not least for his foresight. He saw the future and parlayed his independent record label, Tritone, into one of the most powerful entertainment companies in the world, crushing and then swallowing less savvy competitors in music, film, television, video, live performance, broadcasting, publishing and new media technologies while cultivating a roster of artists and brands that read like a who's who of contemporary pop culture. To be with him was to have the world at your disposal.

Several in the room had partnered with him to change laws, gut regulations, lower standards, finance acquisitions and buyouts, and manipulate public opinion for a variety of purposes. Several, but not Dr Frey, who'd always been wary of the executive's high profile and unbridled ambition.

'The three girls are only part of the problem,' the doctor offered cryptically.

'You could have fooled me,' Less griped. 'There are petitions to re-open Precious Blood circulating through these neighbourhoods with tens of thousands of signatures on them. A year ago they couldn't put twenty people in a pew on Sunday morning. Now there are overflow outdoor services in Prospect Park. Even the Archbishop is astonished, I might even say worried, at the sudden change.'

'Perhaps because the Archbishop has nothing to do with it,' the banker asserted. 'They have been blindsided as well.'

'What else could be the matter?'

Frey approached the other end of the table with his nearly empty wine bottle, pouring the last drops into the latecomer's glass.

'There is a new relic.'

Frey's declaration was met with sceptical stares and confused gasps around the table.

'From the chapel?' the Senator queried.

'No, from the morgue.'

'How?' Less asked.

'Rumours came to my attention that such a thing might happen and I arranged for a few of my staff from the hospital to be present at the autopsy, but they were turned away. It was done quickly and secretly.'

The grumbling in the room was so loud it threatened to bleed under the door and through the walls.

'You've had our friends in the police department twist some arms I presume?'

'Yes, but the body had been cremated by that time,' Frey explained.

'And the heart stolen?' Less chided.

'Yes.'

'And you think the girls did this?'

'No, but it won't be long before they hear about it.' Frey said quietly. 'Once they do, they will be compelled to find it.'

'And lead you to it?' the Senator concluded.

Frey nodded.

'We are watching them closely and working our other contacts in the Medical Examiner's Office.'

'It must be found!' the telecom baron exclaimed.

'I will find it.'

'This is of grave concern.' Less responded, tapping his manicured fingernail on the polished mahogany table. 'The boy is already regarded as a saint in some circles. Saints leave behind relics. Relics inspire cults. Cults grow into movements. The longer the heart remains hidden from us, the greater the danger.'

A brief silence was followed by an alternate proposal.

'This must be of some interest to the church as well?' the banker assessed. 'Have you made them aware?'

'I assume you are reaching out to our colleagues at the Vatican,' Less said.

'Let them deal with this and we can wash our hands of this whole affair,' the banker said.

'Yes,' Frey advised tersely. 'Some in place there are suspicious and perceive a threat to their authority as well. They will share our interest in debunking the relic and the girls.'

'But not killing them,' the investor retorted sceptically. 'They are clergy after all, not Mafia.'

'Once I posses the relic I will take care of the girls.'

Less was not persuaded. 'Doctor, we left this matter in your hands because of your position and your unique background, but our patience is now being sorely tested.'

'Perhaps I could prescribe something for your anxiety?' Frey answered snidely.

'Your arrogance in the face of such failure astounds even me,' Less chided. 'The boy escaped you. The attackers were defeated. These self-styled saints are making their mark. A new relic is in the hands of our adversaries. Our investment in Precious Blood is lost.'

'But not our cause,' Frey pushed back.

'Not *yet*.' Less countered. 'You seek to influence minds, control behaviour. We seek to control attitudes. Influence trends. I tell you this for sure, things are trending away from us. Gradually now, but the floodgates will eventually open unless they are dealt with quickly and decisively.'

'I have every confidence in my strategy,' Frey reassured.

Less pointed in frustration out at the billboard of Lucy in the distance.

'What is that girl saying?' he conjectured. 'Pull back the curtain. Ignore the illusion that's been created for you. Friends, we *are* the curtain!'

'Surely it will take more than signage and words to roll back the tide that has been surging in our direction for centuries now.'

'That billboard was financed with small donations. Kids emptying their piggybanks, college students sacrificing their daily lattes, old ladies lighting fewer candles on Sunday. And that space doesn't come cheap.'

The ad exec nodded. 'True. It was leased from my biggest client.'

'Everybody loves a bandwagon,' Frey observed dismissively.

'Everybody loves a *winner*,' Less parried. 'Ours is a collaborative enterprise, but also a competitive one. Time and our patience is running out. We've tried it your way. Next, we will try it mine.'

'They will lead us to it,' Frey declared with certainty. 'And this matter will be closed for all eternity.'

'Then we are all agreed on the task?' the Senator asked.

Everyone present nodded their approval, even the media mogul, reluctantly.

As the meeting disbanded, the doctor approached Less.

'Is your problem with the girls or with me?' Frey challenged.

The mogul did not mince words.

'Find the heart. Kill the girls,' Less stated. 'The clock, Dr Frey, is ticking.'

5

The Reliquary Heart

Cecilia sat, cross-legged on the wide plank pine floor in her washed-out black tank top and panties, strumming her guitar, staring out at the harbour through the grungy factory windows of her Red Hook apartment. Trying to find her voice for the comeback performance she was planning. The loft space was poorly lit except for the early morning sun, unfinished and unfurnished but for a ratty couch and table and chairs she picked up dumpster diving. Pretty much status quo apartment-wise ever since she'd come to New York. Her eviction from the Williamsburg place turned out to be a blessing in disguise. Red Hook was a place for her to hide. Away from the fans, away from the prying, judgmental eyes of the press and her hipster brethren. It was safe, if a little lonely.

She stood in the window and could see the Statue of Liberty from one side and lower Manhattan from the other. The bay was bustling with ferries and water taxis and tugboats and freighters, their enormous hulls leaving powerful wakes, adding exponentially to the characteristic chop of the restless, unpredictable waters. Behind her was the less picturesque view of the public houses, the onetime epicentre of the crack epidemic in New York City, now just an eyesore, the very definition of an apartment 'block': grim and style-less but functional. An inconvenience to the developers looking to gentrify the peninsula with furniture superstores and big box organic markets most locals couldn't afford to shop in.

The grey and blue suited brokers anxiously boarded the water taxis for their Wall Street offices on one side while the tenement tenants dutifully boarded buses to clean houses and babysit children on the other. Cecilia pondered the 360-degree view of success, of struggle, surrounding her. She left her guitar lying on the floor and walked to the window.

She dropped her head, her sharp black bob meeting her lips, trying to figure it all out, surveying the signs of life amidst the urban blight for an answer. Her eyes played hopscotch over lot after vacant lot, all the way to the ferry piers. Children played hooky in some, making up games from the rubble; others were fenced off and furrowed, transformed into tiny farms of rows of tomatoes and lettuce. Indeed, signs of life were everywhere. A neighbourhood rehabbing if not yet reborn. It wouldn't be long before construction began, she figured. In a few years, she laughed to herself, this place would be worth a fortune.

What is the difference between success and failure? she pondered. Desire. Determination. Diligence. Definitely. But it was something more. Belief. That it was possible. That it could be done, whatever it was. It was the hardest part, and the most essential. You had to believe in it, in yourself, before you could do it. Only you.

'Save yourself,' she whispered and looked up.

Cecilia searched the south side of the sky in vain for some sign of Sebastian. She couldn't stop thinking about him. It was almost impossible to focus on her music. She searched for his smile in a rainbow, his face in a cloud formation. It was unlike her. It was uncool. Desperate even. Like a girl sitting by the phone, waiting for a guy to call, a call that might never come. Oyo said that others saw him everywhere, but Cecilia could only see him when she closed her eyes. Lately, it was so intense, only causing her frustration to grow. She began mumbling to herself, fighting back the rage that was slowly building inside of her.

'What do you want from me?' she erupted, fist clenched in frustration. 'Tell me, goddammit!'

A sudden loud smack startled her, but Cecilia didn't flinch. The windowpane was breaking before her as if in slow motion.

It cracked but didn't shatter.

'Nice ass, bitch!' she heard one of the teenage boys scream out from the lot across the street, still wielding a piece of brick in his hand. 'For a saint, that is.'

Cecilia looked down at him impassively as he laughed.

Still thinking intensely of Sebastian, she suddenly began to feel woozy. Light as a feather. She looked down at her feet and felt herself lift up off the floor. She was petrified.

'Sebastian,' she called out.

The boy dropped the stone and frantically motioned for his posse to leave. Their mouths fell wide open at the sight of the levitating girl in the window. They turned white as ghosts. They ran backwards, afraid to take their eyes off her as the 'leader's' pants turned soaking wet with urine.

She hovered a few inches above the floor in the bay window, knowing that it was Sebastian who'd lifted her up. Lifted her when she needed it most.

'You're here,' she whispered. She was comforted as if he were right there, holding her. 'Inside.'

The boys turned the corner and Cecilia glided gently to the floor.

'I miss you,' she said.

She paused for a moment, closed her eyes and took it all in, gathering herself before returning to her six string. She tore a piece of paper from her spiral songwriter's notebook and began to make something she hadn't made in a while. A set list.

* * *

Martha burst into Agnes's bedroom and pulled back the vintage lace curtains. 'Well?' she fumed, hands on hips.

'Well what?' Agnes groaned, still groggy, squinting her eyes to make out her mother's form in the sunlight.

'Are you coming?'

'Where?'

'To church,' Martha shouted, buttoning her new blouse and tossing on her jacket. 'It's Easter in case you've forgotten.'

Agnes exhaled, considering it. 'I don't think so, Mother.'

'You don't think so?' Martha queried. 'What will people think if you don't come?'

'Honestly, who cares? Besides, I didn't buy a bonnet this year.'

'Don't be disrespectful to me, or to God for that matter.'

'To God? Seriously?'

'It's a mortal sin, Agnes.'

'What is? Me or not going to church?'

'You had no problem going to church when that guy was in it.' Martha said. 'Guess you'll do anything for a boy, even go to church!'

'I'm not boy crazy, Mother.'

'You're old enough now to do what you want. Your soul is your own responsibility.'

'Right. Let's keep it that way.'

'Oh forgive me, I forgot Saint Agnes,' Martha said snidely,

clasping her hands. 'You're too busy being blasphemous.'

'You know all about blasphemy!' Agnes was pissed off. She popped out of bed. 'Going to church for all the wrong reasons. The same way you live your life!'

'You have no idea what my reasons are. You're just a little girl, holed up in her room, pining for some guy she'll never see again.'

'My father?'

'That's it, Agnes,' her mother said. 'Get dressed, you're going to church!'

'You know what happened the last time I went. Ash Wednesday. The nasty stares from the ushers and whispers from the blue-haired ladies in the pews. That uptight deacon who is always cheating on his wife even refused to give me communion. Hypocrites. All of them!'

'He didn't refuse to give you communion. That's so dramatic. He was probably starstruck or something.'

'Oh please. If not for that visiting priest from Kenya I'd still be standing there.'

'I need to put on my make-up and get out the door if I want a seat. The church will be packed, whether you come or not.'

'Hey, maybe I can score you a better seat? Do they have Saint Seating, a whole Saint Section, Mother?' Agnes shouted, trying to get under her mom's skin. 'Make up your mind! Am I a saint or a sinner?'

'Do you think it's easy to be mocked because of who your

daughter is, or who she's pretending to be? Do you think for one second showing up with you in church, with you anywhere, is easy? I'm worried for your soul, Agnes.'

'You don't believe me. You don't believe any of it, do you?'

'I believe that you should go to church.'

'What do you believe about me?'

'I believe you are my daughter, though lately I'm not so sure you weren't taken over by something or someone in that church,' Martha answered, almost breaking down.

'You think I'm brainwashed?'

'I really don't know anymore.' Martha split, slamming the door behind her.

Martha's scepticism, mostly unspoken until now, hit Agnes harder than she would have thought, exposing doubts she herself had been harbouring.

'When you figure it out,' Agnes murmured to herself, 'be sure to let me know.'

Agnes exhaled and fell back on to her bed, transfixed by the rays of morning sunlight blazing through her window, warming the room. Birds were chirping, blossoms on the trees in her yard beginning once again to bloom. Stressed out and shaky from the blowout argument, she reached for the tablet next to her and noticed an alert from a local club flashing on her screen.

JOIN US FOR THE MOST UNBELIEVABLE COMEBACK SINCE THE RESURRECTION!

CECILIA TRENT PERFORMING LIVE! TONIGHT ONLY!
GENERAL ADMISSION. TICKETS ON SALE NOW!

'She's doing a show?' Agnes muttered out loud to herself. She was stunned.

'Now that's an Easter service I won't miss. I need to see her.'

The front door buzzer got her attention as did her mom's shouts from the hallway bathroom.

'Agnes! Get the door!'

Agnes didn't budge. She was glued to her tablet, searching for ticket details, and in no hurry to get back into it with Martha.

'Agnes!' Martha shouted again. 'The door!'

She lifted her bedroom window shade slightly and eyed the small crowd loitering, as usual, near the front of her home. One of them must have got the nerve to ring. 'She's got to be kidding.'

Most of Agnes's followers were especially respectful of her and her privacy. If anything, they'd become a kind of community watch, looking out for her. They gathered in front of the Fremont home, leave gifts on the sidewalk or on the stoop, but never, until now, had one of them come to the door. Cops, reporters, family, neighbours all knew to call or email first. Martha knew this. In fact it had been her rule, which made Martha's 'end of my rope' bitching seem more authentic to Agnes than usual.

'Christ, are your legs broken?' Martha groused, heading for the front door.

'No, are you blind?' Agnes sniped. 'You see those people outside don't you?'

Martha rolled her eyes and reached for the knob. 'Yes, I see them. I always see them.'

'I can't just *get the door*.'

'Nothing's happened, Agnes. No threats. No attacks. You make it back and forth to school everyday. If someone was out to hurt you, they would have done it already.'

'I honestly think you're trying to get rid of me, Mother.' Agnes tone suggested she was only half kidding.

'I don't want to feed into this paranoia any longer.'

'You mean you don't want to be inconvenienced any longer.'

Exactly what Agnes had hoped to avoid was now on deck. The resumption of hostilities.

'They never come to the house,' Martha huffed. 'I would have thought you'd show a little more grace under the circumstances.'

'The circumstances,' Agnes mumbled once more. 'Here we go again.'

She bristled at her mom taking a cheap shot. Of course, it was her fault, all this saint stuff, and now she was complaining. Something else to blame her for.

'What would you know about grace?' Agnes said, fuming as Martha answered the door.

'Can I help you?' Martha said uncharacteristically sweet, the surprise in her voice making Agnes wonder who had darkened their doorstep.

Agnes's curiosity got the best of her and she joined her mother in the doorway. Facing her was a young boy, small boned with dark hair, eyes and complexion, holding a gift. He looked at Agnes in disbelief, like someone would look at a famous celebrity, and held a small box out to her.

'For you,' he said.

Agnes took the cardboard box with the cellophane window. 'Chocolate?'

'For you,' he repeated like someone who didn't speak English very well.

It was an Easter chocolate moulded in the shape of a lamb.

'Thank you,' she said softly. 'But why?'

'Jude tell me. He tell me to bring you.'

'Bring me where?'

'To my house. My grandmother. She sick.'

'How do you know Jude?' Agnes asked, kneeling and taking the boy's hands in hers.

'He live with us.'

Agnes reached behind the door for her wool shawl and brought it over her shoulders. Martha grabbed her arm tightly. Her lips were pursed in anger, and fear.

'You are not going to some stranger's house!' Martha commanded.

Agnes stopped; she heard a voice in her head, clear as a bell. It was his voice, Sebastian's. *Go to her*.

'You don't know if this boy is telling the truth,' Martha said.

'Yes, I do,' Agnes said.

'You won't go with me to Easter mass but you'll leave with a total stranger?' Martha shouted.

Agnes bounded down the brownstone steps on to the sidewalk. Turning back, she touched her heart and blew Martha a kiss.

The small crowd that had gathered in front of her house and across the street parted silently as she walked with the boy. She nodded to them in thanks.

'What's your name?' Agnes asked him after a while.

'Manny. Manuel.'

Church bells rang from every block, heralding Easter as they walked down Union Street past Fourth Avenue, past Third Avenue, over the Carroll Street bridge. The boy couldn't help but stare in awe at Agnes – her brassy auburn hair against the moss-coloured water of the Gowanus actually made it look far less toxic and way more fantastical. The farther they went, the tighter the boy's grasp became until they reached the drawbridge between Nevins and Bond streets, where it became vice-like.

'Are you afraid of something?' she asked.

He shook his head *no*, but his eyes, open big and wide, gave

him away. He pointed at a large double width townhouse at the end of the canal, right before the projects.

'It's a bad place,' Manuel said.

Agnes looked at the building. It was well kept and appeared to have been recently renovated from the construction permits still taped to the windows. In fact, it was city owned and operated according to the signage. A healthcare facility of some kind.

'Let's keep walking,' she said, smiling. 'Take me to your home.'

They continued down Union to Henry Street, deep into Carroll Gardens, and stopped at a small home in obvious disrepair. It was dated, and not in a good way. An eyesore in the rapidly gentrifying neighbourhood. There was, however, an Easter decoration in the yard – a large wood crucifix with a deep purple scarf draped over it. Spotlights pointed to the cross, illuminating it in the night.

The door opened as Agnes and Manuel turned up the front walkway. Another child's face was visible behind the tattered screen of the storm door.

There he was. Standing there, looking at her with his dark black eyes.

'Jude,' Agnes gasped.

The boy ran out to greet her, grabbing her at the waist and holding her tight. She brushed the hair away from his face and kissed his forehead.

'I've been thinking about you,' Agnes said, looking him in the eyes.

Jude made a 'Y' shape with the thumb and pinky of his right hand and positioned each digit so that one was pointing at Agnes, the other back at himself.

'Same,' Agnes said recognizing the word in sign language.

Jude nodded and smiled.

Manuel and Jude each took one of Agnes's hands and led her inside. The home was as modest as the exterior signalled it would be. Outside a room near the end of the hallway a family kept vigil. Agnes and the boys approached, and the man and woman stood and bowed their heads.

'This is my mother and father,' Manuel explained.

The couple smiled at her, the gratitude in their eyes unmistakable, and ushered her into a small bedroom where a woman lay motionless. She moaned in agony. Agnes approached her without hesitation.

'Her name is Theresa,' the woman said.

'Please have mercy on me!' the woman called out in tremendous pain. The family was trying whatever they could to ease her suffering, but nothing was helping her. A vaporizer on a mahogany dresser was pointed to her face, candles and serene music played, and she was dressed in a soft flannel nightgown. The woman was emaciated and frail, her eyes yellowed and sunken, lips cracked and cheeks hollowed by illness and time. Family portraits and photographs of

memorable occasions crowded her nightstand, telling the story of a woman much loved and a life well lived. Beside them, bottles of prescription pills, religious statues, lotions and holy water. The woman held tight to a rosary with clear crystal beads.

At the foot of the bed was an old, carved wooden case. It was open. Rows of small wooden crucifixes and miniature bottles of what looked to be holy water beckoned her.

The woman gasped for air.

Slowly and with great effort, Teresa turned her head toward Agnes and beckoned her to come closer. The woman was praying. Agnes recognized it as a portion of the prayer to Saint Agnes.

'Saint Agnes, you refused to give up your faith; help us to be proud of our faith, to love it, to be strong in it, and to give witness to it daily.'

The smell of roses cut through the menthol mist and filled Agnes's nostrils like they had in the sacristy of Precious Blood, but there were no flowers or vases on display in the room, or anywhere.

'Help me,' the woman pleaded in pain. 'Have mercy on me.'

Agnes stepped closer to the bed and kneeled at the side of it.

Theresa's lips were parched, cracking from the lack of saliva. Her hands and feet were starting to stiffen. But, still, she would not go. 'Please,' she continued to plead.

Agnes stood and left the room without a word. Overwhlemed.

'She's dying,' Agnes said to the couple standing there.

'Yes,' the man agreed. 'We keep telling her it's OK to go, but she's still hanging on. Suffering.'

'Can't they do anything?' Agnes ordered. 'She needs medical help.'

'Her body is beyond care, but not her soul,' the man said. 'You are what she needs now.'

'I can't help her. I'm so sorry,' Agnes said, feeling like a fraud in front of the desperate woman and her family. She began to panic. Doubt flooding her mind. 'I'm just a girl. A teenager. I don't know what to do.'

'She is tormented,' he said. 'As if there is an evil inside that will not let her die.'

'You don't understand. *I don't know what to do.*'

'This kit has been passed down to us through generations, in the right hands these things can help to drive out demons.'

Agnes swallowed hard.

'I'm not an *exorcist*,' she said trying to keep calm in the face of such a request. 'I don't have any such authority.'

'Do whatever you think you should do,' the man answered, gesturing to the open wooden case. 'It will be enough.'

The man mouthed the words, but it was Sebastian's voice she heard. Agnes bowed her head and closed her eyes. She was transported back to the sacristy at Precious Blood. Sebastian gently cleansing her wounds with water filled with rose petals

and fragrant oils, then dressing her wrists delicately with bandages. She had felt cared for, comforted, and loved.

Jude looked at her, eyes fixed on hers as if he were trying to encourage her, communicate with her non-verbally.

Agnes looked at the old woman and asked Jude for a bowl of warm water and a soft cloth.

'I will only take what I need,' Agnes said, echoing Sebastian's words, before heading out into the hallway to look around. She took some white petals with magenta tips off of an orchid and put them in the water. Then she added a few drops of lavender oil from a small bottle on the dresser and returned to the old woman's room.

'Do not be afraid,' Agnes said softly in the woman's ear. Her lips morphed into a trembling smile as Agnes put some water to wet her lips, and her eyes lit up as she reached for Agnes and took hold, not of the girl's fingers, but of the chaplet dangling from her wrist. One by one, the woman fingered the bone beads with great effort, whispering prayers on each, a look of peace coming over her as she progressed along the bracelet.

'*Let us gain courage for our own battle by honouring the martyrdom of the glorious virgin Agnes. Saint Agnes, vessel of honour, flower of unfading fragrance, beloved of the choirs of Angels, you are an example to the worth of virtue and chastity. O you who wear a Martyr's palm and a virgin's wreath, pray for us that, though unworthy of a special crown, we may have our names written in the list of Saints.*'

Agnes stroked Theresa's white hair and fevered forehead gently until she completed her prayers. The woman mustered all of the strength she had left and pulled Agnes's arm, sat up, and kissed the heart-shaped milagro dangling from the chaplet. Then she fell back on to her pillow.

'Let go,' Agnes instructed.

The woman closed her eyes and exhaled while Agnes washed her gently, the sound of dripping water when she rung out the rag the only noise in the room now. The woman was immediately soothed and calmed by Agnes's touch. The aroma of fresh roses grew stronger.

'What is happening?' Manuel asked his mother.

'It is a miracle, Manny. She's washing away her sins and her pain.' The mother said finally at peace. 'She's preparing her.'

The old woman appeared to be smiling. And then the death rattle. The sound of her soul departing. No more moaning. No more suffering.

Agnes stood and spoke. 'She is at peace.'

The family kneeled before her in homage and thanks as Jude smiled.

'No, thank you,' Agnes said, urging them back up to their feet. 'I wasn't called here so that I could pray for her. It was so she could pray for me.'

6

Rogue

The joint was packed.

It looked like a sold out show and it smelled like one. Not an inch of space to find between ticketholders in the sweaty, squealing and expectant general admission crowd. Not on the floor, not on the first balcony or on the second. Burly bouncers pulled double duty. Not only were they hired to keep watch over the headliner, but to keep the aisles and fire exits clear.

Cecilia had on skin-tight leather leggings and mile-high black ankle boots. Her hair was poker straight with the very tips of it evenly dyed a blood red. Her bone chaplet and milagro dangled around her wrist. She was both street and divine. The top she'd chosen for the performance was a rusty, elaborately sculpted wrought iron corset. It was old, an antique that looked Victorian. But it fitted over her slim midriff perfectly. A gift from Bill not long after they first met. He said he'd had a writer friend in Paris ship it over. Cecilia was never absolutely sure if it was a kind gesture from a friend or a payment for a drug debt, but it didn't matter. To her, it was a one-of-kind gift from a man that always supported her. Like Sebastian, a man she hadn't seen for much too long.

Cecilia leaned against the backstage wall. Some of the crowd caught a glimpse of her behind the red velvet curtain and began to scream. She closed her eyes and swallowed hard. She was anxious, but instead of sweating, her hands throbbed on the verge of bleeding like they had in the tattoo parlour.

'They really want you.' She opened her eyes at the sound of a familiar voice cutting through the screams, calling her from the door of her dressing room at the end of the narrow hallway.

Cecilia knew that voice. She knew it in the deepest part of her.

It was Lucy.

She was in a black trousersuit. The only visible make-up on her face was real gold leaf gilded eye shadow, which matched her gold double eye milagro that Sebastian had given her. She was carrying a crushed velvet gold clutch.

'How did you get back here?'

'One of your bouncers knew me from my party girl past,'

Lucy said nonchalantly, holding a ticket. 'Comped.'

'And here I thought you'd burned every last bridge.' Cecilia smirked.

'Hey, those burning bridges are the only things lighting my way right now,' Lucy said.

'I should've known you wouldn't pay.'

'That way I always get my money's worth.'

'Probably spent all your money on that eye gold,' Cecilia said.

'All that glitters,' Lucy joked, pointing to herself.

'How did you know I would be here? I don't remember sending up the Bat Signal.'

'No, just a sniper flyer.' Lucy held up a tattered and rain-soaked piece of eleven by fourteen paper announcing Cecilia's last minute gig. They walked toward each other, slowly at first, and then ran into each other's arms. 'You look divine.'

'I can't believe you're here,' CeCe said.

'Me neither,' a third voice chimed in.

'Agnes,' Cecilia whispered.

'Surprise,' Agnes said, her eyes welling with tears of relief.

The only two people in the world who really knew her, staring right into her own eyes. In the flesh. Agnes looked otherworldly without any effort. She wore a bohemian skirt and her lambswool cowl. The front of her hair was twirled into messy pin curls, bright green and turquoise chandelier earrings dangled from her mane like Christmas decorations in an

auburn tree. The dainty above-the-knuckle gold band rings she sported on one hand with her chaplet, perfectly complimented the mourning ring on the other.

'Don't tell me you snuck in, too?' Cecilia asked.

'She dragged me in,' Agnes laughed, pointing at Lucy.

'I couldn't leave her waiting at the stage door like some pathetic groupie, could I?' Lucy said.

'You didn't have to come,' Cecilia said.

'But we did,' Lucy replied.

'Wouldn't have missed it,' Agnes added.

There was a knowing silence between them.

Cecilia's pre-show anxiety melted away with the two of them there.

'Can we duck back into your dressing room?' Lucy said. 'I don't want anyone to think this is some kind of cheap publicity stunt.'

Cecilia felt Lucy's head to check for a fever. Lucy laughed and then smacked her hand off. 'I'm serious.'

The three of them went into Cecilia's dressing room. It was the coolest place Agnes had ever seen. Rock 'n' roll at its cheapest and dirtiest. A sacred space for musicians.

'So, this is what it's like,' Agnes said in amazement. 'I always wondered.'

'Yeah, this is the good life,' Cecilia jibbed. 'A make-up mirror, a filthy toilet with no seat, and graffiti covering every inch of a cubicle coffin.' Cecilia was only partly joking. Agnes

could see this was where she lived. Where she thrived. Agnes took a minute to read some of the 'markings'. The sayings that people wrote before walking out on to the stage. Last words. It was like a motivational cemetery of angst and anger, filled with the most creative combinations of swear words she'd ever seen. *If you don't like my music, then you just don't fucking get it.*

'I like that one.' Agnes said. 'Reminds me of you.'

Cecilia smiled. 'Church of the poisoned mind.'

'I didn't even know that was anatomically possible,' Agnes joked, pointing innocently at another particularly acrobatic demand.

'You'd be surprised,' Cecilia ribbed back, calling their attention to a pithy maxim above the ratty couch. 'This one's a favourite too.'

Misbehave to the grave!

'Looks new. Like your handwriting,' Lucy jibed. Cecilia didn't deny it.

The one that stood out most to Agnes was the least abrasive. It read simply: *Better to burn out than to fade away.* At that, Agnes handed Cecilia a large plastic bag filled with gold medals.

'What's this?' Cecilia asked.

'A bag of belief,' Agnes said. 'Thought you could use it tonight.'

Cecilia opened the bag and rummaged through hundreds of milagros. Little miracles that people held on to for hope and strength.

'Antiques?'

'I'm sure most of them are.' Agnes said. 'People hand them to me wherever I go. I was saving them for a special occasion. They have so much energy.'

'Thank you,' Cecilia said, placing the bag delicately on the vanity. They glowed like disco balls in the bulbs shining from the make-up mirror, throwing waves of rippled gold light on to the walls and the girls.

Cecilia placed her hands on Agnes's cheeks and kissed her forehead.

'And, what'd you bring me?' Cecilia asked Lucy.

'Myself,' she said sarcastically. 'The gift that keeps on giving.'

'I've seen you on TV and in the papers,' Cecilia said.

'Just doing my thing,' Lucy responded. 'Getting the word out, so to speak.'

'Keeps you busy,' Agnes observed, her tone taking on a bit of a sarcastic edge that was more like Martha's.

'I hope it's not causing any problems for either of you,' Lucy said. 'I know it draws attention to us.'

'No,' Agnes said quietly. 'Sebastian didn't want us to change. Besides, I'm happy to see you online or in person. In person is better.'

'Well, this is as good a place as any for a reunion,' Cecilia observed.

'In my mind, we've never been apart,' Agnes said. 'I've been

thinking about both of you constantly. About him. It's hard to explain . . .'

'I know,' Cecilia said, reaching for her hand.

'I feel him more now then I did when he was standing in front of me,' Lucy added.

'Now he's inside,' Agnes said. 'I don't think anyone but us can understand that kind of relationship. That kind of love.'

'It's the deepest kind. I'm sorry I haven't contacted you,' Cecilia said. 'I just needed some time to myself after the investigation.'

'It was more like an inquisition if you ask me,' Lucy added.

Agnes noticed the glint from the Vaseline spread over Cecilia's forearm. She reached for CeCe's wrist and raised it gently.

'I don't even know how to mourn him,' Agnes said, studying Cecilia's gorgeous black sacred heart and arrow ink. 'I can't let go.'

'Then don't,' Lucy interjected.

Lucy looked around at the small crowd of assistants, press agents, promoters' reps and roadies gathering in the hall, craning their necks to get a look at Cecilia, Agnes and Lucy together. It was the first they'd been seen together since the night they left the church and people were naturally curious. She could almost see the publicists crafting their items for the gossip rags.

Agnes pulled her hand away from Cecilia's and noticed a

stain of blood on her palm. She looked at Cecilia and Agnes.

'Can we shut the door?' Lucy asked.

'Your stigmata, it's bleeding.' Agnes said.

Lucy shut the door and leaned up against it. She shut her eyes and then slowly opened them.

'What?' Agnes insisted.

'Cecilia, why are you playing a gig now? After so long?' Lucy asked. 'And why are you here?' she asked, pointing a long manicured nail at Agnes. 'Why are the three of us here?'

'Are you losing your shit?' Cecilia asked. 'Quit with the riddles.'

'I heard something that I thought you both should know.'

'So you didn't come just to see me?'

'What did you hear?' Agnes asked.

'A priest that follows me around told me something. It's so crazy but I can't get it out of my head. I needed to tell you. Both of you.'

'A confession?' Cecilia asked. 'Well, you've come to the right place.'

Lucy smiled weakly and turned her back to them.

'What?' Agnes asked firmly.

'They did an autopsy on Sebastian before he was cremated.'

'Right.' Cecilia's jaw tightened at the thought. 'And they found nothing.'

Lucy turned toward them.

'Are you trying to say he was high or something?' Agnes quizzed.

'No nothing like that.' Lucy responded tentatively. 'It's worse.'

'He's gone,' Agnes said. 'What could be worse?'

'That's just it,' Lucy said enigmatically. 'He's not. Not all of him anyway.'

Agnes and CeCe stared at her blankly. Dumbfounded. Distraught.

'Now you're scaring me,' Cecilia winced. 'Just say it.'

'His heart,' Lucy began.

'What about his heart?' Agnes asked, trembling.

'It's been taken. Stolen.'

Agnes and Cecilia were shocked. Frozen in place.

'Do you really believe that? Cecilia asked.

'Yeah, I think I do.' Lucy replied.

'You *think* or you *do*?' CeCe pressed.

'I do,' Lucy admitted.

Lucy's certainty was persuasive.

'Who would do something like that? Agnes cried.

The answer was clear to each of them but only Cecilia spoke his name. 'Frey.'

Agnes doubled over in anguish. 'Frey killed him. Isn't that enough?'

'It's never enough for him until we're all gone,' Lucy said.

'And he wins.' Cecilia agreed, her expression turning from sadness to anger. 'Well, if he wanted our attention, he has it now.'

'We need to know the truth,' Agnes insisted.

'I'm going to ask Jesse for help,' Lucy said. 'We're going to need him to get to the bottom of this.'

'You really think he'll help?' Cecilia asked. 'He's still shell-shocked from Precious Blood.'

'I'll throw myself on his mercy,' Lucy said, only somewhat convincingly. 'He won't be able to resist that.'

A loud knock at the door startled them.

'Thirty minutes to stage,' House Security informed.

Lucy paced the room anxiously then cautioned Cecilia. 'I don't think you should go out there tonight,' Lucy warned. 'It's too dangerous, especially now.'

'I have to,' Cecilia said, bringing her hand to Lucy's cheek. 'Especially now.'

'Cecilia, don't,' Agnes pleaded.

'If you don't want to stay, I totally understand,' Cecilia said to her sincerely.

'If you're playing, I'm staying,' Lucy smiled sadly. 'I came to get my money's worth, remember?'

Agnes nodded.

Cecilia grabbed the doorknob and ushered them out with a hug.

'Keep an eye on my friends, OK?' Cecilia instructed the

bouncer. 'And bring me a hammer and a box of nails from the janitor's closet.'

'Whatever you say,' he replied, gesturing for a few of his men to escort Lucy and Agnes out to the floor while he searched for a custodian.

Lucy turned back as she was leaving for a final word.

'Be careful,' she advised.

Cecilia held up her hands so that Lucy could see her palms were dry.

'Frey is doing his job,' Cecilia said. 'I'm gonna do mine.'

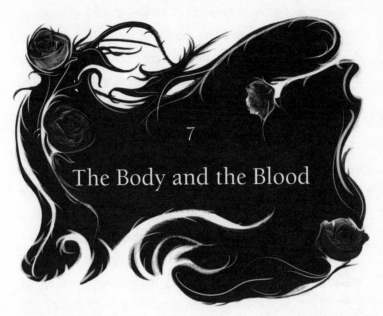

7

The Body and the Blood

The pounding in Cecilia's dressing room was loud enough for the security guard down the hall to take notice.

'Everything OK in there?' he asked, gripping the doorknob in case he needed to get in there quickly.

'Get lost,' Cecilia responded.

'Twenty minutes to curtain,' the bouncer said, knocking nervously on Cecilia's door.

Cecilia resumed her hammering, ignoring him.

She could hear him take a deep breath and then exhale through the crack of the door. Relieved.

'It's going to be one hell of a night,' the bouncer said, laughing. She could hear his footsteps as he walked away.

It sure was going to be a hell of a night, if she had anything to do with it. And since it was her show, she had everything to do with it. The bag of milagros that Agnes brought were coming in handy, helping her add the last little detail to her outfit. The music was most important but this was, after all, show business and she had tremendous respect for her apostles.

One after another she reached for the milagros in the bag, fixed them each with tiny brass tacks and beat them feverishly into her boots until they became a metal mosaic of golden crucifixes, burning hearts, body parts and praying hands – transforming her kickers into sacred armour.

Nearly twenty minutes passed. She admired her work, holding the boots up in the vanity mirror and watching the light reflect off them and on to the ceiling. Both black boots were completely covered.

'Fierce,' was all she could say.

Cecilia reached into her pocket for the sword and bow charm that Sebastian had given her, deciding whether to add it to her footwear decoupage. Turning it in her fingers, like a magic eight ball, she cut her thumb on its edge.

A heavy knock at the door drew her attention.

'Showtime,' the bouncer advised. 'Ready?'

She sucked the blood streaming from her fingertip. Her eyes lit up. She put the sword and bow milagro back in her pocket.

'I'm always ready,' she responded, slipping her boots on,

and then zipping them up. The tips of the tacks inside sliced slowly into her skin as she walked to the door.

'So are we,' he said.

The lights were turned down. The space was pitch black, not even a floor light on the stage was shining. Cecilia pulled out her pocket flashlight, climbed the backstage steps, and cued the sound engineer to start her opening track, 'Seven Souls' by Material feat. William S. Burroughs.

The crowed roared in unison at the sound of Burroughs reading, his old hoarse and spectral voice crackling about death, and began to sway to Material's ambient beat underneath. They were anticipating her, conjuring her like a post-punk genie from a bottle.

Cecilia poked her head through the velvet curtain as a single spotlight illuminated her. She pulled her head back, flashing them, teasing them. Giving them a little, before she gave them a lot. Gave them her all. More screams and even tears from the audience followed. The room was already a sweaty sea of Cecilia acolytes, both old school indie kids who'd been with her from the beginning but also large groups of more mainstream, newly converted fans, and the show hadn't even begun.

'They adore her,' Agnes yelled into Lucy's ear, barely audible above the crowd noise and crackling PA system.

'Without a doubt,' Lucy observed, distilling the essence of it all.

Lucy scanned the room, on alert, white-knuckling the moment. She studied the fans, trying to understand their relationship to Cecilia and hoping to gain more insight into her own followers. As the assembled undulated to the beat, anticipating Cecilia's appearance, Lucy felt the crowd working themselves not so much into a frenzy, but rather a mass hypnosis. There was an inescapable sense of ecstasy in it.

Agnes looked over and saw a familiar guy standing by the bar. Texting. She nudged Lucy, distracting her from her amateur analysis.

'Well, look what the cat dragged in,' Lucy said. 'I'll be right back. Don't move.'

'I couldn't if I wanted to,' Agnes replied, eyeing the wall of security surrounding her, keeping the over-capacity crowd under control.

'Speaking of crazies,' Lucy laughed to herself, approaching the guy in the black shirt and jeans. She walked up behind him and drove her kneecap into the back of his leg, knocking him momentarily off balance. He clenched his fist, cocked it and turned, ready for a fight.

'I should have known,' Jesse said, relaxing his fingers.

He seemed more relieved than thrilled to see her, she thought.

'Don't you have reviewers on staff to handle this kind of thing,' Lucy ribbed. 'Long time no see.'

'That's what the internet and texting are for, isn't it?'

'Spare me the tech lecture, Jesse. I'm just saying you don't get out much anymore.'

'Well, you seem to get out enough for the both of us.'

'Why are you such an asshole?' Lucy shouted, loud enough to hear through the opening song playing.

'Oh, I don't know. Maybe because I have to look over my shoulder wherever I go. You want to know why I don't get out much? That's why.'

'Frey is after all of us, Jesse,' Lucy sniffed. 'Welcome to the club.'

'That's just it, Lucy. I didn't get a membership,' Jesse yelled. 'But I'm paying dues.'

It wasn't like Jesse to whine about being excluded and Lucy took his complaint with a grain of salt. His tone suggested that he was as worried about her as he was himself. He was being sweet, she thought, in his own difficult, abrasive way.

'There are no secret saint meetings, Jesse. No Martyrs Anonymous,' Lucy barked, showing her frustration. 'You know we haven't even seen each other until tonight. We're figuring it out. All this crazy shit happening to us now that you don't even know about.'

'What? You got special powers or something?'

Lucy was silent. Jesse knew not to press, although by the look on his face, it was killing him not to.

'Yeah, well, eternal glory may be your thing, but it's not mine.'

He snapped a few photos of the crowd on his phone, captioned them and uploaded them to Byte, ignoring Lucy.

'I know I haven't been in touch lately. I've been pretty busy.'

'Yeah, I know. Getting The Word out. But not even a selfie for me to post.'

Lucy laughed. It had become a stock response to interviewers and everyone else who asked what she was up to these days.

'That was the old me, Jesse.' She reached out for a hug.

Jesse embraced her and rolled his eyes.

'I agreed to do that Fourth Wall show,' Lucy confided. 'They've been after me for a while now.'

'I begged you to do that show years ago,' Jesse sniffed. 'Why would you do it now?'

'The time is right,' Lucy said. 'I'm sorry I didn't let you know.'

'Yeah, well, that dude's a ratings-whore and a fraud about to enter contract negotiations with his network. He just wants to embarrass you, Lucy, not help you spread your message, or whatever you're spreading . . .'

'I don't expect you to understand.'

'What I understand is that the more you are out there, the greater the danger.'

Lucy could see Jesse getting red-faced even in the darkness. She could tell he was more than worried; he was scared. She took his hand.

'Listen, I have my doubts about whether I'm doing the right

thing. Every day,' Lucy attempted to explain. 'But it's about more than what I think. About what's rational. It's not about me anymore. It's bigger. And that I am sure of.'

'Not about you?' Jesse snarked, 'That's something I never thought I'd live long enough to hear.'

'Or something I thought I'd live long enough to say,' she laughed.

'If you keep making yourself so vulnerable to Frey and those animals he controls, you won't live much longer, Lucy,' Jesse countered, gesturing at the sold out crowd.

'It didn't keep you away,' Lucy said appreciatively, finally understanding that Jesse had risked his own safety to keep on eye on them.

She reached out for a hug.

'You might as well just copy him in on your schedule.'

She held him tight as he struggled to break free. 'It's what I have to do. What we each need to do.'

Their discussion was beginning to attract attention. A few stragglers saw them and wandered over, like hungry zombies catching the scent of living flesh.

'You're one of them,' a girl shrieked, waving her friends over.

'Him, too,' her guy friend noted, pointing at Jesse.

'See what I mean,' he said. 'Shrapnel.'

'There's something really important I need to tell you before the show starts. Let's go where we can talk.'

'More important than your big TV gig?' Jesse said.

Lucy took Jesse by the arm and dragged him out of the club through an exit on the first balcony floor and on to a small fire escape. She jammed her foot between the door and the jamb, keeping the portal open.

'About the size of a confessional,' she said.

'Or a witness stand,' he countered.

She looked around and noticed a small group gathered outside the stage door beneath them. Lucy moved even closer and whispered quietly into his ear. Everything she knew, everything she suspected. About Sebastian's heart.

'What?' Jesse recoiled and stepped as far away as he could on the tiny landing and grip the railing tightly. 'Somebody is totally screwing with your head.'

Lucy calmly sat down on the cold metal step. 'I think it might be true, Jesse.'

'Why? Why would anyone want to do that?' Jesse shot back sceptically. 'Kill you, kill all of us, I get. But Sebastian is already dead. What would be the point?'

'Frey is a soul crusher. He wants to hurt us. Demoralize us,' Lucy said. 'And everyone who believes in us. He needs to discredit us before he tries to kill us. Or we become even more powerful.'

Everyone who believes in us. It took Jesse a second to process what she was saying.

'C'mon, Lucy,' Jesse said, shaking his head. 'This is insane

diva stuff, even for you. Total psychodrama.'

'Don't you see? The threat from Frey is more than just the power he has over some strung-out street punks to attack us,' Lucy explained.

Jesse threw his hands up. 'If you ask me, it seems like you are doing everything you can to die trying. Don't drag me into this again, Lucy.'

'You're already in it,' Lucy replied. 'With Sebastian. With us.'

'A bunch of lunatics,' Jesse mumbled bitterly.

'Now you sound just like Frey,' Lucy railed.

Jesse's face flushed noticeably even in the darkened back alley. She could see he was still smarting from everything that had happened.

'Don't. You. Dare.' Jesse hissed. 'I could have left with him. Avoided all the bullshit.'

'You know what happened,' Lucy insisted, her voice rising. 'You were there, Jesse.'

Jesse continued to struggle, mostly with himself. 'Don't tell me what to believe!'

'You don't need to believe, you saw.'

'Honestly, Lucy,' Jesse sighed, rubbing at his eyes. 'I don't know what I saw anymore.'

The look of rejection in Lucy's eyes was so powerful that he couldn't look at her. He dropped his head in shame.

Lucy relented. 'Then just do me a favour, OK? Find out

what you can. Maybe I am crazy, but I need to know. We need to know. You owe me at least that much.'

'I don't owe you a thing, LuLu. I made you,' Jesse stressed like a media Dr Frankenstein, his voice dripping with contempt. 'I was arrested, thrown in prison, dragged through the mud by prosecutors and the police, humiliated, discredited, my reputation destroyed . . .'

'What reputation?' Lucy scoffed. 'You owe me your life, Jesse. Don't forget that.'

Jesse looked down, still avoiding her eyes. He saw the small group that had been standing there disperse and depart with hugs and kisses, except for one, not part of the group, leaning against a dumpster. The bushy hair and leather jacket seemed familiar, even in the shadowed alleyway. The guy looked up at the fire escape through the darkness, his sharp features silhouetted by the security light above the backstage door, and exhaled what remained of the cigarette smoke in his lungs. Their eyes met for the briefest moment and he walked away, the sound of boot heels clicking gently along the cobblestones and concrete and into the silent night. Jesse was confused, uncertain of what he'd just seen. But moved, deep inside.

'Did you see that?' he said quietly, rubbing at his eyes.

'See what?' Lucy asked.

'Nothing,' he answered.

'I think it's more than coincidence that we're all here tonight, together for the first time in months,' Lucy argued. 'I feel like

we were led here for a reason, you know?'

Jesse was coming around. 'Maybe,' he said.

Lucy's appeal to him was becoming even more urgent. She threw herself on his mercy. Determined but egoless. 'I need your help, Jesse.'

'That's a first,' he said, his resistance waning. 'What do you want me to do?'

'You still in touch with those dirt bags at the Medical Examiner's office who slipped you those celebrity morgue photos for Byte?'

'You mean sources?'

'Whatever makes you feel better,' she conceded. 'We need to find out what happened to Sebastian. Who took his heart. And find it!'

'How the hell do you know someone really took his heart?'

'One of the people that follow me around, a priest, told me.'

'You're going to risk your life on the say-so of one of those psychos?' Jesse questioned. 'How do you know he wasn't just some guy in a priest costume?'

'It's more than that, Jesse. I see things. In visions. In dreams. The heart is key.'

'If you're trying to convince me, you're not doing yourself any favours talking like that.'

Lucy looked him square in the eye. 'I know.'

This time it was Jesse who took a seat on the cold metal

step, running best- and worst-case scenarios through his head, none of them very appealing.

'OK, let's say I believe you. That I'm willing to make a leap of faith,' Jesse posited reluctantly, still unsettled by the figure in the alleyway. 'There has got to be more to it, a larger purpose for Frey then just to embarrass you or piss you off or whatever.'

'Like?'

'What am I, a prophet now?' Jesse retorted.

'Hardly,' Lucy said with a smile.

'Why not just let it go?' Jesse asked one last time, exasperated. 'Things are going well for you and for Agnes and Cecilia. You're out there talking yourself up. Look at that crowd in there. Can't you pitch a reality show or design a fragrance or something? Do you need to revisit all that pain and suffering Sebastian brought?'

'You're missing the whole point, Jesse,' Lucy replied. 'We're doing well because of Sebastian.'

'You're still alive, so far. Are you sure you want to rattle the doctor's cage?'

'There is much more to life than living Jesse,' she said. 'Whatever the endgame to all this is, the reason for everything that's happened, this is the beginning of it.'

'So, that's the game?' he asked. 'Capture the heart?'

'It's not a game, Jesse,' Lucy said. 'It's a war.'

8
Music for the Masses

Cecilia burst onstage like an explosion. She strummed her guitar with an exaggerated windmill motion, the milagros on her boots spitting back beaming rays of light into the crowd.

'She's starting. I'm outta here,' Jesse said, heading for the exit. 'I'll do what I can.'

Lucy blew him a kiss while mouthing a sickly-sweet 'Thank you' and then returned her attention to the show.

Lucy pushed her way back beside Agnes.

'Look at her,' Agnes said, amazed.

'Yeah, but don't forget to look around you, too,' Lucy said, ever cautious.

'Is he in?' Agnes said, looking back at Jesse.

'Whether he likes it or not,' Lucy said.

Cecilia finished her guitar intro and took to the mike through walls of noise and feedback. Shining in the spotlight. She started wailing sorrowfully, as if she were mourning.

Sacrilege by the Yeah, Yeah, Yeahs, one of her anthems, channelled through her fingertips to her guitar and from her throat into the microphone.

'Fallen for a guy,

Fell down from the sky.'

A bittersweet song that spoke to her, to her followers, and one that summoned him. She harkened back to the time she played for him at the church, and he was all she saw in the audience. He watched her every move and hung on her every word, just like he was then. She felt it. And she made the crowd feel it, too. They were transfixed. Everyone but Lucy. Her eyes were on the lighting tech at the side of the stage, loitering behind the curtain. Agnes noticed Lucy getting wobbly, reaching for the edge of the bar to keep herself up.

'You OK?' Agnes asked.

Lucy heard her but couldn't respond. She was trapped in her own thoughts, which seemed to be occurring five minutes into the future. Lucy could actually see his intentions, visualize his actions in advance. In a blink, she saw the lighting rig collapse, the overhead speakers tumble down, the chaos of the crowd running for the exits. She saw flashes of Cecilia lying motionless on the stage in a pool of her own blood.

The tech caught her looking at him and winked, as he climbed the narrow metal ladder bolted to the wall and up to the rig.

Lucy tried to get a bouncer's attention, frantically pointing toward the stage then the lighting rigs, but it was too loud and the floor too jammed. It was like trying to explain a complicated movie that she'd seen but the other person hadn't. It was all getting lost in translation and crowd noise.

Neither was she able to get Cecilia's attention from the back of the room.

Agnes tried to calm her down, taking Lucy's hands in hers, but Lucy pulled away.

'Where are you going?' Agnes shouted.

'Stay here!'

Lucy made a mad dash for the soundboard at the back of the venue. She could see the lighting rig begin to sway, almost in time with the audience and the music. The club staffer was riding it, rocking it gently back and forth like a child on a swing, in an effort to loosen it from the ceiling. It was almost unnoticeable from the floor unless you knew what you were looking for. And Lucy did.

Onstage, Cecilia was lost in the moment, in her song, in Sebastian. Her eyes shut tight. Like the rest of the audience, oblivious to the tumult occurring in the back of the room. No way for Lucy to warn her. Agnes looked where Lucy was pointing and saw the guy atop the steel lattice.

Lucy hopped into the sound booth, pushed the engineer over and began to pull the leads free from the board, cutting the sound and lights in the room completely.

'What the . . .' Cecilia shouted, opening her eyes.

Her microphone was dead and so were the monitors behind her. She couldn't see a thing. The club security assigned to protect Lucy now rushed toward the sound booth to restrain her, angrily clearing a path through the confused fans.

In the brief moment before the boos and complaints from the crowd could fill the room, Agnes cried out her warning. 'Cecilia, up there.'

Cecilia recognized the voice as Agnes's and reached for her crew flashlight, shining it upward. She saw the guy working feverishly at loosening the rig from the ceiling. CeCe bent down and pulled three milagros from her boot and tossed them at him, one by one, like Ninja fighting stars. He was struck on the arm, neck and back, distracted from his task but not badly hurt.

He pulled the milagros from his body and flung them back at her, straight for her heart. The gold medals hit her wrought iron corset and bounced off with a harmless ping, but the assailant had not only thrown the milagros with little effect, he'd thrown himself off balance. The engineer got to his feet and began to insert cables back into the inputs, restoring some of the sound and lights in the house, disorienting the phony lighting tech. He teetered and fell as the crowd gasped in horror.

Cecilia stepped back as he crashed down to the stage along with the rig. Just then, the sound and lights returned but the crowd was literally in the dark about the confrontation that had just taken place.

'Is he dead?' a fan in the front row called out to CeCe.

'No,' she replied indifferently.

'Are you OK?' another shouted.

'Yes,' she replied.

'Thank God,' a voice yelled out from the crowd.

'Thank Lucy,' CeCe mumbled.

Cecilia and the crowd looked on as security quickly carried him off on a gurney and wheeled him backstage to wait for an ambulance. Agnes rushed to Lucy's side.

'She was just trying to stop that guy from falling into the crowd,' Agnes shouted at the bouncers. 'Let her go.'

'Hey,' Cecilia screamed through her mike, finally able to see the commotion at the back. 'She saved my life.'

The crowd broke into applause. A rolling wave of approval cascaded through the venue along with chants of 'Let her go' that quickly became deafening.

The head of security nodded and his men released Lucy. Agnes took her by the arm.

'Let's get out of here,' Agnes said.

Lucy smiled at Cecilia and CeCe blew a kiss back to her.

The lights went down.

The smoke machine powered up, spewing atmosphere

all over the stage.

Cecilia reached down for one of the milagros that had failed to kill her. Using it as a pick, she looked up and out into the crowd, thinking about what had just happened, about what Lucy had told her, about what was to come.

In the crowd, she saw the anxious faces of her apostles and recognized a silhouette in the smoky haze, a backlit figure glowing subtly in the artificial fog. Her heart and soul were filled with joy. He was there. At her show. Just like she'd dreamed since the moment they met.

She brushed the strings of her guitar gently with the milagro and fingered the fret board tenderly. Determined to play the show of her life. She restarted the concert, her career and her mission with a single, simple announcement to the expectant audience that burst through the speakers with commanding power.

'Intermission,' she shouted, 'is over.'

9

Punch Drunk

Lucy and Agnes stood at the back door of the club, not anxious to face the pack of photographers and bloggers waiting for them on the other side. News of the melee was already spreading through the blogosphere.

'Do you want one of us to walk you out?' a bouncer asked.

'No, we're fine,' Agnes answered.

'Who the hell was that lighting guy?' Lucy asked.

'He's not on staff. Just some dude we hired from the halfway house down the street for the night. Trying to be supportive. You know. Now he'll probably sue our asses.'

Lucy and Agnes shrugged, keeping their suspicions about the guy's deadly intentions to themselves as he trudged off.

'I'm sorry,' Lucy said.

'Don't be,' Agnes comforted, taking her hand.

'I see things that are going to happen. I can't help it.'

'Good thing for Cecilia, right?'

'Doesn't that freak you out?'

'Sebastian said we would discover things like that when we needed them, remember?' Agnes said calmly, finding the silver lining in Lucy's predicament.

Agnes was being more than understanding. She was commiserating.

'You too?' Lucy asked.

'Yeah,' Agnes said. 'Sometimes I feel like there's two of me. Literally in two places at once. Or none of me. Like I'm fading away or splitting apart. I can't control it.'

'Yet,' Lucy said. 'Get on it. That talent might come in handy.'

'That was the first attack on any of us,' Agnes observed. 'Why do you think it would be in such a public place?'

'I don't know,' Lucy said. 'It was pretty ballsy trying to attack her in a crowded room like that. Makes me wonder if killing her was the point.'

'What do you mean?'

'Sebastian said we'd be hunted, right?'

'I'm not getting you.'

'I mean that if Frey really wanted us dead, he'd be making more of an effort,' Lucy said.

'You think that stage diver was all about stopping the show?'

'Maybe,' Lucy said. 'Frey's as afraid of the message as he is of us.'

'So why would he want to keep us alive?'

'The heart is the key. I feel it.'

The sounds from the stage began to overwhelm their conversation.

'Ready?' Agnes asked.

'Ready.'

Agnes pulled her hood over her head and Lucy shielded her eyes with a new pair of oversized shades. They walked quickly through the rear exit and into the whirlwind of media types shooting pictures and video, and shouting questions. The doorman had cleared a path to Lucy's waiting car and driver.

'Jump in, I'll take you home.'

'No, thanks. I want to walk.'

'I don't think that's such a good idea,' Lucy said. 'Get in.'

'I'm OK,' Agnes said. 'Really.'

'Careful, OK?'

Agnes waved goodbye and slipped away. Her mind was spinning every which way. She needed some alone time, some peace.

She tried desperately to make sense of what Lucy had told them and what had happened at the show – Cecilia's life at stake, holding on to her sacred heart chaplet and her black and gold mourning ring. Trying to figure it all out. Her life. His heart.

'I can't do this,' she said to herself, her eyes tearing up.

A light rain began to fall as she turned the corner on Smith Street toward Park Slope. The rain felt good on Agnes's face. It wasn't epic, like the weather or its aftermath the previous November, but it reminded her of Sebastian nonetheless. Considering what she just learned, and what had just happened, it was a mixed blessing.

Agnes headed straight to Precious Blood, or what remained of it, for the first time since it all went down. She hoped she would see him there, feel him. She needed him now more than ever. Once she arrived, she saw that the scaffolding and police barricades were long gone, leaving the entire edifice in a sort of spotlighted limbo; it's only purpose now as a stop for morbidly curious tourists or field trip destination for parochial schools. She half expected to find a gift shop erected near the staircase.

Agnes stood across the street staring at the charred walls and shattered windows, away from the prying eyes of the few religious fanatics and die-hard atheists, who regularly congregated and chose sides, pontificating or speculating about what had actually happened there. For some it was a shrine. For others, a monstrosity. For her, it was both a crime scene and the place where she fell in love.

Nevertheless, she had to come, especially now. The only people she could trust, she had met there. It was where their memories stained her forever, where they lived – Cecilia, Lucy and Sebastian. Trust wasn't something she could do easily

anymore. Not in the world she lived in now. It was getting smaller. Closing in on her and she found it hard to breathe. The end, her end, could come at any time.

She heard someone approaching from behind – a man, she figured from the heaviness of his step. He was close enough for Agnes to hear the rain bouncing off him to the sidewalk. She steeled herself, clenching her house keys between her fingers like spikes, just in case, and continued to stare ahead at the church.

'Excuse me, Miss. Aren't you, aren't you . . . one of them?'

Agnes's first reaction was to deny it. To walk away from it. All of it. Go back to her life the way it was. With the exception of school and her neighbourhood, she was the least high profile of the three girls and was more than happy to leave the notoriety to Lucy and Cecilia. It had been a manageable level of attention and harassment, a neighbourhood and school thing, just enough to get her trolled in the high school hallways and online or to get her mother a free cup of coffee or loaf of bread at the local bodega in exchange for a kind word. Just in case it was all true. Ass coverers or believers, the coffee tasted the same.

'No,' she whispered firmly. 'I'm not.'

'But I've seen you with the others.'

'It wasn't me,' she said again, less convincingly.

'C'mon, it is.'

Agnes was more irritated than threatened, hoping to have

some time for reflection. To be with Sebastian again, if only in her mind. She relaxed her hand and put her house keys in her pocket.

'I'm sorry I just want to be alone.'

'I didn't mean to bother you. I must have been mistaken.'

The disappointment in his tone struck her. She felt the distance between them grow as he turned to leave.

Agnes wanted to deny it a final time as he left, scream it out to him, but her instincts took over. She could not deny it. Not here. She removed the cowl from her head and as she did, layers and layers of gorgeous auburn ringlets cascaded down around her pale face, falling to her waist.

'Please. Don't go,' she insisted. 'I'm Agnes.'

He turned back to her and approached slowly.

'All those beautiful things destroyed,' Agnes mused, as if she were talking to herself. 'Never to be replaced.'

'There is no need to replace them. They are here now, in you,' the stranger answered, laying a hand on Agnes's shoulder. 'Alive.'

'Thanks but I'm afraid that brings little comfort to me,' Agnes sighed. 'The world is so cruel. I hate it. And I don't know where to look or what to do.'

She wiped at tears beginning to mix with the raindrops. She was becoming emotional, but instead of her heart beating wildly, it was slowed by the stranger's touch. Calmed.

'Agnes, why are you crying?'

She felt herself begin to open up to the stranger in a way she wouldn't have imagined a few minutes before. As if she were not actually speaking to another person, but thinking out loud, confessing thoughts so personal she was glad not to be facing the stranger.

'So many reasons.'

'Tell me.'

'For a dying old woman I visited today. For a boy I loved and lost there,' Agnes cried, pointing weakly at Precious Blood. 'For myself, I'm ashamed to say.'

'There is no shame in compassion, in sympathy, in love,' came the reply. 'To the woman you gave comfort. The kind of comfort one receives only from true faith. To the boy you gave love. The kind of love that comes only from a pure heart. '

'And what about me? What did I give to myself?'

'Why did you come here?'

'I wanted to be near him.'

The stranger whispered.

'He isn't there.'

The stranger moved in closer behind her, almost touching. Agnes didn't move. He brought his hand to her scarred wrists and turned them gently upward into the falling rain. His touch was reassuring. Gentle. Nearly tranquilizing. She suddenly felt displaced. There, but not. Both unable and unwilling to resist. The kind of feeling she'd told Lucy about. A feeling she'd only experienced in her most private moments. She felt the touch,

the presence, warm and alive, but saw no breath blowing past her in the cold night.

'Who are you?'

'Did you know that the boy, Jude, is named for the patron saint of desperate causes?'

'How do you know him?'

He spoke in a soft but commanding voice, one suddenly familiar.

'*Quid quæritis viventem cum mortuis?*'

'Why do you seek the living among the dead?' Agnes translated out loud. She gasped, raised her head and turned. Her heart filled. She turned to face him, reach for him, but he was gone. Agnes fell to her knees, weeping.

'Sebastian.'

'Need an escort?' a burly voice asked through the thick of the darkness.

'Never did,' Cecilia said, waving the security guard off. 'I can take care of myself.'

'Yeah, I just saw that,' he replied. 'At the show.'

'Keep the faith,' she said, walking away.

'Watch your sweet brave ass, OK?' he called back.

'You can watch it for me,' she yelled back, wiggling as she split.

He kept an eye on her until she'd left the alley and turned on to heavily warehoused and dilapidated Van Brunt Street. It

wasn't a good idea for her or anyone to walk alone at night in the midst of this desolation, but she was preoccupied. Lucy's news weighed heavily on her, and the fact that someone had already tried to kill her once that night seemed to give her a little breathing room in terms of mortality.

Everything loomed over her like the massive cranes towering over the terminals in the distance. There they were, scraping the sky, loading and unloading container after container, even in the dead of night. No respite from the heavy lifting, or the constant threat of a crushing blow. Cecilia could relate.

She hadn't noticed it until just that second but her hands were hurting. From the gig, she figured, but she remained on guard nonetheless.

'CeCe,' a weary voice called out.

She kept walking. Whether it was an apostle or an assassin, she was prepared.

'CeCe,' he called again, this time more forcefully.

She stopped and turned in recognition and amazement. 'Bill?'

The weary voice was familiar, but not the man. 'You were great.'

'What?' she asked, thoroughly confused and more than a little freaked out.

'Your show. You were great.'

'You were there? You?'

He approached slowly, eyes cast downward. 'I wouldn't have missed it.'

Cecilia was almost speechless.

'I almost died,' she said. 'Your corset, the wrought iron relic you gave me. It saved me. You saved me.'

'I can't save anyone, CeCe, not even myself. I'm a junkie. A liar.'

As he approached, the light from the streetlamp above revealed Bill – an older guy, sixty-ish, close-cropped grey hair wrinkled hands but manicured nails, his two-piece suit pressed neatly, creases in the slacks and a noticeable glint beaming from a pair of recently polished lace-up shoes. A sharp-dressed man; an executive out for a nightcap, a Park Avenue lawyer or a Wall Street broker, anyone might have thought.

Cecilia brought her bloody hand to her lips to stifle a gentle laugh. 'I'm sorry,' she said, 'I don't think I've ever seen you upright before.'

He raised his head and smiled. Their eyes met. His were clear, hers turning red with emotion, as if she'd just emptied a bottle.

'You're so dressed up,' she said.

'It's my girl's big night,' he said. 'You bet your ass I'm dressed up.'

Cecilia took in the pride radiating from his eyes.

'I'm totally dry now. Two months,' he said. 'Thanks to you.'

Cecilia let the tear in her eye fall. Black mascara streaked

her porcelain cheek like a dusty raindrop down a windshield.

'That's not exactly a deathbed conversion, Bill,' Cecilia observed. 'I haven't seen you in three months.'

'Well, it wasn't my deathbed that did the trick, it was yours.'

'But it still took you a month.'

'I never said it was easy. None of it,' he said.

She closed the distance between them. They hugged, holding each other tightly. He was still thin, still frail. She could feel his bones through the designer threads that hung on him, the slow beat of his heart and the wet, rumbling breaths of a lifelong smoker. All was well on the surface, she thought, but there was no hiding the damage that had been done inside. She stepped back after a long while, still holding his hands. He squeezed hers gently; with what she figured was all the strength in his body.

'Where are you living? What are you doing?'

'Well, I gave up my penthouse,' Bill joked. 'Traded it in for a cot in the shelter.'

'Still writing?'

'Not so much,' he replied. 'Doing a lot more talking these days. To kids mainly. Runaways. Addicts. Hopeless cases. Aspiring writers. Thinkers. You know, like me. Small bites. One day at a time. One person at a time.'

'One at time,' CeCe repeated thoughtfully.

'I feel like I'm finally earning my keep. Making up for wasted time.'

'They'd be wise to listen. About how to be real. To be true. Like I did.'

The compliment brought a humble smile to Bill's face.

'On the contrary, lady.'

Cecilia didn't know what to say. It was all too much. Being on stage, seeing Bill again. Like old times, only it wasn't. Not in the least. Those days of looking up at the stars and wondering what they'd turn out to be were over. The innocent fantasies, dreaming, delusions of grandeur. Over.

The man took a long, deep, crackling breath.

'I'm so sorry, CeCe,' he confessed, shaking. 'It was the addiction. I had no idea Ricky meant to hurt . . .'

She cut him off, reaching for his hand. 'All's well that end's well, right?'

As she took her hand from him she noticed the blood from her palm had been transferred to his. She reached back to wipe them.

'Oh, Bill, I don't want to stain your suit.'

'Not stained,' he said, wiping his hand across his breast pocket. 'Cleansed.'

Cecilia held both her palms up to him, displaying the seeping wounds.

'It's so scary,' she admitted, breaking down. 'I'm just oozing out drop by drop.'

He held her under the smog and stars on the abandoned Brooklyn Street.

'You mean something,' he said. 'That's what's scary.'

Cecilia held him back. Tight.

'Whatever is happening to you means something,' he said. 'It's what we all want. Need.'

His words connected with her. Right down to her soul.

'It definitely means something to me,' she said.

'Can you ever forgive me?' he asked.

'Ego te absolvo,' Cecilia said, raising her hand up over her head in a gesture of mock absolution. 'You genius son of a bitch.'

'I believe in you, Lady of Sorrow,' he whispered in her ear. 'Sing your song for the lonely girls, so everyone can hear it. Until you can't sing no more. And then, keep singing.'

Cecilia felt a sharp pain in her hands, followed by a sharp pain in her head. She fell backwards, almost losing consciousness. Cold-cocked. As she looked up, dizzy and finding it hard to focus, she saw Bill struggling to catch his breath. A black-sleeved arm tightening a chokehold around his slender throat. The assailant was big, ski-masked. Typical mugger dirt bag on the prowl for a well-to-do older gentleman and his young girlfriend, she figured. Give him what he wants and he'll go away.

'Where is it?' the attacker asked, addressing not Bill, but her.

'I don't know what you're talking about,' she responded groggily, struggling to get to her feet.

'Tell me now, or he's a dead man.'

Bill's eyes were bulging and his facing turning as white as his hair, but he hadn't lost his fight.

'Fuck you,' Bill growled, biting at the forearm that immobilized him, to little effect. 'Don't tell him shit, CeCe.'

Cecilia watched him struggle, unable to help him, the street-lamp above throwing a fuzzy halo over his head.

'Last chance. Where is it?'

'Where is what?' she screamed.

The assassin frowned sympathetically, as if she'd taken too much time to guess the final Jeopardy question.

'Aaaaaaaaaah,' he wailed, crudely imitating a buzzer. 'Time's up.'

'Bill! No!' As her anguished screech faded off into the dark night, a single thrust of a sharp blade through flesh and bone broke the silence. Bill crumpled and fell toward her, blood pouring out his mouth and down the front of his starched white shirt. Her instinct was to chase the murderous bastard but she knew she needed to stay. In the moment it took to get to Bill's side, the vicious beast who'd done it was already gone.

'I'm ready,' Bill whispered to her with his last breath, holding on to the forgiveness she just granted him.

She held him, rocking him back and forth. 'I'm sorry, Bill. I'm so sorry.'

'Thank you,' he said. 'For loving such an unlovable man.'

His voice trailed off and his eyes became fixed on hers and then to the sky.

'No!' Cecilia screamed over his lifeless body.

A few heads popped warily out of loft windows to spy the commotion and in seconds the air was filled with the sounds of sirens. She lingered over the old man, kneeling beside him, crying, her blood-soaked palms turned upward, resting on her thighs.

'What happened?' a passerby said, waving at the squad cars fast approaching.

'He's gone.' Cecilia wailed. Still holding him tight. The blood from her hands mixing with the blood draining from his neck.

'Do you know who did it?'

'I do,' Cecilia whispered.

Agnes entered the front door and retreated quietly to her bedroom, still reeling from her night.

'Agnes?' Martha shouted sharply.

'Night, Mother,' she called back, confirming that it wasn't some random intruder traipsing across the living room.

'Morning, you mean,' came the grumpy and disapproving reply.

She closed her bedroom door without further explanation. She expected a follow-up knock but it never came. The fact that she was home seemed sufficient for Martha on this night.

Agnes didn't want to talk anyway. After all, what could she say about where she'd been and what she'd been doing?

Oh, Mom, I was just out helping a terminally ill woman die tonight and then I went to Cecilia's show and she almost got killed . . . Oh and then I ran into my dead boyfriend. Good night. Love you.

Agnes stripped off her clothes and put on a cream robe with a delicate grey feather print. She grabbed the tablet from her desk and sat down on the floor in a corner of the room, her back to the wall. This way she could be sure no one could see her through the curtained windows, a sign of both increasing paranoia and heightened caution. However, the sensation she was feeling most acutely now was curiosity. Curiosity about the boy, Jude.

Agnes's fingertips swiped and tapped at the glass screen as she filled the search box with the words 'Saint Jude'. Results for hospitals, charitable organizations and churches filled the page, but it was the biography that she was most interested in.

'One of the twelve apostles . . . farmer by trade . . . preached the gospel throughout the Middle East . . . martyred in 65 A.D.

'Patron saint of lost causes and desperate cases,' she read aloud, just as Sebastian had said.

Lost causes. Desperate cases.

Which was she? Were they? Was the situation? The heart? A desperate case? A lost cause? Maybe both and all of the above. She wondered how Lucy and Cecilia were coping with what went down. Her frustration grew deeper the more she thought about it. Maybe the Precious Blood thing was some kind of cruel joke Sebastian had played on them. Inviting them to attend his suicide party. Had he cast her as the virgin sister-wife? Was there a message in there for them? For her?

She continued to read aloud. 'Jude Thaddeus is the Miraculous Saint.' That was it, she thought. Jude gave her the chaplet, which led her to Sebastian, to love, and tonight, to the dying woman. To her purpose. He had interceded in her life in a miraculous way. Maybe he was the one that could lead her to Sebastian's heart again. 'And a little child shall lead them,' Agnes murmured softly.

Lucy's Vision

'You can come in.'

Lucy entered. The room was white, misted over and smelled of ether. She was enveloped, her vision obscured, eyes burning. She tried to follow the voice calling out to her. 'Where?'

'This way.'

'I'm coming.'

She could barely see.

Lucy moved forward, tentatively at first, her hand thrust out defensively in front of her, trying to sweep away the dense vapour. Each time she took a step she found her way blocked, stopped in her tracks, dead-ended. Exasperated, she turned around and ran, smashing her head into yet another wall.

She rubbed at her forehead and wiped at her eyes, tearing from fog and frustration, trying to clear them. Looking down, she noticed that her chaplet was missing.

'Don't touch your eyes.'

'Why?'

'This room is sterile. Pure.'

'I'm sorry,' Lucy stammered. 'I'm having trouble seeing where I'm supposed to be going.'

'You are getting closer.'

The fog thinned slightly. She spied a sign on a door that read MORBID ANATOMY. Lucy followed the voice through the haze and through the door to a table with a water basin, a towel and a pair of latex gloves.

She washed each of her hands and dried them quickly.

'Put them on.'

Lucy complied, slipping her hands inside one and then the other, stretching each over her fingers and rolling it down to her wrists.

Jars, boxes and labelled display cases lined the walls.

Saint Philomena, Virgin and Martyr – ex ossibus*

Saint Barbara of Nicomedia, Virgin and Martyr – ex ulna brachi deptri**

Saint Clare of Montefalco – ex velo***

Saint Teresa of Avila – ex veste****

And on and on. Relics. Pieces of wood, cloth, garments, nails, dust, dried flesh, body parts and other oddities presented as if in some maudlin museum. Lucy moved past each, eyeing them as best

*   bone
**   muscle
***   veil
**** vestment

she could with her clouded vision until she came upon the last four displays and stopped. Four empty antique cylinders crafted from bent glass labelled: Cecilia. Agnes. Lucy. Sebastian.

'Follow me,' she was ordered.

She continued forward, tentatively, arriving at a set of double doors. Lucy pushed one side and entered. The mist receded as she entered, revealing the sterile environs of an operating theatre. A privacy curtain stood in the centre of the room. The overhead light was blinding. She could barely make out the faces of the photographers positioned behind the glass in the observation gallery above her.

Lucy shielded her eyes and dropped her head downward, reflexively checking her outfit. She was dressed in hospital scrubs. Cameras flashed as she approached the curtain.

'Lucy! Here!' they shouted, their muted voices barely reaching her through the glass.

'Is there something wrong with me?' Lucy asked, raising her head. 'Am I sick?'

She saw a motionless, toe-tagged body lying prostrate on an operating table. The privacy curtain partially blocked her view. She strained to see the face, but couldn't.

'Are they . . .' Her voice trailed off.

'Dead?' the paparazzi yelled down to her in the operating theatre.

Lucy approached her patient.

The closer she got the better she could see.

A set of crude and primitive surgical instruments was set out on

a steel table. Saws, knives of varying blade lengths, clamps, scoops, ice pick, and spreaders dripped fresh blood. If it wasn't for the medical setting, she might have mistaken them for weapons, or instruments of torture. Behind them was her chaplet and an elaborate headpiece, made of dripping pearls all set in a spider web pattern surrounding bird skulls. It was gorgeous, fit for a queen. Or a saint.

'Put them on, Lucy!' the photographers shouted. 'Pose for us!'

Reluctantly, she reached for the crown and placed it gently on her head. Pearls draped around the sides of her face and under her chin like chainmail, framing it, and the razor sharp beak of the bird skull in the centre sat perfectly over the bridge of her nose. She did likewise with the chaplet, sliding it over her hand and on to her wrist, the gold double eye milagro dangling toward the floor.

Lucy raised her eyes to the gallery and the photographers went wild, screaming her name, cameras buzzing. Flashes sprayed the room like bullets from a firing squad. She stood immobile, braving the pictorial invasion, until their manic thirst was sated and the room fell silent.

A shrill beeping followed, filling the air. Lucy looked at a heart monitor with leads running toward the body behind the privacy screen. It showed a flat line. A chill ran through her, freezing her momentarily in place.

'What am I supposed to do?'

The voice, now clearly emanating from behind the curtain,

responded. 'Seek and you shall find.'

She reached for the curtain and pulled it away revealing the body of the patient. Lucy recoiled, speechless, at the sight of the man; a man she knew, his chest cracked completely open, split at the breastbone, an empty cavity. His body defiled. Heart missing.

'No, it can't be,' she stammered.

He reached for her arm, but only managed to grab her milagro, pulling it from the chaplet.

'Heartless,' he whispered ominously, pointing at the gaping hole in his chest, and dropping her charm into the gaping wound.

'Dr Frey!'

Lucy screamed as the dismembered doctor howled with laughter and cameras flashed from above, waking her.

Her eyes snapped open. She was hyperventilating. She pressed the shift button on her phone, checking the time, still groggy, her consciousness trapped halfway between the operating room and her bedroom. She breathed in and out, hoping to get control of her anxiety and shake off the effects of the awful dream like a bad hangover.

'Lucy,' a familiar voice calmly called out.

It was not Dr Frey's.

She saw a figure, illuminated by the cool blue glow of her touchscreen, dressed in shadows, at the foot of her bed. Familiar, yet not. Lucy kicked off her sheets and propelled herself back against the headboard, shouting.

'Who the hell are you? How did you get in here?'

She fumbled for her phone on the nightstand and raised it, ready

to wing it at the intruder.

He spoke again, his voice coming at her in surround sound, from everywhere, resonating deep within her. 'Lucy.'

'Sebastian?'

She slowly moved the phone toward him, screen side out, shedding more light on him.

He nodded.

'Am I still dreaming?'

'Are you?'

Sebastian walked around to the side of her bed and opened his shirt.

'Don't come any closer,' she demanded. 'How do I know it's really you?'

He stopped. 'Do I need to prove it to you?'

'But you're dead. Ashes!' she screamed at the top of her lungs, pointing at the small silver urn that sat on her nightstand.

'Death is not the end.'

Lucy could barely bring herself to look. He held out his hand, reaching out to her. Lucy took it. He pulled her closer.

'No,' she moaned, pulling back. 'This is not real.'

She reached for the light switch on her lamp and flicked it on. He was still there. Big as life.

'It's no trick, Lucy,' he said.

'You're a zombie or a ghost or something. You must be.'

'No,' he said, reaching out to her again.

Sebastian took Lucy's hand. It was steady, firm. He brought both

their hands to his chest.

'What are you doing?' Lucy shuddered.

'So that you will know.'

One by one, he brought her fingers to the wounds in his chest and stomach. She felt the jagged edge around the fleshy rim of each gunshot. He pushed her finger in deeper. Inside of each bullet hole. The crack of gunfire echoed in her mind and the scream of Cecilia and Agnes as he fell to the marble floor. She smelled smoke and incense, saw the subtle smile of victory cross Frey's face. The reality of him and the reality of his sacrifice gradually taking hold of her.

'I'm so sorry Sebastian. So sorry for doubting you.'

'Seeing,' he said, a note of sadness in his voice, 'is believing.'

Lucy wept bitterly. As if she'd been caught cheating. She threw aside the trappings of comfort dressing her bed, the alpaca throw and Egyptian cotton sheets, and curled up in pain and shame.

'I don't deserve the gift you've given me.'

'You are the gift, Lucy.'

He got into bed with her and held her close, his eyes, and his mouth inches from hers, resting in the comfort only his arms could provide.

'Wasn't there another way?'

'You think there are other ways, but there aren't. What happened had to happen.'

Lucy nodded and wiped at her eyes. She cleared her throat, putting on a braver front for him.

'People say they see you.'

'They see what they want to see,' Sebastian said.

'But I haven't. Why haven't you come to me?'

Sebastian smiled. 'Sometimes the hardest things to see are the ones right in front of us.'

'Please forgive me.'

'You have nothing to be sorry for.'

She brought her head against his chest, pressing her ear against his skin. It was warm but there was no beating heart. Her eyes filled again with tears.

'They stole your heart.'

'No, Lucy. no one can take what has already been given away,' he said. 'My heart belongs to the three of you, only and always.'

'What happens next?' she asked.

'You will do what you need to do,' Sebastian said. 'For the good of all.'

'I don't know what to do,' she said. 'Who to trust.'

'Trust yourself,' he stressed. 'The answers are within you.'

'There were so many things I wanted to say to you and now . . .' Lucy's voice trailed off.

'There will be a time for that, Lucy.'

She closed her eyes tightly, tucked her head under his chin and opened them, noticing his chest was repaired. Unscarred. Whole. He rose.

'Please don't go, Sebastian. Not again.'

'I'm never far away.'

He touched both of her eyes and she closed them reflexively.

When she opened them she was alone in bed, only the scent of him remained. She was rested for the first time in a long time, the doubt that had burdened her replaced with resolve. The alarm sounded and she reached for her smartphone, swiping at the alarm app, to turn it off. The shrill beep reminded her that a day of interviews lay ahead.

10

Prayers for Rain

Cecilia burst through the emergency room doors of Perpetual Help hospital under her own power, not on a stretcher like she had the last time she was here. She wore streaks of Bill's blood on her face, in her matted hair, on her stained clothing. War paint. Even the cops who questioned her at the station couldn't get her to clean it off.

The busy waiting area, full of broken arms, cut fingers, minor burns and anxiety attacks masquerading as heart attacks, went silent as the girl with the blood-soaked tee approached the desk clerk stationed in front of the lifts. He eyed her cautiously, suspiciously. He'd seen her type before, wild-eyed, aggressive, unreasonable, looking for a ride up to the penthouse. Needing one.

'Visitor or patient?' the attendant asked politely, not wanting to rile her.

'Neither,' she replied.

'Is there someone you are here to see?'

'Alan Frey,' CeCe said tersely.

She couldn't bring herself to use his title, to say Doctor.

'Your name?'

'Cecilia Trent.'

The clerk pored over the list.

'He's not expecting anyone. There's not a soul on the list.'

'There wouldn't be a soul on his list, would there?' she said through gritted teeth. 'Call him.'

The attendant reached for the phone somewhat reluctantly and dialled the doctor's extension. It rang and rang. He placed the receiver back in the cradle and shook his head.

'No answer,' he said. 'I'm not sure he's up there. You're welcome to wait in reception if you like.'

'He's up there,' she snarled, walking by his desk.

The clerk reached for her. 'Don't make this difficult.'

'Don't touch me,' she ordered.

The clerk hit the alarm at his desk and three burly security guards promptly arrived armed with Tasers and billy clubs. A crowd was slowly gathering, whispering, oohing and aaahing in recognition, filling in the hallway between the entrance and the reception desk. She felt like a runaway tiger from the circus.

She was cornered, her back to the lift. Ordinarily, she would take comfort at being in a public place, where there were witnesses, but not anymore. Now, anything was possible. Anywhere at anytime by anyone. The show was proof of that. Bill was, too. Her hands were throbbing, trickling blood again. She wiped them on her jeans.

'Step away from the elevators,' one of the security guards demanded, placing a hand on the Taser at his hip.

'Make me,' she said, mocking him like a child.

They took one step forward. She took one back, her spine coming up against the 'up' and 'down' plate on the wall. The guards were closing in when a ringing at the desk broke the anxious silence.

'She says her name's Cecilia something. Looks like she's been making out with a lawnmower.' The clerk waited for a response, seeming surprised by the one he received. 'Are you sure? OK, then.'

He waved off the guards and returned the receiver to the cradle. 'Send her up.'

'You serious?' one asked. 'This girl is dripping blood.'

'Then she'll be right at home up there. Let her go.'

The lift came, but not necessarily to her rescue.

'Up?' the operator asked perfunctorily.

Cecilia backed into the lift slowly, her eyes fixed on the guards and the crowd that continued to linger, waiting for something to happen.

115

'Floor?'

'Top.'

She remained with her back to the wall eyeing the jittery operator warily. He did likewise, more than suspicious of the sweaty, bloodstained girl behind him, pushing the limits of his peripheral vision until he almost literally had eyes in the back of his head.

'Psych,' he said, as the car arrived at its destination.

He pulled the handle. The cage opened and Cecilia was released into an unsettlingly quiet, white-walled reception area. The lift door closed quickly behind her. She saw a desk a few feet ahead, situated behind thick, soundproof glass. It was empty. Unattended. She approached it and through the pane she saw nothing. No papers, no folders, no logs. The desk was totally clear of clutter, spotless. Beyond it all she could see was a dimly lit hallway bordered by closed doors.

'Must have had an influx of OCD patients,' she whispered to herself.

Another buzzer startled her, like a morning alarm clock ringing after an all-nighter. It was followed by the sound of a metal latch clicking open. She walked to the door and pushed it into an even more oppressive silence.

She continued slowly past door after door toward a faint glow coming from an office at the end of the hallway. She stood in front of it, unsure whether to knock or just kick it in.

Before she could decide, a voice called out to her.

'Look who's here; the local stigmatic.' Frey's voice was filled with condescension. 'Won't you come in?'

Cecilia spread her fingers wide and pressed them against the office door, opening it inch by inch until the man in the white overcoat was fully revealed. Her face flushed in anger at the sight of the doctor merrily going about his business.

'You work late,' she said, trying desperately to keep her anger at bay and her emotions in check.

'I find it easier to get things done.'

'That's what I heard.'

'Lovely corset you're wearing, by the way,' he said. 'That thing could stop a bullet.'

'Yeah, it's a real life saver,' she hissed.

Cecilia was seething but did her best to keep her composure, at least until she got the answers she'd come for. She entered the room, closing the door gently behind her. Whatever happened in Frey's office would stay there. In the full glare of his overhead light, Frey could see the drying blood covering the dishevelled girl's clothing.

'Well, it's nice to see you in a more professional setting,' he said, standing. 'What can I do for you?'

His reference to their last moments together at Precious Blood, which also happened to be Sebastian's last moments, did not escape her.

'You can start by telling me why you had my friend murdered tonight.'

'Oh, I'm sorry,' he replied wanly. 'Did somebody Kill Bill?'

'How'd you know it was Bill?'

'Lucky guess.'

The self-satisfied smirk on his spectacled face sent chills through Cecilia. He had the whiff of movie villain about him – effete, erudite, obnoxious, cold, calculating. Perfect casting. All that was missing was the hairless cat.

'I should end this right now.'

'You've killed before,' Frey observed undaunted. 'Why stop with Ricky?'

'Don't tempt me.'

She was certainly angry enough to kill him, and the circumstances seemed favourable. They were alone, at least she thought so. But then, there had been witnesses in the lobby. If Frey turned up dead, they'd come for her. She'd be tried and jailed. Vilified. Nullified. A supposed saint committing the ultimate sin. Even his own death would be a victory for his cause. It was his trump card. And he knew it. It emboldened him.

'I'm honoured to have the starring role in your revenge fantasy, Cecilia,' Frey countered.

'Not revenge. Justice.'

'Vengeance is easier.'

'You would know.'

'What I know is the murderous mind, Cecilia. It's what I do. A person with bad intentions in your present state would come in here guns blazing. Full of righteous anger. Shooting to kill, not shooting the shit, so to speak.'

'A person like me?' she asked. 'You have no idea what I'm like.'

'They say that we stop looking for monsters under the bed when we realize they're inside of us,' he paused. 'Just as we stop looking for evil. There's evil inside all of us, Cecilia. You are no different.'

'The only reason you're still breathing is because you have something I want.'

'And what is that?'

'You know,' Cecilia seethed. 'Where is Sebastian's heart, you sick bastard?'

Frey laughed, pulled open the drawers of his desk, unfastened his lab coat and raised his arms as if preparing for a frisk. 'If it makes you feel any better, look around,' he invited.

Cecilia didn't bother. Frey would never keep the relic where it could be easily found. Instead, she moved closer, around his desk, stopping inches from his face. For the first time, she could sense fear in him. She, on the other hand, wore a blank expression. One probably familiar to a doctor who spent his life dealing with the emotionally disturbed and unpredictable.

'We were defending ourselves, Doctor,' Cecilia said. 'As you well know.'

'Defending yourself or killing to satisfy the delusional demands of your bi-polar boyfriend?'

'We loved him in a way you will never understand. We did what we had to do to protect him and ourselves,' she said, glowering, 'from you.'

'Love? Frey laughed derisively. 'Lucy loves only herself. Agnes is in love with love. And you . . .'

'Tell me, Doctor. What about me?' Cecilia opened the top drawer of his desk and ran her fingers along the blade of a long, sharp letter opener.

'You, Cecilia, are in love with pain, not people. Rejection. It's why everything around you suffers and dies. It's why you are here. You're clinical. Textbook.'

'Sounds like you've spent a lot of time thinking about me,' Cecilia scoffed.

'You're the focus of a lot of attention, for better or worse,' he added. 'For worse in my view.'

'Not very insightful,' she said. 'Since the source of my suffering is you.'

'Maybe, but I've heard even the Vatican has an eye on the three of you.'

'Don't change the subject.'

'They don't take kindly to blasphemers.'

Cecilia laughed. 'What would you know about that?'

'I'm not the one you have to fear.'

'I'm no angel,' Cecilia countered, rotating the letter opener

like a knife in the palm of her hand, as if she might be preparing to plunge it into him. 'But I'm no killer.'

'Let me help you, Cecilia,' Frey asked. 'Rid you of this delusion.'

'Like you wanted to help Sebastian?'

'I was cleared of any wrongdoing,' Frey boasted. 'The authorities chose to believe me instead of you three and that blogger. Have you forgotten?'

'Dead men tell no tales, unfortunately,' Cecilia countered. 'The most powerful witness against you was never heard from. I'm honoured to be his voice.'

Frey slammed his fist down on his desk in an uncharacteristic show of emotion, staring down Cecilia and the blade.

'Look at yourself!' he shouted. 'You come here flashing your teeth, dripping blood. Angry, bitter, full of threats. Making accusations without a shred of evidence. Saint Cecilia! What a joke.'

'Yes, I should have learned to mask my true intentions like you have.'

'I'm afraid you've learned nothing from me, Cecilia.'

Cecilia suddenly brought the point of the letter opener to the base of his throat. He didn't flinch.

'How did you become such a soulless prick?' she spat.

'Google me,' he said snidely.

She pressed the point deeper into his flesh, nearly drawing blood before pulling it away. Frey remained impassive.

'There is one thing I have learned from you.'

'Now you have me curious,' he said. 'What might that be?'

'That evil is real.'

The doctor smirked. 'We are beyond good and evil, Cecilia. We exist in a post moral world now.'

'Thanks to you and those like you,' she said. 'Speak for yourself, not for me.'

'Nobody wants to be judged a sinner or a saint, Cecilia, certainly not by the likes of you.' Frey smirked and raised his hand in a heavy metal, devil-horned salute.

'I don't judge, Doctor,' CeCe replied, glaring at him. 'I embrace differences, not treat them.'

'People say they want to be different, but what they really want is to be the same.'

'So just take two and call me in the morning. The easy road.'

'The easy road,' he agreed.

'Then it all depends on who they choose to be like, doesn't it?'

'There is a lot of Sebastian in you.'

'Not nearly enough,' Cecilia said, turning her back on him to leave.

'Remember, Cecilia,' Frey insisted. 'No good. No evil. Only choices.'

'And consequences,' Cecilia reminded through gritted teeth.

'The three of you can choose to stop this.'

She turned quickly toward him, raised her hand with the letter opener above her head.

He looked her square in the eye. 'I want to see your face when you kill me,' he said.

She brought her hand down without hesitation, hard and swift, and drove the sharp point of the letter opener into his desktop, right between his pointer and middle finger, barely missing both. She left the opener standing upright, like Excalibur in the stone.

'No,' she said. 'We can't stop this.'

'A choice. And a consequence.'

'When I find what I'm looking for, I'll be back for you.'

'I'll be here, Cecilia,' he said. 'For now, I'll let you leave.'

'For now,' she replied, 'I'll let you live.'

The bell rang. The hallways filled. Lockers slammed open and shut. Signs of spring were everywhere – relaxed attitudes and clothes, blaring music, and sexual tension. Agnes took a deep breath, still smarting from the verbal abuse she tried to ignore. She had her auburn hair loosely tied back in a gorgeous fishtail and her lips were stained a cherry red. She wore a vintage rust, purple and teal Indian tunic-style top as a mini dress with rust opaque tights and her worn-out brown biker boots.

'Have you seen that hot new guy?' Hazel asked urgently.

Agnes just smiled and shook her head. 'No, but it sounds like *you* have.'

'He's amazing looking,' she continued. 'Lives in the Heights, I think. On the promenade.'

'Why are you telling me all this?' Agnes asked.

'Um? Because he's . . . hot?' Hazel said. 'Can't I help my best friend?'

'If he's so great, why don't you want him?'

Agnes wasn't interested, but she needed to make the point that she wasn't a charity case. It wasn't like she had trouble getting guys. If she wanted.

'Because I think you might have a lot in common.'

Agnes stared at her sceptically. 'What might that be?'

'I hear he also tried to . . .'

'Tried to what?'

'You know . . . hurt himself,' she said.

'Jesus, Hazel!'

'He just got out of the hospital.'

'Perpetual Help?'

'Yeah,' Hazel replied.

Hazel took Agnes's arm, escorting her down the hall.

'I just thought he could use a friend. Someone who could relate to him.'

'Are you starting a suicide survivors' club or something?' Agnes huffed.

'No. You're both alive. Very alive,' Hazel said, thrusting her hips back and forth.

Agnes rolled her eyes. 'If I run into him, I'll say hello.'

'Well, that won't be long.'

'How do you know?'

'He's in our next class.'

11

Miss Anthrope

Jesse wandered through East Flatbush past several boarded-up houses and shops on his way to the morgue. He approached the non-descript building, a glass-fronted two-storey construction with less character than the average elementary school.

He pulled at a few of the heavy metal doors and found them all locked. Mayfield, the guy he'd come to meet, his 'source' as he'd identified him to Lucy, was nowhere to be found; at least he didn't think so. They'd never met face to face.

One of the doors on the end of a loading bay cracked open and Jesse could see in; there were stainless steel tables stacked up in front of the double doors marked Personnel Only. A young man, not much older than Jesse, stepped out. He was dressed in scrubs, the standard morgue technician gear, but also stained paper booties and a nylon cap that hid a tight Afro. He smelled intensely of cherry. Jesse recognized the odour from biology class. Formaldehyde. He walked straight for Jesse.

'Lookin' for someone, man?'

'How'd you know it was me?' Jesse jibed.

'You stick out like a sore dick around here.'

Jesse wasn't used to criticism from his stoolies, but he knew the guy was right. His whole Smith Street shades-and-soul patch indie vibe didn't cut it in Crown Heights. Besides, Jesse could tell Mayfield was not a man to fuck with.

'What's with the whole Mayfield bit?' Jesse taunted, trying to be hard before he got completely run over. 'Some Seventies' B-movie pimp shit?'

'Way too deep, son,' Mayfield explained. 'Mom told me I was conceived to the SuperFly soundtrack.

'So she named you for Curtis?'

'It fits, too, don't you think? I'm fly, so the ladies tell me.'

'More like fly on the wall if you ask me. '

'That works. I hear shit. I see shit.'

'Don't flies eat shit, too?' Jesse pressed.

'Not this one,' Mayfield replied coolly, patting at a bulge under his armpit that looked a lot like the outline of a glock holster.

'Chill, dude,' Jesse said. 'Is this the morgue?'

'What's it look like?' Mayfield replied. 'They kill 'em, we chill 'em.'

'Can I check it out?'

'Nah,' Mayfield said, pulling a smoke from his front pocket and lighting it. 'We can talk here.'

Jesse gagged a little as Mayfield blew a nicotine cloud in his direction. He looked around and saw no one. The coast was clear, which was either a good thing or potentially a very bad thing. 'You know that kid the police shot a few months ago?'

Mayfield's expression changed. 'You mean that dude that thought he was the messiah or some shit. Jesus Christ Superstar?'

'Yeah,' Jesse said. 'Sebastian.'

'What about him?'

'I heard some things,' Jesse said.

'Like?' Mayfield asked, giving him nothing.

'Like somebody did a little heart surgery on him before he was cremated.'

Mayfield looked at him silently.

'You accusing me of somethin' bitch?' Mayfield said, pushing Jesse backward with two fingers.

'Not at all,' Jesse said, showing some balls and walking back toward him. 'I just want to know if you saw anything.'

'I don't know,' Mayfield said, looking at the ground.

'You don't know?' Jesse said, getting more aggressive. 'A

heart just disappears from a dead body and you don't notice anything? Hear anything about it?'

'All kinds of creepy shit goes on here, man. You remember a few years ago when a bunch of dudes got busted for taking pictures with frozen heads. Shit happens. It's just another day at work around here.'

Jesse remembered the stories. He wondered if the rumours about Sebastian were nothing more than the urban folktales church mice in the neighbourhood told among themselves. Still, there was something in Mayfield's tone that said otherwise. Jesse had learned to read the signs of people hiding something. 'Sorry, dude. I don't believe you.'

'What-cha mean? I ain't ever lied to you.'

'Until now,' Jesse corrected.

Mayfield took another long drag on his cigarette. 'What's that in your pocket?'

'I don't have a weapon,' Jesse answered nervously.

'No doubt,' Mayfield said, puffing his chest. 'But you did bring something for me, right?'

Mayfield snapped the butt of his lit cigarette at Jesse's front pocket. It landed with a dull pop and ricocheted away. Jesse caught his drift. He reached into his pants and pulled out a pocketful of cash. He handed it over.

'Let's talk,' Jesse said, as Mayfield counted the roll and slipped it in his back pocket. 'For real.'

Mayfield lit another cigarette.

'Chain smoking?' Jesse asked, trying to loosen the tech's tongue. 'It'll kill you.'

Mayfield laughed out loud. 'It's living that kills you, man.'

'Give me one of those,' Jesse said, reaching out and grabbing a smoke from his pack.

'When you work around here, you see ain't none of us gettin' out of here alive.' He took a long drag. 'You figure out it's not death that's scary. It's life you gotta be afraid of.'

'What about Sebastian?' Jesse pressed.

'Body parts go missing around here all the time, bruh. Sometimes it's black market shit; sometimes it's voodoo. You know. Everyone's got their thing.'

'You mean their price,' Jesse said.

'Why do you care? Ain't celebrities your beat? This guy was a murderer.'

'No, he wasn't.'

'Listen, I saw the orderly they found at the bottom of The Perpetual Help elevator shaft. He was beat to shit. Looked like a raw piece of meat sent through a grinder. He didn't get that way from a fall. And the dude did escape the mental ward right afterwards, you know what I'm sayin'?'

'Leave the CSI shit to the experts. Tell me what happened here.'

'Like I said, I didn't actually see anything.'

'But?'

'I heard that what you said happened, happened.'

Jesse took a step back, and flicked his cigarette to the side. A nervous sweat broke out above the top of Mayfield's lip, and he removed the nylon cap containing his 'fro. Jesse could see relief and anxiety in the man's eyes. Jesse had just been poking around, not really believing there was anything to Lucy's story. Now it was different.

'His heart was stolen?' Jesse said, cringing. 'Why?'

'Now, how the hell would I know? People do crazy shit like this for fucked up reasons.'

'Why would Frey do it?' Jesse wondered out loud.

'Dr Frey?'

'You know him?'

Mayfield dropped his butt, consumed almost to the menthol filter, to the ground and stamped it out without answering.

'Frey didn't take it.'

'What?'

'He sent a team down from Perpetual Help to supervise the autopsy, but they arrived late and the detectives were already out searching for coffee and doughnuts. The tech in charge refused to let them in. The next day, the heart was gone.'

'Did he ever do something like that before?

'Nah.'

'None of this was ever reported?'

'No shit, Sherlock,' Mayfield cracked. 'When the higher-ups discovered the heart was missing, the orderly was fired. The cops scrubbed the record clean so none of them would get

131

screwed for leaving, and the rest of us were told to shut up or we'd be the next pink slip. I got kids, man.'

'They had to know it would come out somehow.'

'I guess they just figured that if word got out, they'd say it was some kind of crackpot story made up by the superstitious old timers who wanted the church to stay open.'

'Where is it?'

'Nobody knows.'

'Bullshit. You know.'

'Back the hell up man,' Mayfield spat. 'Before you dig a hole you can't climb out of. You ain't the only one looking for it.'

'Don't worry about me. What about the heart?'

'Look, I'm trying to turn my life around. I don't want to get involved.'

Jesse wasn't convinced. The more they talked the better he was able to size up the guy in front of him. Yellow bloodshot eyes, greying skin, scratchy forearms, runny nose. He looked sick, but not with the flu. It was hard for Jesse to tell if he really knew or was just fronting for some quick cash.

'That's not what it looks like to me. I see a dude that needs a fix.'

'I said *trying*,' Mayfield admitted.

'Frey's people asked and you told them, didn't you?'

'I ain't told them shit.'

'I don't believe you.'

'We got a relationship, you and me,' Mayfield joked. 'Don't I always save the best for you.'

'Yeah, we go way back,' Jesse said sceptically. 'Why didn't you tell them?

'They didn't *ask* me right.'

Mayfield rubbed his empty fingers together. Jesse took the rest of the bankroll he'd brought with him and held it up for Mayfield to see.

'But you *do* know?'

Mayfield pulled a pen from behind his ear and tore off a piece of his paper lab coat. He scribbled a name and an address on it and handed it to Jesse.

'This is the last I heard.'

Jesse handed over the cash.

'Now that's the way to show appreciation,' Mayfield said, stuffing the bills in his pocket.

'Just wondering, but the tech in charge that turned Frey's people away during the autopsy, that wouldn't have been you, would it?'

'I'll take the fifth, my man.'

'Yeah, I'll bet. A fifth, a litre, a pint, a flask.

The morgue worker smiled.

'Sorry to see you fall off the wagon,' Jesse said sarcastically. 'Don't spend it all in one vein.'

Mayfield sniffed hard and wiped at his nose.

'You ain't gonna report this are you? Because it won't be

hard for them to figure where this came from. These people, they don't like losing.'

'It's all off the record man,' Jesse mumbled, almost totally lost in thought. 'Background.'

'Listen, I gotta go; a fridge-full today. Good luck.'

'Thanks,' Jesse said. 'I think.'

Jesse watched the tech walk back to the re-enforced door and thought about all the secrets the place held inside, and about the one secret that just managed to escape.

'One last thing,' Mayfield called back to him. 'Just because he didn't take it don't mean he stopped looking for it.'

12

Evangelista

'Security!' a woman yelled at the gatekeeper near the Brooklyn Navy Yard entrance. Suddenly, two guys in uniforms came out to get Lucy and escort her through the small crowd gathered at the gate. They took her to the check in.

'Name?'

'Lucy Ambrose.'

The woman behind the glass scrolled down her list. 'I.D.'

Lucy poked around inside her Chanel bag and pulled out her wallet. She handed over her New York State driver's licence. Her picture looked like a publicity headshot, unlike everyone else's the guard had ever seen.

The woman reviewed it, looked at her and paused for a moment, obviously starstruck. She instructed Lucy to step back and look at the camera. Lucy knew the protocol for entering media outlets. She looked at the camera and gave it her best face. The woman quickly snapped, ran off a low-res sticker with her name and photo and handed it to Lucy to wear. Lucy took the badge, but didn't want to put it on, didn't want to ruin her look, so she just acted like she did. The woman quickly snapped another photo of Lucy.

'You need another photo?' Lucy asked, knowing it wasn't typical.

'For the file,' the woman said, a little tense.

The woman called for a pickup in her walkie-talkie. 'Lucy Ambrose is here.'

Before long, a cart arrived carrying a production assistant wearing the blasé expression and indifferent attitude that all PAs somehow manage to perfect. Lucy was ushered into the dark, cavernous television studio, crowned with massive lighting rigs and public address system suspended above the set.

'Anyone else joining you?'

'Just me.'

The production assistant crossed Lucy's name off a guest list and handed her a laminate to hang around her neck. 'This way.'

The studio was buzzing. A lion's den of activity. Writers

arguing over cue cards, make-up conferencing with wardrobe, directors arguing with lighting, producers interfering with everything. A typical day at work for them. People preoccupied with little things. All of them making a casual but concerted effort to get a look at her. Craning their necks, shooting a quick sideways glance as she walked by. Judging her.

The smirks from the media types inside were in stark contrast to the reverent stares she'd encountered outside, but she was getting used to it. Here she was, on enemy territory yet again. But there was no point in preaching to the converted. No point at all, she figured, and Lucy was determined to practise what she preached.

Be yourself.

Still, there were the haters to contend with. Before they used to hide in the nooks and crannies of the local nightclubs, former classmates waiting for a wardrobe malfunction or any unguarded moment to capitalize on. Friends to her face just waiting for the chance to take her down a notch. Put her in her place. It was the same now, except it was professionals doing the dissing.

Today's booking was a huge get for her. It was her biggest interview to date. And it was different. It was live. And rather than the typical sit-down with the typically hostile talking heads, the 4th Wall was more like a town hall, controlled by the audience, than a chat show. The audience submitted questions and could even place the guest in a challenging

situation. For Lucy, it was a chance to go over the head of the media gatekeepers and reach out to the younger teen demographic of the country's biggest video music channel.

But the biggest difference was that they picked a special interviewer for every guest. You didn't know who'd be interviewing you until you got there. This both terrified and excited her. She hoped it would be Cecilia or Agnes waiting for her in the other chair, but she was pretty sure it would be Jesse. He knew the booker and had been opposed to her doing the show. She thought there might be a bit of reverse psychology going on.

Lucy was shown to the green room, a pseudo-comfortable area decorated to look like some idyllic nineteen-sixties' sitcom living room. She wore a flesh-coloured trousersuit with garnet bead embellishment on the shoulders that dripped down on to the front, sleeves and back in the shape of droplets and shades of blood. Gorgeous rhinestone haute couture faux gore. Her eye make-up was charred black and her lips were painted a matt flesh.

She took some of the colourful gumballs out of an apothecary glass urn and threw them in her mouth, admiring the Saint Lucy statue they had painted over in a superwoman motif.

'Super Saint,' Lucy laughed to herself. 'Very funny.' She tucked it in her bag.

'Can I get you anything?' the PA asked hurriedly. She left without waiting for a reply.

Lucy helped herself to a bottle of water from the mini fridge and looked around at the framed celebrity pictures who had been prior guests of the show. She couldn't help but wonder if she'd make the wall, too.

'Someone will be in shortly for your touch up and to mike you,' a girl said, popping her head in Lucy's dressing room and then disappearing. Everyone looked like they'd just rolled out of bed, scurrying around, noses to their clipboards.

The door slammed shut and Lucy sat alone, wondering exactly what it was they'd be discussing, and more importantly, who would be interviewing her. She saw some pretty cool shows where guests were interviewed by their idols or people they really loved. It was a kind of a gift to the guest, and it made the whole thing fun and even touching. You really got to know the person.

'Ready?' the tech asked, holding her microphone pack.

'I am.'

Lucy knew the drill. She lifted her halter unreservedly for the thirty-something audio tech, who seemed nervous to be in such close proximity to her tight and toned belly. He attached the pack at her waistline and handed her the chord to snake it up through her top. She pulled it up and then handed back the little black mic. He clipped it to her top and tucked in what was left of the chord. A girl came in, heavily made up, and began powdering her face and blushing her cheeks. She was chewing gum and cracking it in Lucy's ear, distracted and

barely interested in the task at hand.

'You know what? I'm good,' Lucy said to her before the girl could take a brush to her hair.

'You think so?' the girl asked, scrunching her nose.

The colour bars came on the monitor bracketed to her wall and the stage manager counted down. Showtime.

Another knock and Lucy was escorted to a hallway that exited on to the set, right beneath another monitor where she watched the opening credits both live and on TV, experiencing the oddest kind of dissonance. The camera panned feverishly over the audience, zigging and zagging, music blaring and lights strobing. Everyone was busy doing their part, talking into headsets, riding on camera dollys, and operating lights.

'Our guest today needs little introduction. In just the span of a few months, she has gone from socialite to, some say, a saint.'

'When the announcer says your name, just walk to the X mark in front of the couch and sit down there. You will be perfectly framed in camera. Make sure you are on the X.'

'Yes.'

'Oh, and one last thing,' the producer said right before walking on to the set. 'You're going to be interviewed by . . .'

Lucy anxiously waited to hear, like a kid waits to open a present on their birthday. She was almost sure it would be Cecilia or Agnes. Jesse was a long shot, but then again he could have been faking his opposition to the show to keep her off-guard.

'. . . *What do you think, and more importantly, what does she think? Welcome, Lucy Ambrose!*' the announcer said, drumming up excitement.

'Who?' Lucy asked the producer.

'*And welcome the woman who looks like she could be her sister . . .*'

Immediately an 'I was right' smirk washed across her face. She waited for either Cecilia or Agnes's name to be called. Or both.

'*The woman who helped make her . . .*' the announcer screamed. '*Clare Ambrose! Lucy's mom!*'

Lucy's heart sank. A stranger with the same blood coursing through her veins stood before her. She was nothing short of shell-shocked as the lights and cameras moved maniacally around them and the audience shrieked in surprise and satisfaction. They knew the story. Everyone did. Lucy's mom left her when she was born for something better – the spotlight. Lucy felt like someone had punched her in the chest.

'*Go!*' the director ordered from the control room, so loudly that Lucy could hear the command through the producer's earpiece.

The producer nudged her out into the spotlight. Lucy walked out, disoriented. She hit the X marked in gaffer tape in front of the centre of the couch just as her mother made her way from the other side.

Lucy sat, leaning over and whispering as the audience burst out in applause. 'Why are you here?'

'For the same reasons you are, honey,' Clare said in her direction. 'To get the truth out. I am your mother.'

'Now you are,' Lucy said.

'I have always been your mother and I always will be, Lucy.'

'I don't have a mother,' Lucy said, taking her seat and regaining her composure as to not give her mother, or the audience, the reaction they were hoping for. The reason for even more attention and a Where Were You My Whole Life? item on page six.

'The apple doesn't fall far from the tree,' Clare replied into the microphone, taking in Lucy's flawless appearance. 'You look divine.'

'You might have made me who I was,' Lucy said confidently. 'But not who I am.'

The audience was left with little doubt that this was truly mother and daughter as they turned toward the camera, straightening their outfits and their postures identically, smiling to mask their obvious discomfort.

Lucy looked like she'd just seen a ghost, and in many ways, she had.

'Doesn't she look gorgeous?' Clare said, trying to win over the audience.

Lucy's smile tightened to a clench-toothed grimace.

The applause light flickered on and off.

'How and why are you here?' Lucy asked.

'I called the show.'

'You called the show?'

'Yes, I got you on!' Clare said. 'I thought this would be the best way for us to reconnect.'

'You mean, you got yourself on the show using me?'

'Lucy,' Clare said. 'We're on TV.'

'Well, I am delighted to be here to interview my only daughter,' Clare asked, trying to get the interview on track. 'How have you been?'

'What do you care?' Lucy asked. 'Oh, right, you care because you're on TV.'

'You know, when you were little, I used to take you to church every Sunday.'

'Yes, you did,' Lucy said. 'Before you left and never came back, you loved to dress me up on Sundays.'

'And you loved the attention,' Clare said. 'Like mother, like daughter.'

'I am nothing like you.'

'Oh, my darling, but you are.'

The applause light flickered on and off and the audience burst out into thunderous claps and catcalls.

'We can help each other.'

'You mean now I can help you.'

'Lucy, let's get to the viewers' questions,' the host chimed in. 'What the people want to know.'

He handed a blue card to Clare to read. 'Mariana from Bay Ridge asked, What really happened inside the church?'

'I don't think there is anything I can add.'

'But you were there?'

'Yes, I was there,' Lucy said, trying to slice into her mother. 'Between the investigators, the lawyers and the press, I think you have a pretty good idea.'

'Ah, yes, the lawyers,' Clare ruminated. 'I'm sure Daddy has the cheque in the mail.'

Lucy felt like a little girl again, at her father's mercy, not good enough. Starving for his attention. Just like her mother.

'It was a traumatic thing. Not something I want to relive for ratings.'

'Well, then, why are you here?' Clare asked.

'To tell the truth.'

'Well, then tell it.'

'You can't tell the truth unless people are willing to hear it,' Lucy began. 'Sebastian . . . He was the truth.'

'He was sick in the head,' Clare said. 'Wasn't he?'

'Takes one to know one, Mother,' Lucy said angrily.

'I'm just quoting what was in the papers,' Clare said, with an oversize shrug for the crowd.

The sight of her mother playing devil's advocate for the cameras, to the audience, at Sebastian's expense was galling to Lucy.

'And you believe what you read?'

'I've found that most of what people tell you not to believe in the papers is because they actually don't want you to believe it. Isn't that the truth?'

'That was me,' Lucy said. 'Before.'

The producers loved every minute of the shrinking violet before them.

'Some say that something mystical happened in the church. That you and the others were transformed into some kind of holy people?'

'People say a lot of things.'

'What do you say?'

Lucy thought for a moment about how best to answer her. 'It wasn't what happened inside the church that is important. It's what happened inside of me.'

'Which was?'

'We can't help but be changed by love,' Lucy answered. 'By death. By both.'

'And you were changed?

'Yes.'

'Did you love him?' her mother asked.

'Sorry, I don't share intimate details with strangers.'

'I want to know.'

Lucy was silent.

'The people want to know,' Clare added.

'Have you ever met someone who knew you better than you

145

knew yourself? Who really understood you? Loved you unconditionally.'

'You loved me,' Clare said. 'When you were a baby.'

'But you didn't love me,' Lucy said. 'Not enough to stay.'

'I loved you enough to know it was best for me to go,' Clare said. 'Do you know how hard that was for me?'

'I am not interested in how hard anything was for you,' Lucy said. 'I don't even know you.' Lucy paused, answering her own initial question. 'Sebastian was that person for me. For us. Take it as you want to.'

'So what's next? The way people follow you around now; it's like some sort of cult. What is it they expect to hear from you?'

'I don't know what they expect.'

'Are you starting a new religion, a clothing line, or . . . what?'

'I think there are enough religions,' she said. 'And clothing lines.'

'Then you fancy yourself as some kind of shaman or priestess?'

'I'm no prophet,' she said. 'That's for sure.'

'Well, you must have a message for them you'd like to tell all of us?'

'I just want them to open their eyes.'

'To see what? Who? You?'

'To see what a mirror can't show them. To see someone they love with all their heart and soul. Themselves.'

'Is this Sebastian's message or yours?

'Sebastian put it this way,' Lucy answered. 'Know yourself. Accept yourself. Be yourself. That's all.'

'So, love yourself? Seems we've heard that before.'

'Yes, people have heard it. But do people listen?' Lucy asked. 'The biggest haters are the voices in your head.'

'Did you learn that from Sebastian or Dr Frey?'

Lucy's eyes turned to angry slits. 'Dr Frey is a personality pimp, selling people more acceptable versions of themselves in ten milligram chewables.'

'Oh, I think we've touched a nerve,' the interviewer said, turning directly to the camera.

'You and the other girls accused him of murder, but he was cleared.'

'Of killing Sebastian, yes, he was cleared,' Lucy admitted grudgingly. 'Not of killing souls. He'll answer to a higher court someday.'

'Sounds like threats. Aren't you worried about libelling him? He is a powerful man.'

'If you think I'm worried about him sending an attorney after me, you've got to be kidding. He's done a lot worse.'

'Why should they listen to you? All of this new found self-awareness seems hypocritical coming from such a material girl.'

'They should listen to themselves, not me.'

'A simple enough pitch, I guess?'

'We're all selling something,' Lucy answered. 'I'm a high concept girl.'

'With a monthly allowance,' Clare said. 'I guess it's easy to preach when someone is paying the church bills?'

'You will not speak to me like that. You have no right.' She could see the crew reaching for their mouths to stifle their judgmental giggles.

'Your entire image has been built around flitting from one red carpet to another, one product endorsement to another, one nightclub to another,' Clare said. 'On someone else's dime.'

'Jealous.'

Clare sat there speechless and fuming.

'Anyway, I didn't know you were keeping a running tab,' Lucy continued. 'On your own daughter.'

'Someone has to,' Clare said.

'You don't have to do anything,' Lucy quipped. 'Except be my mother, which you failed miserably at.'

'You have your father to bankroll your dreams. At least you got that working for you.'

'Has it worked for me?'

'Well, I think you proved to everyone today that you are a martyr.'

The producer was getting increasingly anxious as Lucy turned the tables on her mother. Exploiting the truth, but Lucy's truth, not the truth they were hoping to get on the airwaves.

'I just wanted a mother.'

'You always had a mother.'

'You were just a gestational surrogate.'

The audience was shocked. Shocked at her vulnerability on display. They started clapping. For Lucy. For baring her soul. For telling the truth – a truth which so many of them wish they could say. Lucy didn't even notice the standing ovation and uproarious applause. She only noticed her mother. Sitting stoically next to her.

'Well, I hope you find whatever it is you are looking for,' Clare urged.

'It's true, I am looking for something. Something I'm desperate to find.' Lucy said to the camera before turning back to her mother. 'But you, you aren't it.'

13

The Saint and the Serpent

'That's him,' Hazel whispered, leaning toward Agnes's desk.

Agnes tried to ignore her, but Hazel kept poking her in the back with the bejewelled nail of her index finger.

'OK!' Agnes growled.

'Is there a problem you'd like to share, Miss Fremont?'

'No, sir,' she answered.

'Look!' Hazel giggled.

Agnes turned around. 'You're going to get us thrown out of class.'

'Who cares? What will they do? Make us say ten Hail Marys. You got that!'

Agnes rolled her eyes. 'I said OK.'

She dropped her pen. When she bent to retrieve it, she saw a guy with dirty blond, tussled hair. He was dressed in a crumpled blue blazer, jeans, loafers and a V-neck sweater; starched button-down collar shirt poking through it at the neck and the sleeves. Preppy, except that on closer inspection, his tie was loosely knotted, and one-side of his shirt collar was unbuttoned. A fashion statement? Or minor act of rebellion in the conservative environment? Possibly both, she thought. He had a faraway look in his eyes as he tapped his pen against the desktop, waiting impatiently for class to end. He was somewhere else.

'Definitely hot,' Agnes said to Hazel. 'Is that what you want to hear?'

'Told you,' Hazel said proudly.

'But . . .'

'Oh, c'mon, Agnes. No buts. Lighten up. I'm not trying to marry you off or anything.'

'You sound like my mother,' Agnes moaned.

'Hey, I thought we were friends,' Hazel joked, pretending to be slighted.

'Things are different for me. I don't have a lot of patience for chit chat anymore.'

'Did you ever?'

Agnes was frustrated. It wasn't just social interaction with friends and classmates that had changed for her. It was

everything. The class seemed interminable. Not just because Agnes was dreading what Hazel might do when it was over. Everything was interminable now. In fact, she wasn't even sure why she was still enrolled. The parish, the principal and the faculty were split on whether she should be allowed to attend and she could feeling herself losing ground every day. The only kids she could relate to were the ones who'd enlisted in the military or gone to jail. She took a deep breath and tried to explain.

'It's like someone going off to war,' Agnes said. 'They're not the same when they come back. They see the world differently, you know?'

'So Precious Blood was like boot camp for you?'

'Something like that,' Agnes explained, 'Except my uniform is on the inside. You can't see it, but I can't take it off either.'

Hazel paused for a second to let it sink but it was clear to Agnes it hadn't.

'Like PTSD?'

'I guess,' Agnes griped, exasperated. 'Should I have to be some kind of robo-saint for everyone, Hazel? A stoic?'

'Jesus, Agnes, can't you just act your age?'

'For me, that's what all this stuff is now, school, grades, homework, boys. An act. I don't really expect you to get it.'

'Now I really am insulted,' Hazel moaned.

Agnes checked herself. 'I'm sorry,' she said, reaching for her

friend. 'I just get so frustrated sometimes. Mostly with myself.'

'You're a young girl. A human being,' Hazel argued. 'You are flesh and blood.'

Agnes laughed. 'Thanks for reminding me.'

'And, he . . . is very flesh and blood.'

The bell rang and teacher finally stopped talking. Before she could scoop up her books, Hazel grabbed her and dragged her to the back of the classroom. To the new guy.

'Hi,' Hazel said effusively, extending her hand.

'Hi,' the boy said shyly.

'I'm Hazel. What's your name?'

'Finn. Finn Blair.'

'Very nice to meet you, Finn,' Hazel continued. 'This is my friend, Agnes.'

Agnes was mortified. It was funny, she thought, how after all she'd been through, this kind of thing could still make her blush. 'Hey.'

He smiled, and then looked quickly away. 'Um, I gotta go, so . . .'

She sensed the nervousness in him but something more, too. He was broken. Wounded. Gun-shy. Like an abused animal that had just escaped and needed to be rescued. It was in his eyes, his body language, and the tone of his voice.

'That went well,' Agnes laughed.

'Oh, my God! He's totally into you,' Hazel shouted.

'He practically ran away.'

'Hook 'em, then reel them in,' Hazel said, making flapping fish gills with her hands behind her ears. 'He won't get far!'

'Now you really sound like my mother.'

Lucy and Jesse walked uphill from DUMBO through Brooklyn Heights, through Cobble Hill along Smith Street almost to the end, talking about the attack at the club and her talk show appearance.

'I told you not to do that show,' Jesse criticized.

'Please, no I told you sos.'

'Your mom? Really,' he continued, shaking his head, 'you should have seen the look on your face.'

'It's just like her to do something like that in public.'

'You handled it,' Jesse said.

'Yeah, but it was still humiliating.'

'Well, that was the point. A total psychological and emotional blindside.'

'I wouldn't be surprised if Frey was a silent investor in the show.'

'Don't kid yourself, I'm looking into it,' Jesse cracked, only half-joking. 'What about Cecilia's gig?'

'What about it?' Lucy asked. 'Some jerk on furlough tried to take a cheap shot at CeCe. I wasn't having it.'

'Now that sounds more like Frey,' Jesse replied. 'I should have stayed. Maybe I could have helped.'

'I saw you still managed to run the story with pictures.'

'A guy's gotta eat, Lucy,' Jesse chided. 'I can't sit around waiting for juicy gossip from you anymore.'

'True. You'd be waiting a long time.'

'It was a warning shot you know.'

'Well, it definitely got my attention.'

'Can't the cops protect you?'

Lucy shook her head. 'Don't trust them.'

Jesse nodded. 'Hard to know who to trust right now.'

'No, it isn't,' she said flatly, looking him straight in the eye. 'We can't trust anyone.'

A few silent blocks later they arrived at their destination.

'This must be the place,' Jesse said to Lucy, glancing down at the address Mayfield had slipped him at the morgue.

It was an address on a Carroll Gardens side street, and not a very nice one. The smell from the Gowanus canal was intense here, wafting over what remained of the immigrant neighbourhood. The scrap heap sitting in the junk yard across the street provided the perfect visual of decay and the clatter from the F train overhead was maddening.

'Are you sure about this?' Lucy asked.

'Mayfield doesn't lie when there's money involved.'

They started to walk up the path to the front door, past the weathered statue of the Madonna stepping on the head of a snake in the front garden, adorned with fresh, lush roses. Lucy stopped briefly to admire it.

'My grandmother had one of those in her yard,' Lucy recounted.

'Old timers,' Jesse said, nodding his head.

'I was always afraid of it. It terrified me. But now . . .' Lucy began. 'Now, it's terrifying and beautiful. Inspiring.'

She knocked on the heavy wooden door and waited. From the cracks that ran through it and the rusted doorknob, it was obvious it hadn't been painted or tended to in a while.

'Maybe nobody's home?'

'No. Somebody's home.'

After a while a woman answered. Lucy met her gaze, surprised, yet not.

'You're the woman from the Brooklyn Ball, and the parade,' Lucy said. 'The one who helped me? Perpetua.'

'Yes,' the old woman confirmed. 'I knew you'd come.'

Jesse and Lucy exchanged glances. Confused. Perpetua ushered them in, offering them a drink and something to eat. A few people, dressed in their Sunday best, hovered around a coffee table in her dining room. The mood was serious. No music playing or loud chatter. The sound of the ticking grandfather clock filled in the silent gaps. Jesse noted there was plastic on the living-room furniture. 'I knew it. Old timers,' he mumbled to himself.

The whole place seemed from a different time.

'I have pastries. Cookies. Please help yourself.'

'Thank you,' Lucy said sincerely. 'I feel like we're crashing a party.'

'Or a wake,' Jesse said, nudging Lucy.

'You are welcome here,' Perpetua said sweetly. 'My home is your home.'

'I think you were right about Mayfield,' Jesse whispered. 'What was he thinking give us a phony address? Of someone you know, no less.'

'Don't be in too big a hurry for a refund, Jesse,' Lucy urged to his surprise. 'If anyone might have answers for us, it's her.'

The group of visitors noticed Lucy in their midst and stood back. They crossed themselves.

'Awkward,' Jesse whispered.

'Shhhh,' Lucy instructed.

Some of them looked familiar from outside her condo or from news stories about protests in front of the church. One in particular. The priest who'd told her about Sebastian's heart. He caught her eye and smiled, raising his piece of almond biscotti in salute.

'Who is he?' Lucy inquired.

'One of us,' Perpetua said.

'One of who?' Jesse asked.

'One who believes,' Perpetua replied.

'I was so angry with him I smacked him on the street,' Lucy admitted contritely. 'He told me something awful and I just flew off the handle.'

'What did he tell you?' Perpetua asked.

'I can't even bring myself to say it,' Lucy demurred.

The priest smiled at Lucy through his cut and swollen lip, with forgiveness in his eyes.

Lucy smiled back at him, at all of them, both in greeting and to acknowledge their respect for her. Jesse was taking it all in. Lucy wore the look of a girl who'd been elevated from the lower classes to royalty. Accepted. Comfortable in her own skin. A girl who suddenly understood her role. It was in stark contrast to the self-satisfied smirk she'd defensively worn as she climbed her way up the nightlife ladder not so long ago.

'Holly GoHeavenly,' he whispered.

Lucy reached out her hand to Perpetua. The woman took hold, the twisted bones of her arthritic fingers squeezing Lucy with surprising strength.

'You said you knew I'd come. How did you know?'

'Come with me.'

'I'm going to hang out here OK?' Jesse said, digging into a cannoli from the pastry tray.

'Free food,' Lucy said jokingly to Perpetua. 'No club kid can resist.'

'Mangia. Eat!' the old woman said, in her warmest, most hospitable voice.

Perpetua walked Lucy down a short dark corridor toward the back of the house. The old woman opened a door to a small, austere room with a steam radiator and tiny window

facing out on a vegetable garden, marked by rows of tomatoes and a handmade pergola overrun with vines and bunches of red grapes hanging from them. A twin bed, neatly made, with a crisp white sheet and green wool blanket, sat against the white side wall with a single closet door. It was warm and smelled of latex paint, recently redone, unlike the rest of the house. It seemed less a bedroom than a hiding place. A secret stopover on the way to somewhere else. The radiator came to life, knocking and hissing, as Perpetua spoke.

'Before he came to you, he slept here.'

Perpetua stepped aside and Lucy entered. Slowly. She could feel Sebastian's presence, as if he were still there. She walked to the bed and sat on it gently, running her hands along the coarse and tightly tucked military style blanket beneath her. She stared out at the shaded, fertile garden and imagined Sebastian sitting in the same place.

'How long was he here?' Lucy asked.

'Not long.'

'Did you know him well?'

'We took him in when his grandmother died. He stayed with us. Until Father Piazza moved him on the doctor's advice.

'To Perpetual Help?'

'Yes,' Perpetua said sadly. 'We weren't permitted to visit him or communicate in any way. When he escaped from that madman, he came here.'

Lucy wasn't surprised. Despite the spartan quality of the

room, Perpetua's home was warm and hospitable. Safe. Comfortable. Quiet. A place, she imagined, where love and loyalty was prized above all else. A world with which she regrettably had far too little experience, as had Sebastian, according to what Perpetua told them. What must he have been thinking, lying in this bed, knowing that Frey and the cops were out to find him? To take away either his freedom or his soul. Or both. It was almost too much for Lucy to bear.

'I can't stand that his death will have been in vain.'

'It wasn't. He did what he set out to do. There are the three of you,' Perpetua said.

'He was so young. Just a boy.'

Perpetua held Lucy in her arms, comforting her as she had that night on the red carpet. 'You don't need to mourn for him. His life was short, but complete. You understand?'

'I'm not sure I do anymore.'

'He did what he was meant to do. Fulfilled.'

Lucy wasn't so sure about that anymore.

'Something terrible has happened,' she blurted out, distressed.

'Tell me,' Perpetua said, sitting next to the anguished girl and taking her hand once more.

'We've been looking for something that was stolen. My friend was given this address and was told we might get help finding it here.'

'What are you seeking?'

'I can't even bring myself to speak the words to you.'

'You can speak freely to me.'

Lucy took a breath. 'I think that Dr Frey . . .' Lucy paused, her words catching in her throat at the thought. 'I think he stole Sebastian's heart from the morgue.'

Lucy was shaking and Perpetua placed her hands on the girl's flushed face, holding it still.

'Faccia bella,' the woman said, praising Lucy's beauty. 'Dr Frey didn't steal the heart.'

Lucy was shocked. 'How do you know?' she said, half-fearing the answer.

'Because it is with us.'

'What is with us?'

'What you are looking for. He is here.'

Lucy was confused. 'I don't mean Sebastian is with us. Inside us.'

'Nor do I. It is here.'

'I don't believe it.'

'Seeing is believing,' Perpetua responded.

Perpetua stood and took a few short steps to the closet door. She opened it and revealed a tiny altar. In front of it was a gold kneeler, padded with a garnet crushed velvet cushion. Perpetua struck a match and lit a myrrh-scented votive before the golden jewelled box with two side-by-side doors in front. The flame from the candle illuminated it, throwing beams of light outward. Lucy almost felt the need to cover her eyes. Perpetua reached for the clasp on the casement door, unfastened it, and

pulled the doors open. Behind a glass pane, it was revealed.

A heart.

A human heart.

Whole.

Incorrupt.

Lucy approached the shrine as if in a trance. 'Oh my God. Frey didn't take it. You did,' Lucy murmured in astonishment. 'Why would you do something like this? Why?'

'Calm yourself,' the woman said. 'Like the relics of the past it will inspire many.'

Lucy took hold of the milagro dangling from her wrist and fell to her knees and sobbed. 'I feel him here. This is him.'

'This is your faith,' Perpetua said. 'And your burden.'

Lucy bent over and brought her face to rest on the floor, heaving tears.

'Sebastian. Sebastian. Sebastian.' Over and over she cried out his name in joy and sorrow.

Jesse heard her shouts and ran down the hallway to the room. 'Lucy!'

He stopped in the doorway, shocked and awed by the beautiful, grisly scene.

'Holy shit,' he muttered, grabbing his phone and snapping a few pictures of Lucy kneeling before the organ, proof to himself or evidence for others if it came to that. 'Unbelievable.'

Perpetua held up her hand, signalling him to come no further, and Jesse complied. After a while, Lucy's weeping

subsided, and the woman reached down to lift her up. But it wasn't her hands Lucy felt. It was a grasp she remembered from her first moments at Precious Blood. Sebastian's grasp.

'Do not be afraid,' the woman said.

The words were from Perpetua's mouth but Lucy heard only Sebastian's voice.

'I'm not afraid,' Lucy said.

'*This* is why I knew you would come.'

'I have to tell Cecilia and Agnes. Will you keep it here?'

'It is safe with us for now,' Perpetua said. 'Out of the control of the Ciphers who covet it. Until it can be safely returned to Precious Blood and restore the church.'

'Lucy,' Jesse said, turning pale as a ghost, 'this is creeping me out. Let's go.'

'Does Frey know you have it?'

'I don't know, but he is aware that it's gone.'

'Anyone else?'

'No,' Perpetua reassured her. 'Nobody knows outside our small circle and it is a secret they would not reveal on pain of death.'

'He'll find it.'

'And we will guard it, with our last breath.'

'And with ours,' Lucy said, taking her hand.

Agnes was hanging at her locker, lost in thought. A gentle whisper broke her concentration.

'Agnes, right?'

She turned. 'Finn?'

'I didn't mean to be rude yesterday,' he said apologetically. 'It's just hard for me to know who to trust around here.'

'I understand,' she said.

'Can I walk you to your next class?'

'No,' Agnes blurted.

'No?' Finn asked.

'I mean, no, this is lunch for me,' Agnes explained, holding her brown bag up and wiggling it. 'We can talk in the courtyard if you want.'

They headed silently out the back exit and sat down at a shaded wooden picnic table on the grass. Dogwoods flowered all around them, a few of the blossoms dotting the tabletop.

'This is my favourite tree,' she said randomly. 'It's peaceful here. Not like inside the building.'

'Or inside my head,' he smiled.

Agnes wasn't sure how much she should tell him she'd heard from Hazel, but looking at the pained face of the boy across from her, she decided to jump right in.

'I heard you were at Perpetual Help?'

Finn was slow to reply. 'Yeah,' he said quietly. 'I heard you were, too.'

'Yeah.'

Finn saw Agnes's expression change. Darken. 'Sorry, I shouldn't have said anything.'

'No, it's fine. We can talk about it if it will help you.'

'I don't know if anything will help.'

Agnes moved in closer, and the closer she got, the more relaxed he became.

'What happened?' she asked. 'Don't worry, I won't judge you.'

Finn looked away and closed his eyes tightly, his lids fluttering nervously as if he were in a deep sleep, reliving the past couple of months, years, maybe even his entire life. He began to speak in fragments.

'You know? My parents. They . . .' He hesitated searching for the right words. 'They have certain expectations of me.'

'You feel you've disappointed them in some way?'

'Yes, you get it,' he said relieved. 'By not living up to what they expect of me.'

'I do get it,' she said.

'Do you . . . do you ever worry they don't love you?' he asked.

'I believe my mother loves me,' Agnes confessed. 'But I don't believe she likes me.'

'Yes,' he agreed. 'But doesn't that mean we're more like obligations?'

'So you took it upon yourself to rid them of their obligation?'

'Yes. Pills. Unsuccessfully.' His eyes reddened with guilt. And shame. And sadness.

Agnes pulled up the sleeves of her lambswool sweater and bore her scars to the boy. 'A lot messier,' she said. 'And just as unsuccessful.'

'Lucky thing,' he said, looking away awkwardly.

'For both of us,' Agnes added.

'Who knows where I'd be without Dr Frey,' Finn continued. 'He saved me.'

Agnes bit her lip. It suddenly occurred to her that he was 'away' when everything went down at Precious Blood and knew nothing about it. He might have been the only person she'd met in the last few months who didn't.

'Yes, he has quite a reputation,' Agnes said.

'Did you know him? Did he treat you?'

'Not really.'

'Then how did you get better?' Finn asked. 'You seem so together.'

Agnes allowed herself to be flattered. It felt good for a change. She had to be so defensive about herself since Precious Blood. Even to her closest friends and family.

'Believe it or not, there was another patient from the ward that helped me. I owe it all to him.'

'You're lucky it wasn't that dude, Sebastian,' Finn said. 'I heard he was totally insane.'

'Who did you hear that from?'

'Dr Frey.'

Agnes was shaken, but kept her cool. 'Don't believe

everything you hear, Finn. You of all people should understand that.'

'Well, I don't know why anyone would need to escape,' Finn said. 'Frey is getting patients released in droves now.'

'Really?'

'Yeah, to the Born Again halfway house on Bond Street. No one dangerous of course.'

'Of course,' she said.

Agnes imagined an army of Sicariuses, a legion of hardcore sociopathic murderers controlled by Frey, let loose on Brownstone Brooklyn.

'The day I was released, the police commissioner and the mayor were up on the ward taking pictures with him for winning some community award.'

Agnes checked the time on her phone. 'I've got to get to class.'

'Thanks for taking the time, Agnes. I know you don't know me at all.'

'I know you better than you think, Finn.'

'Maybe we can get a coffee after school sometime?'

Agnes picked up her books and smiled. 'Maybe.'

14

Star Crossed Liars

There was no memorial service for Bill.

No next of kin that could be located.

The only contact number the city could find was Cecilia's. She received a voice message from the homeless shelter administrator's office giving her a location at which she could claim his ashes if she chose to do so. She was informed that she had two weeks or they would be disposed of. She knew where to go. She'd been there before. Recently. The souvenir from her trip now worn proudly on her tattooed wrist.

Cecilia arrived at the morgue dressed in a short black skirt, black velvet platform pumps framed in studs, dainty matching black crosses painted lightly on each shin, and a tank top with a delicate chain link bra over the top. She walked in, gave her name, and an open cardboard box with a small metal can inside, too inelegant to be called an urn, was handed over to her. No waiting. No fuss.

'Sorry for your loss,' the clerk said in a thick New York accent, barely looking her in the face.

She was amazed at how light the box felt. A grown person reduced to a handful of powder; dehydrated like those food rations they used to take to outer space or sell in candy stores. An entire life – hopes, dreams, struggles, triumphs – all of it boiled down to its essence. Bill would have appreciated it, she thought. At least the writer in him would have.

She was hoping they might have some of his personal effects to transfer as well, but Cecilia knew the greatest likelihood was that his stuff had been stolen. She was right.

'That's it,' the person behind the desk said. 'All except for this hat.'

Cecilia put the old, dapper fedora on her head, took a deep breath and headed to the subway. It was a long ride home, but she had little sense of time passing. Like an athlete waiting for the game to begin, she was in the zone and ready, come what may.

As she escorted Bill's ashes up the steps to her Red Hook loft, she spied another box in front of her door. The address was written large in a shaky hand, but it was one she recognized even from down the hall.

To: Cecilia Trent
From: Bill

Agnes navigated the hallway, hugging the lockers along the wall, trying her best to avoid her classmates and ignore their nasty chatter.

'Oh, look! It's Carrie!' one girl shouted, flapping her arms in faux fright and running away.

'Saw your soul sister preaching on TV again,' another mocked about Lucy's interview.

'Hey, Agnes,' a boy called out, his back turned to her. 'Check it out, I'm like you.' He turned, slowly revealing a piece of tyre rubber wrapped around his head like a head band with darts sticking into it, creating a fanned head piece.

A firm but sweet voice called from an office doorway behind her. 'Agnes?'

Before Agnes could process what the boy was doing, and the crowd that was gathering around them, she stopped and poked her head in the door. 'Hi, Sister.'

'Do you have a moment?'

'Ah? Sure?' Agnes stepped in and closed the door, shutting out the abusive, gossipy noise from outside.

'I saw your friend Lucy on TV.'

'Hasn't everybody?' Agnes sighed.

'Don't listen to them, Agnes,' Sister Dorothea said.

'It's hard to turn the other cheek, Sister.'

'It's supposed to be hard.'

Agnes looked out the classroom door and saw the strangest thing. It was she inside the room watching herself get mocked outside in the hallway. Agnes closed her eyes tight and opened them again. The image of herself was gone.

'I feel like I have a disease, you know? Funny, but that's how Frey described it,' Agnes said.

'Well, I don't agree with him about much, but he might be on to something.'

'What?'

Agnes was surprised that the sister would claim to have anything in common with the psychiatrist.

'Recent behavioural studies show there is such a thing as cognitive vulnerability,' Dorothea explained. 'That depression and perhaps other mental illness may actually be contagious.'

'Faith is a communicable?'

'In a sense. And some, like Frey, think those that suffer from it, to use an analogy, need to be quarantined, isolated. Managed until they are cured or die off.'

Agnes's thoughts flew to the penthouse floor of Perpetual Help, imagining Dr Frey's domain more as petri dish than psych ward.

'Confine and eliminate the infection at the source.'

'Yes, or the message spreads, the movement grows, virally, by words, by deeds, over the airwaves and the internet and takes hold, until it can no longer be contained.'

'So Sebastian was like patient zero?'

'Yes, and now there is the three of you. And Jude.'

The discussion was bringing a new clarity to Agnes and the threat they represented to the Ciphers.

'How do you know so much about this?'

'The cult of Saint Agnes is an old and devoted one. I believe in you,' Sister Dorothea said humbly.

Sister Dorothea pulled the necklace from under her dress, revealing a sacred heart milagro dangling from it, one identical to Agnes's.

'Agnes? Are you OK?' the sister asked.

'No,' Agnes answered. 'No, I'm not OK.'

'I know this seems impossible, but it isn't.'

'Thing are happening,' Agnes said. 'Things I don't understand and probably will never understand.'

'I can't imagine what you're going through, but I do know something about how you're being treated. When I made my decision to go into the convent, I heard the snickers, too. The ridicule. I got the looks. From my own family, mind you.'

'Really?'

'You know the joke I'm sure: "Nun today, none tomorrow".'

Agnes tried to contain herself but burst out laughing instead. 'That's a good one.'

'I know,' the nun said, joining her in an uncontrollable giggle. 'But don't tell anyone.'

'We are misfits,' Sister Dorothea said. 'You, even more so. If

it's true, if you are a destined to be a saint, and I believe you are, then you really don't fit in on this earth or in the heavens. Saints are the biggest misfits of them all.'

'I saw Jude,' Agnes said.

The nun smiled. 'I know. What you did for that family was wonderful.'

'I don't know. Is that it? Is that what all this is for? What Sebastian chose us for?'

'What could be more important than to offer solace and compassion at the hour of death?' Sister Dorothea said, coming around her desk to take Agnes by the wrist, revealing her chaplet. 'She had no need for gifts, or medicine. All she needed was what you brought. Peace. That comes from the power of belief.'

'It's all projected on to us. How can others believe in me when I don't even believe in myself?'

'Don't worry, you will.'

'When?' Agnes asked, sobbing.

'There is something extraordinary inside of you, Cecilia and Lucy,' Sister Dorothea said.

'You have no idea.'

'Is there something you want to tell me Agnes?'

'Ever since Precious Blood, I feel different inside. It's more than just a change of heart,' Agnes confessed. 'Sometimes when I sleep, or dream, I feel myself slipping away. Separating in two.'

'These things happen when we are troubled or anxious. Our mind's way of helping us make sense of things. You have been through incredible trauma.'

'That's not what I mean, but you know that, don't you?'

The nun returned to her desk and sat, searching for words. 'Such phenomena are noted in the biographies of the saints and martyrs. We call them hagiographies. And in tales of their suffering called Passionaries.'

'What things?'

'Many regarded as saints are believed to have displayed supernatural abilities. In fact, these have been both signs of their sainthood in life and a verification of it after death.'

'Superpowers? I'm sorry, Sister, but I'm about the furthest from the X-Men a girl can get.'

Sister Dorothea laughed and continued. 'What you are experiencing is called bi-location. The sensation of being in two places at the same time.'

'It's more than a sensation. I am in two places at once.'

'You are in good company. Saint Anthony, Saint Martin, Saint Ambrose, Maria de Leon Bello y Delgado all recounted similar experiences.'

Agnes opened up, hoping for answers. 'Lucy and Cecilia, the two girls who were with me at Precious Blood, are also different. Lucy can see things before they happen and Cecilia has marks on her hands that hurt her whenever danger is near.'

'Bi-location, levitation, stigmata, telepathy, clairvoyance . . . these are all gifts that others may know you for your true self. Gifts not always used for peaceful ends. Joan of Arc was a warrior. Saint Margaret was a dragon slayer, for goodness' sake.'

That last fearsome image reminded Agnes of Cecilia and her fierceness and fighting skills.

'And Jude?'

'He is an ecstatic.'

'But he is classified as autistic, non-verbal?'

'His outbursts are diagnosed as seizures, his behaviour as ADHD, oppositional defiance disorder, or whatever the clinical flavour of the moment may be,' the sister explained. 'This is how Dr Frey is able to keep him in his care.'

'Jude is so good. So innocent.'

'And so dangerous to Dr Frey,' the nun informed. 'As are you all.'

'He seems to have it all figured out.'

'Not all of it,' Sister Dorothea proposed. 'But he is very good at recognizing certain qualities in his patients.'

'Like Sebastian?'

Sister Dorothea smiled. 'This is all for a reason. Only God knows what that is,' she said. 'Have faith and put it in his hands.'

'I don't seem to have a choice, Sister.'

'God be with your soul, Agnes.'

* * *

Cecilia jaywalked across busy Hamilton Parkway against the light, dodging cars and trucks and the occasional curiosity seeker on her way to the Carroll Gardens Library. She dodged the omnipresent puddles of dog piss as she made her way along the uneven slate slabs that doubled as Clinton Street's sidewalk, arriving after a while at the imposing late nineteenth century red brick building ensconced in the tree-lined neighbourhood. The wrought-iron gate and arched windows brought to mind Precious Blood, which she took as a good omen. For her, both were places of learning.

She hadn't seen the inside of a library since she dropped out of high school but they had computers there and archived stacks of books and periodicals and she needed some information. She flashed her ID, signed up for a desktop and waited her turn. CeCe noticed a plaque above the unused fireplace mantel. 'Donated by Andrew Carnegie. 1897.' As a native of Steel town, his name carried particular weight with her. The wealthy, the powerful, had always tried to soften their image with gestures of largesse, she mused. In that sense, Frey was no different. Though in the doctor's case it was more smokescreen than publicity ploy.

The library was a public place but quiet, especially during midday, except for some crying toddlers, so Cecilia wasn't particularly worried about her privacy or safety. She took a seat as soon as a desktop became available, settled in and did as Frey suggested. She googled him. The search results were impressive, which she expected. Page after page of citations. Studies, lectures, news reports, op-eds, press releases, photos, video. His every promotion, award, charitable donation, every move chronicled in the greatest detail. A digital avalanche of praise and admiration.

Headlines screamed his importance.

Doctor Know!

Psych Bard!

Perpetual Help's Frey: Friends in High Places

A Shrink Grows In Brooklyn

Mayor 'Committed' to Alan Frey's Outpatient Rehab Centre

From his reputation as a world class physician and hospital administrator to his earliest humanitarian efforts, focused mainly on substance abusers, appointments to positions as head of psychiatry at hospitals around the city, and finally his elevation to head of psychiatry at Perpetual Help, transforming the most cash-strapped hospital in city into its finest. The record was one of undeniable achievement. Many claim to stride the hall of power, Cecilia thought, but in Frey's case, the halls only became powerful if he strode them.

Archival newspaper editorial pages she clicked on lauded his courage, his willingness to take on the hard cases. Single-handedly credited with keeping the institution going in the midst of the worst financial crisis in New York City's history, earning him the respect of city hall and the Archbishop himself. The goodwill for which made it easier to get the controversial

Born Again facility approved on the outskirts of gentrifying brownstone Brooklyn. As a physician, his patient list was second to none, an enviable roster of corporate, political and financial A-listers. The authoritative image he presented was beyond reproach.

For someone with more intimate knowledge of the doctor, like Cecilia, however, another thread appeared to present itself. This was a man with a plan, tirelessly working his way into a position of control, climbing the ladder both professionally and socially. Rubbing elbows with other masters of the universe for nefarious purposes. And as the psychiatrist of choice for the city's rich and famous, he was also the keeper of their secrets, owed an unspoken debt, lest certain embarrassing morsels mysteriously find their way into the columns or court filings.

Cecilia knew the type from the local dog-eat-dog music scene. Chameleons, showing a different face as situations dictated, relentless, duplicitous, competitive, mercenary. His reach seemed to extend to every corner of the city, to every big shot – corporate, financial, political, municipal, even the clergy. His power and influence becoming more concentrated and simultaneously more widespread, like the radioactive fallout from a nuclear core.

The search engine answered the how of Frey, but not the why. Even if a man could consolidate such power and hide his true self behind such a pristine image, why would he? Frey was nothing if not rational, but reason seemed to have nothing to do with any of this. Why the animus towards Sebastian, towards them? He was a psychiatrist after all. Why wouldn't he just dismiss their 'sainthood' as the delusion of lunatics and wait for it to go away? Even Sebastian said the Ciphers had been winning for years, gradually turning people away from faith and from their best selves. Instead, he was on some mission – self-appointed or otherwise – to medicate them, commit them, silence them, and destroy them.

She searched the printed archives for everything she could find; thumbing through study after study, lecture after lecture. Until at last she found what she was looking for. An answer. A transcript of his 'job' interview with the board of Perpetual Help. She speed-read through the introductions and niceties, the resumé and the recommendations from former patients and colleagues, and got right to the heart of the matter. The former Archbishop Jensen, near the end of his life, blamed for the hospital's pitiful financial straits at the time, but still active on the board and reluctant to cede control to the ambitious physician. His questions were surprisingly antagonistic for an applicant clearly regarded as a shoo-in.

Archbishop Jensen: Good afternoon, Dr Frey.

Dr Frey: Your Eminence. *Nodding his head slightly in deference.*

Archbishop Jensen: We are honoured to have such an

esteemed candidate for this most important position, but we are also most curious.

Dr Frey: How so?

Archbishop Jensen: Why would a man with such a clear antipathy toward traditional religion want to practise in a hospital such as ours?

Dr Frey: I don't understand.

Archbishop Jensen: Didn't you leave the seminary as a young man?

'Seminary?' Cecilia gasped, loudly enough to disturb the person in the cubicle next to her.

Dr Frey: I did. I preferred to heal sick brains.

Archbishop Jensen: Instead of sick souls?

Dr Frey: I didn't realize there was a litmus test for this position, your Eminence.

Archbishop Jensen: We are not here to judge, Doctor, simply to inquire.

Dr Frey: There is no great mystery in it. Dealing with clergy and seminarians experiencing deep crisis of faith was both disheartening and enlightening.

Archbishop Jensen: How so?

Dr Frey: It gave me permission to question my own views, my own beliefs.

Archbishop Jensen: And so you fell away?

Dr Frey: That is your analysis, Archbishop.

Archbishop Jensen: Don't let me put words in your mouth, Doctor.

Even on paper Cecilia could feel the session getting testy.

Dr Frey: As I pursued my career in psychiatry, I met others who thought as I did. Who found other ways to help the troubled, the addicted.

Archbishop Jensen: The sinful? Some people see these problems as a moral failing.

Dr Frey: Some do.

Archbishop Jensen: But not you?

Dr Frey: No.

Archbishop Jensen: So I return to my original question. Perpetual Help is on the verge of bankruptcy, funded primarily by an institution whose values you disregard and yourself discarded. Why would a person with such a promising future want buy a ticket on a sinking ship, so to speak?

Dr Frey: With the right guidance, I believe Perpetual Help will be the centre for a great change.

Archbishop Jensen: Your guidance.

Dr Frey: Yes. In order for minds to be healed, minds must be changed. From the inside. Old thoughts, old ways replaced. It is the same for institutions.

Archbishop Jensen: Then it all depends on the kind of change one brings or one finds?

Dr Frey: Some change must be facilitated, some must be stopped.

'That's it,' Cecilia murmured. 'Kill the baby in the crib.'

Archbishop Jensen: You see this neighbourhood as an epicentre of such change?

Dr Frey: Not just in the neighbourhood, but in the city and the world beyond.

Cecilia closed the document, still reeling from its contents. 'If they only knew.'

15

Bohemian Sabbath

Agnes left the room in silence. Through the doorway at the end of the long walk, she spied a girl facing the doors, waiting. 'Lucy.'

Agnes hurried to her. 'Are you OK?' she said, embracing her. 'I've been texting you!'

'I know, I'm sorry. I needed to talk to you face to face. I have something to tell you.'

'And I have something to tell you,' Agnes said.

'You go first. I'm going to take a while.'

Agnes smiled. 'I met this guy.'

'Oh,' Lucy interjected.

'No, not like that,' Agnes replied. 'A boy in my class who

recently came out of Frey's ward at the hospital.'

'Another one?'

'He's nothing like Sebastian,' Agnes said.

'No one will ever be.'

'He said that there's some crazy stuff going on up there. Real hard cases Frey is getting released into halfway houses and then out to the streets. One after another. It's like an assembly line of wackos.'

'Did your friend have any idea why?'

'No, but I'm pretty sure I do.'

'Vandals?'

'Vandals,' Agnes replied. 'Looking for us.'

Lucy nodded and looked over both shoulders; fearful they might be being watched.

'It all makes a sadistic kind of sense,' Lucy said. 'Especially with what I have to tell you.'

'What is it?' Agnes said with a lump in her throat.

'Let's find Cecilia.'

Jesse scrolled through his phone's photo app, studying the pictures he'd taken at Perpetua's house. Creepy didn't begin to describe it. Sebastian's heart. Sitting there on display. It hadn't decomposed so far as he could see. But then again, that didn't prove anything. He'd got press releases about fast food burgers with cheese that hadn't grown mould and didn't even smell after a year on a windowsill.

Still, he had to admit, there was something incredibly powerful and yet undignified about it. He could see both sides of it. To the faithful, it was a material, anatomical, actual symbol of courage, of strength, of faith. A holy relic. To the sceptics, perverse at least, a horrible crime at worst, evidence of organ piracy. Grave robbing.

On trips to Europe he'd seen such things visiting churches and cathedrals. Hair, teeth, bone, extremities, all manner of body parts, enshrined. A constant reminder of mortality and immortality. The fact that these items were now more interesting to tourists than pilgrims was not lost on him. He wished that the 'Saints of Sackett Street' as he'd coined them, would become such a novelty, their fifteen-minute shelf life nearly spent as well. But the fascination with Lucy, Cecilia and Agnes was growing more intense, not less, and becoming increasingly disconcerting to him. And terrifying.

He scrolled through file after file of photos and videos chronicling Lucy's transformation from high school hellcat to table-dancing party princess extraordinaire. He reached for a cigarette and a beer, toasting her success. Their success.

'To the bad old days,' he mumbled, cracking a sinister smile.

Reminiscing, however, only led him back to a less celebratory place. The present.

What had she got herself into? The girls had been lucky to escape Precious Blood and Frey with their lives. Jesse, too. Frey's invitation left a sulfurous taste in his mouth and in his

conscience that he had yet to shake.

'Coming with me?' Frey had asked. With or against? Frey's intentions were clear as a bell and so were Jesse's. He was against. He'd been offered a deal with a devil and managed to resist. One of the few things he could be proud of in this whole chaotic, murderous mess. But it was a certain, if unspoken, truth that Frey's was a one-time offer. Jesse had seen and heard too much, no matter what the investigators and the DA chose to believe. He was no better off than Lucy, Cecilia and Agnes. Seeing the end result of Sebastian's confrontation with the doctor at Perpetua's home, no matter how noble, was a sobering reminder of the real reason for his anxiety. There were people out to kill them. And him. Which led Jesse to wonder.

Why weren't they dead already?

It wasn't like Frey to get cold feet, so there had to be another reason. The easy answer was that there were too many people watching. Shrines popping up in front of Agnes's home, sell-outs at Cecilia's concerts, crowds trailing Lucy wherever she went. Not to mention the media attention which had barely waned in the months since Sebastian's death. Apparently, living saints were good copy. Ratings winners. He reached for a thumb drive on his desk and fitted it in the USB port of his desktop. Scan after scan of newspaper and magazine stories popped up as he scrolled through the folders.

The mastheads shouted.

Saints Alive!

Cult teens survive cultish murder/suicide.

Holy Haute Horror!

Psych Ward escapee suffers death by cop.

Inquisition!

Construction Halted At Brooklyn Church.

Top Doc Cleared in Precious Blood Incident.

Bishop declines to comment on Blasphemy Charges!

Holy See Mum On Holy Three.

Vatican't Confirm Authenticity of Sebastian Sightings.

As an eyewitness, Jesse had been advised not to comment publicly on anything he'd seen and heard inside the church, so Byte was unusually silent on Lucy and the others. Whether it was to cover his own ass or out of respect for Sebastian and the girls he didn't really know. He'd reached the point where the whole thing felt like a terrible nightmare. Lucy and Agnes seemed to have the easiest time dealing. They just went about their lives, ignored the haters and the inconveniences as best they could and tried like hell to figure out what it was they were supposed to be doing. Cecilia took a different path and hid away. He was somewhere in between.

In many ways, all the publicity generated from the reporting, the rumours and gossip about Sebastian's death and about the girls was good for him. How ironic for him to be a beneficiary. People flocked to Byte and to him like never before, either as 'content providers' offering exclusive inside tips, or as end

users, or subscribers, relying on him to tell them what was really happening in the world. He was an influencer now, starting to make real money. His reputation for credibility and authenticity overshadowed the weaselly ways he was known for just a few months earlier. Funny how a few murders and a few headlines could change public perception.

Jesse plugged in his phone and downloaded the most recent jpegs and .mov files to his laptop, including the images and video he'd shot of Perpetua and Lucy talking at the end of the visit. He put the phone down and went to his refrigerator for something to eat. The video finally uploaded and began to play automatically. He rummaged through the slim pickings in his freezer, not really listening, and then he heard it. He slammed the door and ran back to his phone and replayed the clip. And replayed it. And replayed it again, just to be sure of what he'd just heard.

Perpetua saying nobody knew.

But that wasn't true. *Mayfield knew.* And it was a good bet there were others who *knew* that he knew. Who had their eye on Mayfield.

Jesse slammed the heel of his palm into his forehead violently.

He was so impressed with himself at getting the tip for Lucy, staying one step ahead of Frey, so caught up in the truth or fiction of it all, the chase, that he'd allowed himself to be careless, suckered. One step behind.

'Shit!' he cursed and speed-dialled Lucy. 'Double-crossed by a junkie!'

Agnes and Lucy waited nervously in front of Cecilia's apartment. Not anxious from the threats that seemed to be gathering around them, but because what they had to tell her. This was the kind of neighbourhood where nobody cared much about fame or celebrity unless it was their own.

Agnes was still shaking from Lucy's vivid description.

Lucy's phone rang. She checked her caller I.D. and sighed.

'It's Jesse,' she said declining the call.

'Could it be important?' Agnes offered.

'Not more important than this,' Lucy answered.

'Can't you just tell me what's going on?' Agnes said. 'You're driving me crazy.'

'Oh, honey, we passed crazy several exits ago,' Lucy said.

Right then, they saw Cecilia approaching from down the block, leather guitar case slung around her body like a quiver. She was dressed in black; the necklace of hypodermic needles dangling from her neck that Bill made her. She fit right in with the Red Hook backdrop.

Cecilia stopped a few feet in front of them. Like Lucy, she looked very much like she had something to say. She and Lucy burst out simultaneously with their secrets.

'Frey was a priest,' Cecilia said.

'Frey doesn't have his heart,' Lucy said.

'What?' Lucy and Cecilia said in unison, this time Agnes joined in.

'Frey was priest?' Agnes asked. 'That makes no sense.'

'Fallen away,' Cecilia explained. 'It makes perfect sense,'

'He knew who Sebastian was. He knows who we are,' Lucy added.

'He believes.' Agnes asserted.

CeCe continued. 'I went to see him at the hospital. It was almost like he wanted me to know.'

'Why the hell would you do that?' Lucy asked.

'To confront him, about Sebastian's heart and about Bill.'

'What about Bill?' Lucy asked.

'He's dead, murdered right in front of me,' Cecilia said, fingering the necklace. 'Frey was definitely behind it.'

'Fucking monster,' Lucy spat.

'I'm so sorry, CeCe,' Agnes said.

Agnes and Lucy each moved in for a long embrace. CeCe acknowledged their condolences sombrely but with clear eyes.

'I would have bet my life he had the heart,' Cecilia said, as they separated.

'Me too,' Lucy said. 'Until I saw it.'

Cecilia was floored.

'Take us there.'

16

Bloodmilk

It was late. Car services were booked and cabs were scarce.

The G train from Metropolitan Avenue to Carroll Street was long but better than walking. Lucy, Cecilia and Agnes entered the subway, drawing an occasional stare or whisper or giggle from passing locals.

'Oh my God!'

'Is that them?'

They ignored it and continued down the flight of slick cement steps into the bowels of Brooklyn's commuter rail system.

It was damp, dark and dirty. The token booth was closed and the platform empty except for a homeless guy or three slumped over at the exits. The rush-hour crowd was long departed, likely in the middle of their second after-work cocktail at some Bedford Avenue boite or another. The overhead fluorescent lights buzzed and crackled, threatening to blow at any moment, and the sound of trains on other lines clacking in the distance faded into nothing. Not a stop-and-frisk cop in sight.

Lucy, Agnes and Cecilia waited wordlessly.

They eyed the beer cans and candy rappers littering the tracks, floating in oily leftover puddles of yesterday's rain. Rats traversed the guard above the electrified third rail, testing their own mortality. Boards and beams from an ongoing repair project were partially tarped and piled up, unbound against the graffitied white tiled walls.

'Some work is never done,' Lucy observed impatiently.

Then finally, it came. The headlamp from the front car blazed brightly at them through the musty tunnel as it approached the station. The letter G, encircled in green, rushing at them. The train was coming, but none of them were sure they wanted to get on. The train raced through the station and passed the waiting women without slowing, without stopping. They could barely make out the digital 'Out Of Service' signs blinking their red-lighted warning on the side of each car.

'Spare some change for a sinner, sister?'

CeCe was startled. She had been so distracted by the noise

and her destination that she'd barely noticed one of the homeless guys from the other end of the platform approach. She reached into her pocket as Lucy and Agnes looked on. She knew what it was like to depend on the generosity of passers-by. They usually just tossed a few coins in her guitar case without even a glance in her direction. It irked her. CeCe wanted to show him more respect as she handed over the last few bills she had on her.

'You look familiar,' Cecilia noted, fixating on the area around his eyes. 'Do I know you from somewhere?'

'Around the neighbourhood,' he replied, the ingratiating smile leaving his face.

He held up the bill to study the denomination and she noticed blood on it. Her blood. She felt a sharp pain.

First from the wound on her hand.

Then from his hands around her throat.

Before Lucy and Agnes could reach her, they were restrained from behind, held back. Lucy struggled, but Agnes seemed to wilt, almost fainting into a trance in the vandal's arms. Cecilia could see Lucy immobilized and Agnes swooning but could do nothing about it, locked in a desperate struggle of her own.

'Don't worry, they're next,' her attacker assured, foaming like a rabid animal.

He grunted and threw Cecilia down on to the cement platform, keeping a firm hold on her throat. She tried to use her knees and elbows to strike him as he sat above her but she

was pinned, her head dangling over the edge of the platform. She turned to look down the tunnel and was met by a light breeze, a tell tale sign that a train was on the move. Approaching.

On the verge of blacking out, Cecilia felt for the hypodermics hanging from her necklace, and wove them in between each of her fingers, makeshift brass knuckles, and made a fist. She punched him as hard as she could in the neck, driving the middle casing into the soft spot in his throat. She slammed it upward through the bone of his bottom jaw into his mouth.

'You were saying?' she asked bluntly.

He released her, blood gushing out of his nostrils and through his teeth, collapsing as Cecilia pulled the stalk from his throat. With the other hand she reached for her cello bow belt buckle and unsheathed it, revealing a blade the length of a kitchen knife.

Agnes's assailant rushed her, leaving her in a heap on the subway platform. Cecilia sidestepped him and grabbed him around the neck, putting a knife to his chest. 'Who sent you?'

'The devil,' the arrogant assassin replied.

A few yards away, Lucy fought for her life. Suddenly, she felt cold metal against her temple and froze. The look in CeCe's eyes told her all she needed to know. It was a gun.

'Drop the knife, bitch!'

CeCe's attention was suddenly diverted by a sight she could scarily believe. It was Agnes, walking up behind Lucy and her

attackers, with a two by four in her hands. CeCe looked down and there was Agnes also, still lying on the ground. A double take. Agnes raised the wooden stud, brought it back behind her shoulder and swung it with all her strength against Lucy's attacker's skull. The force of the blow freed Lucy and sent her sprawling forward, nearly over the edge of the platform. Lucy pulled herself off of the cement. There was no one there but Agnes, still out cold.

The screech of metal wheels against carbon steel rail signalled to all of them that a train was fast approaching. The platform was a scene of carnage.

'Two down,' Lucy said, glaring at the third.

He was unimpressed.

'See you soon,' he said, backing away and running up the exit staircase.

'Get Agnes,' Cecilia screamed, circling her malefactor and keeping him atknife-pointt distance from them.

'Agnes,' Lucy whispered, kneeling beside her. 'Agnes, wake up.'

Lucy touched her face and stroked her hair, which seemed to rouse the sleeping girl. Agnes stood slowly with Lucy's help. Lucy slid along some unctuous tissue on the ground beneath her but kept her balance, kicked aside some shards of broken skull and dragged Agnes along with her. Just in time to bolt inside the train as the doors were closing.

'You OK?' Lucy asked Cecilia.

'Yeah. You?'

They both looked at Agnes.

'What the hell was that?' Lucy asked.

'I don't know,' she mumbled. 'But I've been having these weird out of body experiences ever since Precious Blood.'

'No shit?' Lucy added, in a state of semi-shock.

'I think about being somewhere and I'm there,' she explained. 'I can't control it.'

'Until you need to,' Cecilia said.

The three of them sat silently watching the stations go by out the windows, keeping a close eye on every entrance and exit in and out of their car.

The lights blinked on the ceiling as the train clacked along, strobed the fingermarks on Cecilia's neck which were turning from red to a nasty black and blue. They exited at the Smith-Ninth Street station and Lucy led them to Perpetua's house. To Sebastian.

The streets were quiet. Lucy, Agnes and Cecilia arrived at the modest three-storey brownstone and immediately sensed trouble. The Madonna statue that Lucy had admired was toppled over, its outstretched hand broken off and turned to painted rubble. The snake portion, the one that the Madonna was stepping on, was gone.

The lights were on in the parlour and Lucy climbed the steps and knocked. She grabbed the knob and found the door unexpectedly unlocked. She almost fell inside the house.

'Perpetua,' Lucy called. 'It's Lucy.'

'Look,' Agnes said, pointing to the dimly lit hallway walls just in front of them.

There were splatters of reddish brown everywhere. Handprints, as if a toddler had been let loose with a set of finger-paints.

'It's still wet,' Cecilia said, moving in for a closer look.

Lucy reached for the light switch on the wall. It clicked lifelessly as she snapped it up and down. They moved cautiously down the hallway into increasing darkness, Lucy leading the threesome. Suddenly, she yelled out and fell to the floor.

Lucy was face to face with a dead man.

Cecilia pulled out her cigarette lighter and raised it, illuminating the narrow space. Agnes helped Lucy to her feet and they continued down the hall toward the bedroom at the back of the house. It was a mess of broken furniture and window glass. Sheets torn, crosses splintered, photos ripped and knickknacks, accumulated over the course of a lifetime, strewn carelessly about. Lucy's lighter revealed scratchy phrases, Biblical ones, along the walls, handwritten in blood. Still wet and dripping.

Sobrii estote vigilate quia adversarius vester diabolus tamquam leo rugiens circuit quaerens quem devoret.*

---

* Be sober and alert: because your adversary the devil, as a roaring lion, goeth about seeking whom he may devour. 1 Peter 5: 8–9

A woman's body lay in front of the open closet door, her head bashed mercilessly in.

'No!' Lucy cried at the sight of her murdered mentor, who'd obviously tried with her last breath to protect the relic.

Above her head written mocking words of despair:

Cum me interficerent in ossibus meis exprobraverunt mihi hostes mei dicentes tota die ubi est Deus tuus. *

'Lucy!' Cecilia shouted. 'Where is it?'

Lucy pointed at the open closet door. Cecilia approached with her lighter and looked inside, illuminating the altar.

'It's gone!' Cecilia cried.

Agnes was transfixed by the bloody words above Perpetua. 'Where is your God?' she repeated silently to herself.

Surveying the carnage all around her, she was wondering the same thing.

A rumbling at the front of the house startled them. Cecilia was doubly surprised because she had no inkling from her ever-present stigmata that danger was near. The only exit in the tiny room was the shattered window, and it was too small for a single one of them to climb through, let alone the three of them at such short notice. They were trapped. Whatever, whoever was coming, they'd have to face it together. Live or die.

---

* My bones suffer mortal agony as my foes taunt me, saying to me all day long, 'Where is your God?' Psalms 42:10

Lucy stood up and joined Agnes and Cecilia, shoulder to shoulder, facing the doorway. The footsteps slowed as they got closer until the intruder suddenly revealed himself.

'Jesse,' Lucy said, relieved.

'What happened here?'

'His heart is gone.'

Jesse hung his head. 'I'm too late.'

'If you knew something why didn't you stop it? Call the police or something?' Lucy railed.

'The police?' Jesse laughed. 'I tried to call you. To warn you.'

'How would you know anything about this?' Agnes asked.

'I listened to the video of Lucy and Perpetua when we were here yesterday.'

'She said nobody knew they had Sebastian's heart here,' Lucy reminded him.

'Frey knew?' Agnes asked.

'No. If he knew, he would have sent his creeps for it long ago.'

'What are you saying, Jesse?' Lucy pressed.

'Mayfield played me. We were followed, Lucy. We led him here. You and me.'

'That's why we're still alive. He knew we'd come eventually,' Lucy said.

'So that's why we were attacked tonight,' Agnes said. 'He doesn't need us anymore.'

'How could I be so stupid?' Jesse repeated, inconsolably.

'He has Sebastian's heart. These beautiful people, who believed in us, who had faith in us, are dead!' CeCe cried in anger.

Lucy nodded in a devastated trance-like state, staring at Jesse. 'It's all because of us.'

17

Streetwalking Superstars

The crowd gathered quickly in front of the police precinct house on Union Street. Lucy, Cecilia and Agnes were escorted in one after another. It wasn't exactly a perp walk, but it was close. To the faithful, it was nothing short of a thrill to see the three of them march in together, just as they'd marched out of Precious Blood through haze and fire a few months prior. To the sceptics, a relief to have these dubious latter day saints off the streets and their minions corralled behind police barricades.

'Free them!' some supporters in the crowd shouted, worried that they might be blamed for what had happened.

The three were ushered into a small, drab room with a

frosted-glass door. They were seated at a rectangular table with a single chair at the head of the table left empty.

'Don't tell them anything,' Lucy whispered angrily. 'They can't be trusted.'

'Maybe they can help?' Agnes wondered. 'Protect us? Or something?'

'Remember what Sebastian said: save yourself,' Cecilia reminded them, closing the button on her vintage black Victorian lace high-necked collar to cover her bruises. 'It's up to us.'

The door opened and a harried-looking officer stepped through it, sixteen-ounce coffee firmly in hand.

'Back so soon?' Captain Murphy asked, taking a seat.

Even he reacted to the three of them together. In one room. They were a sight, whether you believed in them or not.

'You're right, it's much too soon for another interrogation,' Cecilia said to the other girls. 'It's basically the same shit we said before. Are we done here, then?'

'What's the rush?' the captain asked. 'Lose something?'

The girls settled back down into their chairs. Whether he knew something or was just being a wise-ass was still up for debate.

'Yeah,' Lucy answered, taking the offensive. 'I've lost my patience with this charade.'

'This is getting to be a habit,' Murphy said, eyeing Lucy.

'First the church, then the TV studio, and now this. Let's forget about the number of complaints we deal with from those nuts that follow you around, blocking traffic, trespassing, loitering around the neighbourhood. I've had to assign half the precinct just to deal with this hysteria. Do you know how much you three are costing the city? The taxpayers?'

'We had nothing to do with this,' Lucy shouted.

'I'm not accusing you of anything. You're not charged with anything.'

'Then why are we here?' Cecilia said. 'Why were we fingerprinted and taken into custody?'

'Standard operating procedure. More importantly, it was for your own safety.'

'How considerate of you, Detective, to come to our aid,' CeCe replied, batting her lashes. 'By jailing us overnight.'

Murphy was unimpressed. 'There was another incident last night. Two junkies dead on the G train platform in Red Hook. A fight most likely.'

Cecilia fiddled nervously with her collar. 'Shit happens.'

'Nothing ever just happens,' he said angrily. 'You're always in the wrong place at the wrong time. You're going to get hurt. Badly hurt.'

'Is that a threat?' Cecilia asked.

'No,' he said. 'A warning.'

'You're a little late.'

'If you see something, say something,' Lucy mocked.

'We've been lucky so far,' Cecilia said. 'Blessed, you could say.'

'Not everyone takes kindly to that sort of sentiment,' Murphy advised. 'Especially the Church.'

'It's not the Church we have to worry about,' Agnes quipped.

'The three of you have a lot of influence. Is this really the image you want out there?'

'Public relations isn't our biggest concern either.'

'Do you know why anyone would want to kill the woman?'

'No,' Lucy replied.

'What were the three of you doing there?'

'Visiting a friend,' Agnes said.

'If you want to know who killed Perpetua, ask Dr Frey,' Cecilia shouted, unable to contain herself any longer. 'And ask him about Bill while you're at it.'

'Still trashing Frey? What in the hell would he have to do with that old woman?'

The girls were silent. The last thing they wanted was for the police to find the relic before they did.

'If the straitjacket fits . . .' CeCe retorted.

'He's the one releasing lunatics into the streets,' Lucy said. 'Into that halfway house along the Gowanus.'

Murphy pushed back. 'Born Again is a joint community initiative between the hospital, the city and the Church,' Murphy informed. 'Everyone in there is pre-screened for violent or anti-social behaviour.'

'Who screens them?' Agnes asked.

'Psychiatric department at Perpetual Help.'

'So, Frey?' Cecilia concluded sarcastically for him.

'Smells almost as bad as the canal,' Agnes said.

'It's the most successful rehab programme in the city. Getting people back on their feet,' Murphy said. 'The place is monitored 24/7.'

'Look at you. Spitting back talking points from a goddamn city press release.'

Lucy was unimpressed. She chipped away at the detective's defensiveness. 'Funny how everyone gets to do fundraisers for it and score political points and congratulate themselves.'

'Isn't that how you make a living?' he replied snidely.

'Only if there's a photographer.'

'Saint for sale,' he said. 'How holy.'

'I think you have saints mixed up with angels,' Lucy rejoined.

'It makes sense if you just let it,' Agnes said, interrupting Murphy and Lucy trying to one-up each other.

'Put it in writing,' the captain snorted. 'Write to the mayor. Or the Archbishop if you got a problem. I'm not the zoning board or the complaint department.'

He picked up his coffee and his files and started out. 'I'm watching you,' Murphy said, frustrated. 'That is a threat.'

He slammed the door.

'I think we might be getting through to him,' Agnes whispered.

'Do you think he's in Frey's pocket?' Lucy asked.

'Who knows?' CeCe said wearily. 'Either way, I think Agnes is right. We made our point.'

'Let the cops sniff around for a while.' Lucy agreed. 'Time to put some pressure on the doctor for a change.'

The old man in the white skullcap kneeled, deep in prayer, after hours in the Sala Dei Santi, Room of the Saints, of the Borgia Apartment. Long robes trailed over the backs of his red shoes, symbolizing the blood of the martyrs, and down to the marble floor.

'Holy Father!' a voice called urgently from behind. 'Me dispiaci.'

He raised his head and slowly opened his eyes, focusing on the large fresco of The Disputation of Saint Catherine by Pinturicchio before him. He rose and turned to face Cardinal DeCarlo, Prefect of the Congregation for The Doctrine Of Faith, the oldest of the nine congregations at the Vatican.

'Che cosa?' the Pope asked.

The slender man with the sharp nose, thin lips and sunken eyes untied the leather binder in his hands and rifled through the papers inside, displaying them for the pontiff. Now that Easter week was over, it would be easier, he surmised, to gain the Pope's full attention.

'The situation we've been following in New York has taken a turn,' the Papal Nuncio explained. 'A bad turn.'

'How so?'

'The cult around the boy and the survivors has grown.'

'This is not necessarily a problem, is it?'

'I fear our silence in this matter has only made things worse.'

The Pope was cool and dispassionate in his assessment as he again reviewed the headlines of Sebastian's death and subsequent investigation.

'This is not the first time we have observed such circumstances. Surely the local authorities and clergy are involved.'

The Nuncio, feeling he was not getting through, handed the Pope a brief of the latest news reports.

'There has been a murder.'

The Holy Father clasped his hands behind his back and began to walk. The Prefect took his arm, whispering the circumstances of the crime and the disappearance of Sebastian's heart.

'What do you propose?'

'That we investigate this blasphemy before more are deceived or injured or killed.'

'Blasphemy? How do you know it is blasphemy? The intervention of God in the world is the very basis of faith, is it not?'

The cardinal was silenced by the Pope's challenge,

remembering to whom he was speaking. 'Of course we believe such things are possible, in miracles . . .'

'I didn't ask what you believe,' the Pope interrupted sternly. 'I asked how you know.'

The Nuncio continued to argue for his views. 'I know that things are spinning out of control and will worsen without our intervention. This is a challenge of the highest order to the primacy of the Church. To your authority.'

'Yes, we must identify the true enemy and put a stop to this before more are injured or worse.'

'Then you concur, Holy Father? Someone must be sent.'

'Yes,' the Pope agreed. 'Someone reliable.'

Jesse bit into an apple that he bought at the deli across the street from the morgue. He stood around; waiting for Mayfield to take one of his regular cigarette breaks, but there was no sign of the tipster. After a while, one of the doors popped open and, Ronnie, a lanky mortuary worker, stepped out.

Jesse waved and walked over. 'Mayfield around?'

'Who wants to know?'

'A friend.'

'You don't look like someone he'd be friends with.'

'Well, not exactly a friend. More like an acquaintance.'

'Uh-huh.'

Jesse handed over a crisp fifty. 'Is he around?'

'Nah,' the guy replied, pocketing it.

'Is he working the night shift today or something?'

'Nah,' the guy said again. 'Didn't show up. Yesterday or today. Boss says he's toast if he doesn't turn up.'

'Did he say anything? Was he in trouble?'

'You know the type,' the guy said. 'Drugs. Robbery. In and out of jail. Nuthouses.'

'Nuthouses?'

'Rehab. Matter of fact, that's where I thought you might be from. You look like one of the douchebags that come around here to see him.'

'Rehab. Like at Perpetual Help?'

'Yeah. I thought you said you knew him?'

Jesse ignored the question and pulled out another fifty-dollar bill. 'Know where I can find him?'

Ronnie looked down and tugged at the bill. Testing its authenticity. He held it up to the light, snapped it a few times and slipped into the pocket of his scrubs.

'He's been living in that group home on the Gowanus. Near where that crazy shit in that church went down a while back. You heard about that right?'

'Yeah,' Jesse said. 'I heard.'

'Let's just say he's not the most reliable type,' Ronnie smiled. 'Plays everybody.'

'Let me know if he turns up,' Jesse puffed. 'Tell him Jesse is looking for him.'

'I'll be sure to tell him,' Ronnie mocked, laughing and

shaking his head as he made his way back inside. 'Whatcha gonna do when you find him?'

Jesse smiled back at him and winked. He sensed a chance at redemption. For being fooled. Putting the girls in danger. For Perpetua. For losing the heart.

'I'm gonna kill him.'

18

Worship for the Wear

Martha pushed her way through the expectant crowd outside the precinct, shouting for her child. Agnes didn't need to be notified that her mother had arrived; she could hear her through the barred and tinted windows of the station house.

'Agnes!'

Agnes looked at Cecilia and Lucy for some moral support, but their sympathetic frowns did little to relieve her anxiety. The closer Martha came to the doorway, the louder her shouts became.

'Did she have to be notified?' Agnes asked of the officer assigned to her.

'Sorry, it's the law,' the woman said. 'You're still a minor.'

Martha barged in. Red faced and nearly hyperventilating with anger.

'Please, Ma'am, keep it down,' the desk sergeant advised as she entered the building. 'She's fine.'

'Don't you tell me to keep it down. I demand to see my daughter!'

Agnes was escorted out and into the vestibule by one of the female police officers, with Lucy and Cecilia close behind. She stood silently, waiting for her mother to notice.

'I'm here, Mother,' she said, her voice barely audible over Martha's wretched racket.

'What are you doing?' Martha screamed. 'I'm called down to the police station. Is this what it is has come to?'

Agnes stepped closer to Martha. Cautiously. 'Stop it, Mother. You're embarrassing me.'

'You're sitting here in a jail cell and I'm embarrassing you?' Martha spewed.

'Are you done?' Agnes said calmly, trying to defuse the situation.

'No, I'm not done,' she fumed, pointing her finger accusingly at Lucy and Cecilia. 'I blame you two for this. For dragging her into this, filling her head with this nonsense.'

Cecilia and Lucy swallowed hard, feeling badly for Agnes.

'Mrs Fremont,' Lucy began to explain in Agnes's defence, 'we—'

'Not another word. I've heard about the two of you,' Martha said, turning away from Lucy and toward the desk sergeant. 'Show me your friends and I'll show you who you are!'

'I'm so sorry,' Agnes mouthed at them, as her mother took her by the arm and dragged her out of the precinct house.

Lucy and Cecilia stared out at Agnes and Martha as the crowd parted to let them pass.

'Tough bitch,' Cecilia said.

'Yeah,' Lucy remarked. 'Wish I had one.'

Dr Frey nodded to the overnight janitor as he approached the lift. Frey was his usual spry self. One arm full of folders, the other carrying a black satchel. The janitor looked up from his mop and bucket. 'Good Evening, Doctor.'

'Good evening,' Frey replied.

'You have a visitor.'

'Yes, I know.'

The janitor returned to mopping and Frey stepped into the lift and rode it to the top floor.

He walked past reception, down the long hallway to his office. He could see a man sitting, his back to the office door. Frey rushed into the room and placed his folders and bag down on the desk before taking his seat. 'Captain.'

'Doctor.'

'What can I do for you a this late hour?'

The doctor shuffled through some papers, all but dismissing his visitor.

'I thought this might be a good time to talk,' Murphy suggested, 'since you haven't returned any of my calls during office hours.'

'Office hours? This is a hospital not a bank, Captain. I'm paid to attend to my patients and the business of the facility at all times. One must prioritize.'

Murphy chaffed at the suggestion that a call from law enforcement wasn't very high on Frey's list. 'Has anyone ever told you that you are an arrogant man?'

'Yes, but I assume you didn't come here to insult me.'

'We're having trouble with Born Again.'

'You mean you are. It seems to be working quite well for the rest of us.'

'Not exactly. Two of the patients released are dead and a horrific crime in the vicinity of the house also raises questions.'

'Yes, I read about that. Awful.'

'There are a lot of sick people in the world.'

'I understand you brought the girls in for questioning?'

'Informally, yes.'

'I didn't realize the police did anything informally.'

Murphy shrugged off the doctor's diss. 'You sound disappointed. Do you think they actually had something to do with it?'

'It wouldn't be the first time that ritual murders or even

suicides, human sacrifice and the like occur under circumstances like these, where cults are involved.'

'That's quite a leap Dr Frey. Ritual killing. Cults. I've seen no evidence of that.'

'Well, that might be because you're not looking.'

'With all due respect, you have no idea where I'm looking. Every possibility is being investigated.'

Frey looked away from the detective and out his office window at the top of Perpetual Help. He gazed over at what remained of the tower of the Church of the Precious Blood. 'People expect psychiatrists to be magicians, Detective, but my job is not that complicated. It requires neither the years of training demanded by the medical board nor particular insight into the human mind. What it does require is the ability to see what is in front of you, plainly, dispassionately, without bias.'

'And what is it you see, Doctor?'

'In Cecilia, Lucy and Agnes, I see three very sick girls. I've made no secret of that.'

'Well, word on the street is that some see three saints.'

Frey smiled. 'And the difference is?'

'Careful, Doctor. You're talking to a parochial school graduate.'

'My point exactly, Captain Murphy. The fact that you could repeat such a ludicrous observation with any seriousness is why those three are still on the street and not in treatment.'

'Under your care of course.'

'Ideally, yes. I do have an ego and they present a unique challenge.'

'The same challenge as Sebastian?'

'Do you know where saints would be today, Captain? Right out there,' Frey pointed to the ward just beyond his office door. 'Committed. Observed. Medicated. Cured in most cases. Prevented from becoming a danger to themselves or others. Not talking to animals, vomiting as retribution, or standing on one leg for years to prove the existence of God to the uninformed and superstitious. They would be treated.'

'That was the plan for Sebastian, I assume. Personality management.'

'Indeed, for his own good and the good of the general public. And you see what happened once he escaped? Mayhem. Death.'

'Which brings us back to Born Again.'

'I'm sorry but that has nothing to do with me.'

'The girls seem to feel differently.'

'And you believe them?' Frey huffed. 'If you intend to accuse me of such things, you'd better have good evidence, and a good lawyer.'

'Those addicts were released on your authority.'

'No, those former addicts were released based upon an established set of criteria, approved by the hospital board, the city and even our community sponsors.'

'Is there anything you can tell me about either of them?'

Murphy asked, handing over a file on each.

Frey thumbed through them casually. 'Not really,' he said. 'The usual. Bad habits, bad choices.'

'Then what are they doing out on the street?'

'We don't warehouse substance abusers anymore, like returned packages in a dead letter office, Captain. We treat them to the best of our ability, with the best medical technology, medications, and cognitive therapies at our disposal and return them to society. We seek to rehabilitate them.'

'Not everyone can be rehabilitated, Doctor, or should be,' Murphy countered. 'The jails are full of the consequences of their bad decisions. And the cemeteries.'

'You were saying there was a murder?'

'An old woman in the neighbourhood. Odd thing is, she knew Sebastian. She was one of the protesters outside the church.'

'Tragic, but some of these people are attracting a lot attention to themselves. It's not difficult to imagine them being followed home, robbed, killed.'

'This wasn't a robbery homicide, Doctor. This was personal. Whoever did this was gloating, wanted to send a message.'

'Are you sure you aren't reading too much into this, Captain?' Frey said. 'Getting caught up in it all?'

'Hmm? 'Reading too much into this?' That's a strange comment coming from a psychiatrist,' Murphy said.

'Not everything is a mystery,' Frey said.

'I just can't figure what those girls were doing there.'

'Can't you?'

'What are you getting at?'

'Those girls are delusional. As bad as Sebastian. Probably worse. And they are walking around scot-free.'

'They aren't guilty of anything criminal. If anything, they are victims of Sebastian. Traumatized. Sick. You just said so yourself.'

'Don't you see, Captain? They are contagious. Every day their following grows. The weak-minded, the depressed, the lonely, the confused, the unstable, they flock to them.'

'Are you saying they are bad for your business, Doctor?' Murphy said. 'That they and their followers should be here instead?'

'I'm saying they are charlatans. The latest in a very long line of them. And that the answer to your questions might more likely be found in their world, not mine.'

'Maybe they offer something you can't.'

'Is there anything else, Captain?'

'No. Not for now.'

'Good night.' Frey watched the detective walk down the hall, wait for the lift and get in. He took the files of the two men Murphy had left, rolled his chair back and dropped them in the bin. He pulled himself closer to the desk and eyed the satchel sitting on the desktop. His initials had been stamped in gold leaf on the black calfskin

casing. The bag was elegant and cool, but unassuming.

He reached for the gold clasp and turned it. The frame snapped apart with an audible pop, the pressure released. The doctor reached into the bag and placed his fingers around the metal canister and lifted it out gently, holding it momentarily above his bag, tilting it to one side and then the other, inspecting it in the light as a jeweller might evaluate a gem about to be pawned. He could see the organ through the glass pane, somewhat surprised it had not been the least bit cracked or damaged in its acquisition process. Sebastian's heart was intact, unusually so, given that few steps had been taken to properly prepare and preserve it. Incorrupt.

'Welcome home, Sebastian,' Frey whispered. 'You are finally back where you belong.'

Jesse walked along the fetid waterside, waving away at flies and the stench that penetrated his nostrils. The still water was the most unusual shade of industrially tinted grey-green. For years, there had been talk of cleaning it up, turning it into some kind of Brownstone Riviera, but for the most part, it remained what it had always been – a polluted dumping ground. A place to drown secrets. He'd heard all the old Mafia jokes that had formed the Gowanus' reputation; that it was ninety per cent guns, that it was the best place to catch 'gowanorrhea', all of that. All of it back-to-back with some of the priciest real estate in the city.

The canal was nestled between the family friendly neighbourhoods of Carroll Gardens and Park Slope, tucked away but sticking out nevertheless. An appropriate place to put a halfway house, especially if you wanted to blend in, Jesse thought.

For the city and the project's supporters, turning a crack house into a halfway house was good politics, especially since it had been re-branded an outpatient facility. Money was invested, the streets around it were cleaned up, business and stores were encouraged to open up and police presence was increased. All good things designed to calm the nervous neighbourhood nellies who typically opposed these sorts of things. They signed off, in exchange for the hope of increased real estate values which was the big picture in the end anyway and an assurance that the residents were guaranteed to be harmless. It was part of the same deal that allowed the conversion of Precious Blood, Jesse recalled. Frey's deal. The connection was suddenly becoming clearer and clearer to him. There was nothing harmless about this place, especially if Mayfield was living there.

As Jesse approached Born Again, he could see a spate of unusual police activity buzzing near the recently renovated four-storey brownstone. The street was taped off and police stanchions dotted the canal side. Emergency vehicles choked off the street and traffic in either direction had been brought to a halt.

'Want to find a traffic jam, look for a traffic cop,' Jesse moaned.

Curious, he walked as close to Born Again and the commotion as he could, just in time to see the police divers fishing a lifeless body from the water. The police radios crackled with details, all offered in code. 'OD' and 'suicide' were the signal codes he recognized.

The body was bloated and grey. Eyes and tongue bulging, like a sick molly Jesse had once found at the bottom of his fish bowl. Jesse wanted to turn away but couldn't. He recognized the corpse. And the bulge of money, his money, in the front pocket.

'Mayfield.'

The lights were burning brightly in the Fremont home long after midnight, passersby glued to the angry shadow play screening on the curtained windows. Fingers pointing, arms outstretched in frustration, feet stomping.

'You will not put me through this again!' Martha bellowed.

'You?'

'I'm not sorry for you, Agnes. Not anymore.'

'I'm not looking for your pity,' Agnes shouted,

'Don't you care about the future?'

'Yes, the future is the thing I care most about.'

'You could have fooled me,' Martha railed. 'You are becoming an embarrassment.'

'Not everybody feels that way, Mother,' Agnes said, pulling the curtain from the window and pointing to the candles, flowers and the assortment of Park Slope pilgrims camped outside their door.

'Something to really be proud of, dear, a motley crew of life's winners gathered in your honour.'

'They are people, Mother! And I don't care what you think or what your friends think.'

Martha took a step back and sat down. 'I'm not trying to insult you, Agnes. I'm just worried sick about you.' Martha explained, nearly slumping, exasperated, into the cushions. 'The police, the newspapers, those people out there. I don't know what happened to our lives.'

'Sebastian happened.'

'All that boy brought to us is danger. Death.'

'Speak for yourself, Mother.'

'Not just him either. Those two girls, Cecilia and Lucy, I blame them, too! How you ever got mixed up with these people.'

'Mixed up?'

'They are beneath you, Agnes. Dropouts and drug addicts. Fame whores. I thought you would choose better than that.'

'I didn't choose.'

'Now you are really scaring me,' Martha said. 'I swear I should just have you . . .'

'Have me what?' Agnes fumed. 'Committed?'

'You are behaving like a crazy person. I don't even know you anymore.'

'You never knew me.'

Agnes bolted for her bedroom and slammed the door. Martha trailed after and stopped in the hallway.

'One of these days it will be the morgue I'm picking you up from, Agnes!'

19

Twisted Lamb

Lucy and Cecilia left the police station and headed toward Lucy's Vinegar Hill apartment. Heads turned, some walked by, laughing under their breath, others followed, praying silently under theirs. They continued to stroll along Court Street, the rebel rocker and the sometime socialite, past the baby strollers and the double-parked delivery vans, a mismatched pair that somehow fitted perfectly together. They looked fierce. Fearless.

They came across a local park with children playing and sat on a long bench.

'What do you think he wants with it?' Cecilia asked.

'To keep it hidden,' Lucy said. 'Out of sight, away from

those who would revere it.'

'Why wouldn't he just destroy it?'

'Because it's a trophy for him. It's power.' Lucy offered. 'It represents everything Sebastian was. Strength, courage and truth.'

'Everything Frey isn't.'

'Now that he has it, he doesn't need us anymore, so life is about to get a lot more dangerous.'

'I know.'

'And he knows we will come for it,' Lucy added. 'No matter what.'

'He's been goading us,' Cecilia said. 'First it was the club fight, then Bill, then those subway jerk-offs.'

'And now, Perpetua,' Lucy said, sadly.

'He has the cops and just about everyone else fooled,' Cecilia said.

'Not everyone,' Lucy said, reassuringly.

'We need to get it back.'

'We will get it back.'

'Eight dollars,' the gypsy cabbie croaked, his scanner full blast waiting to pounce on his next fare.

'Here is fine,' Dr Frey instructed, requesting to be let out a few door ahead of his final destination. 'Put it on the hospital account.'

The town car rolled to a stop. There was no mistaking he'd

arrived at the right spot. Several rows of candles and bouquets of flowers bordered the wrought-iron fence and dotted the foot of the stoop leading up to the Fremont home.

'You know her?'

'Why do you ask?' Frey sniffed.

The driver eyed his passenger in his rearview mirror, making him for another well-heeled cheapskate too distracted by his own life to dig into his pocket for a tip.

'You don't look like a lot of the people I drive over here.'

'How do they look?' Dr Frey asked, reaching into his pocket for a fifty-dollar bill.

'Desperate,' the driver said.

'Looks can be deceiving,' Frey said, handing the money over. 'But then again, you didn't drive me here.'

'Whatever you say, boss,' the cabbie agreed, flicking the bill upright in his fingers and bringing it to his forehead in salute.

The sidewalk in front of the house and across the street was empty, a sure sign that Agnes wasn't home, as Martha had promised him. Frey studied the pop-up shrine, complete with votives, letters, cards, flowers, pictures, pleas and other offerings. The glow from the candles lit the cuffs of his wool slacks, reflecting off the tops of his recently polished black Italian loafers. It was almost blinding. He looked away, rubbed at his eyes and proceeded up the steps.

He reached the top and turned to face the street, unable to

shake the feeling of a familiar but unfriendly presence. He surveyed the block from left to right, one side of the street to the other. Instead, all he could recognize was a bell ringing. Not the ominous tolling of a church bell or the frenetic warning of a car alarm, but the thin ting-a-ling of bicycle.

Frey strained to see the source of the sound through the twilight. Before long, it revealed itself. A boy, riding toward him as fast as his feet could pedal along the grey slate sidewalk. The boy stopped at the foot of the Fremont staircase and looked up at him.

'Hello, Jude,' Frey greeted, showing none of the surprise he felt. 'Sounding the alarm, I see.'

The boy remained silent but stared directly up at him. Confronting him as best he could.

'You are a long way from home at this hour.'

Once again, Jude did not respond but kept his eyes fixed uncomfortably on Frey's.

'Such good eye contact you're making,' Frey observed. 'I always knew you had it in you. Something for us to discuss during your next visit.'

Jude shook his head no.

'We'll see about that, son,' Frey said. 'Now you run along.'

The boy mounted his bike, popped a wheelie over the kerb into the street and pedalled off into the darkness.

'Be careful, Jude,' Frey called after him. 'You could get hurt.'

The doctor returned to his original business and knocked at

227

the door. A vine of lush magenta roses crept up the side of the brownstone. Gorgeous, like nothing he'd ever seen. The scent of flowers filled his nose as he waited.

'Oh, Dr Frey. Thank God,' Martha said welcomingly.

'Your roses are quite something,' Frey said.

'Yes, this is the first time they've actually flowered. The vine has been here since we have, but it never produced roses. Until now.'

Frey was impressed, but didn't want to show it. 'It's been a while since I've made a house call.'

Martha held the door open wide and ushered him in. 'I am so grateful, Doctor. I know your responsibilities at Perpetual Help keep you very busy.'

'Yes, there is always a lot to do,' he agreed, 'But Agnes is a very special case.'

'I'm so relieved to hear you say that,' Martha offered. 'Please come in.'

Frey handed off his coat and studied the home admiringly as Martha hung it in the foyer closet. The decor was eclectic with a vintage feel. A crucifix hung near the entrance to the hallway, and several plaques with prayers of Saint Francis and other generic but beautiful hand-embroidered 'when life gives you lemons make lemonade' type motivational sayings dotted the living-room wall. He took a seat on the couch and waited, as he had been trained, for Mrs Freemont to open up. She fidgeted for a moment or two and grabbed for a tissue from a

decorative box that sat on the coffee table between them, dabbing at her eyes.

'I don't know what to do anymore,' she began sobbing quietly. 'I'm at the end of my rope with her.'

'When I didn't hear from you about a follow-up, I assumed things were improving. For Agnes and between the two of you.'

'Not at all,' Martha answered. 'She was so resistant to see you because of everything that happened with the investigation and I guess I was in denial, too.'

'Understandable. I know she blames me for Sebastian's death.'

'I'm sorry about that, Dr Frey. You were the first one to bring her problems to my attention. If I had only listened.'

'One spends a lifetime building a career, Mrs Fremont,' Frey explained. 'And to see it called into question, especially by those I sought to help, was disconcerting to say the least.'

'I hope you won't hold it against her, Doctor. She's so headstrong.'

'All is forgiven,' he said.

'She is very sick, I see that now.'

'Only now?'

'I thought the attempt that brought her to the ER was impulsive, but now I'm worried that there is something much deeper going on.'

'Yes, much deeper,' he agreed.

'She barely speaks to me, and when we do, it's only to argue,' Martha complained.

'May I see her room?'

'Yes, of course.'

Martha led him down the hallway to Agnes's private space.

'The inner sanctum,' Frey said with a smile as he entered.

'Please don't touch anything. She's very sensitive about anyone being in here.'

'Of course,' he agreed.

The doctor walked straight to the foot of her bed and took in the homespun, bohemian environment Agnes had created for herself. In many ways, it was from another era, apart from the computer that hummed quietly on her desk. It looked idealistic and romantic, like Agnes. But it also painted a picture of a more complicated, more subtle, more independent girl.

He stepped to her dresser, checking the rug for his footprints, and ran his fingers along the edge of the top, noting her pictures and perfumes and framed photos of her parents with her as a child. He stared out her window at the old dogwood tree beginning to flower in the yard. Her closet door was open and he pulled each hanging garment closer, studying them. Vintage lace dresses, long flowing skirts, her school uniform, dry-cleaned and ready to wear. All tasteful, all quality fabric and stitching, all – apart from the uniform that she had to wear – romantic. A handwritten note was pinned to the inside of her closet door. It read:

All truth passes through three stages.
First, it is ridiculed. Second, it is violently opposed.
Third, it is accepted as being self-evident.

Martha watched the doctor pour over it. He tipped his head back and pursed his lips.

'It's some sort of Biblical saying, from Jesus or a prophet, isn't it?'

'No, actually, an atheist. Schopenhauer.'

Frey was intrigued and alarmed. If he and Agnes agreed on nothing else, they could agree on this one philosophy. It demonstrated that she had a much more comprehensive understanding of her circumstances than he had given her credit for, and a much tighter hold on reality than Martha imagined. It was, he thought, a perfect mission statement.

He turned to her desk. 'Do you mind?' he asked, pointing to her drawer.

Martha nodded, still dabbing at her eyes. 'No, it's OK.'

Frey reached for the top drawer and pulled on the handle. It was locked.

'Is there a key?'

Mrs Fremont reluctantly shuffled through Agnes's jewellery box – past oversized turquoise and moonstone rings, vintage bracelets, chunky necklaces and lockets – and finally produced the key. She handed it to Frey who fitted it into the slot and opened the drawer. He wondered what she was keeping so

closely guarded, expecting a diary, press clippings of Sebastian's murder and the investigation that followed. Perhaps even notes, special requests from those psychos who elevated her to sainthood.

To his surprise, there were only three things in the wooden drawer: her patient wrist tag from Perpetual Help, an ornate gold vial and a single vellum page illuminated in hand, the page of Saint Agnes, taken from the Legenda in the old chapel. The police had found a page like it with Sebastian. He'd been shown it during questioning.

Frey lifted the artifact out carefully, removed his glasses from his shirt pocket and put them on. In the dim light of Agnes's bedroom, the paper became almost translucent and the gold, green and red ink seemed to glow, giving the appearance that the words were floating in air before him. As he held the page up closer a shock ran from his fingertips down his arm and he dropped the vellum to the desk, shaking his hand to regain some feeling.

'Static electricity,' Frey explained.

Martha took the page and placed it back in the drawer.

Frey then picked up the vial to examine it.

'It's exquisite, isn't it?' Martha said of the gold vial. 'I have no idea what it is, but she holds it sacred.'

'It appears to be a Victorian tear catcher,' Frey explained.

'Oh?' Martha asked.

'In Victorian times, a woman, usually a widowed bride,

would capture her tears for an entire year, the tears she cried over the loss of her husband, and on the anniversary of his death, she would pour the preserved tears on to his grave. It marked her mourning period.'

'Well, Agnes collects all kinds of things. She's certainly not a widow.'

Frey gently gave the vile a shake and noticed there was indeed water inside.

Martha felt unsettled, watching Frey fondle Agnes's prized possession. She grabbed it and put it back, locked the box and returned the key.

'We shouldn't be in her private stuff like this,' Martha said.

'I agree,' Frey said. 'But if those are her tears, I should probably take them with me.'

'I can't let you do that,' Martha said definitively.

'It would only be for testing. So I can see if she's taking anything,' Frey said, wanting desperately to leave with the fluid.

'I'm sorry, but I can't let you take her things.'

'As you wish,' Frey said, finally focusing on Agnes's desktop. He hit the space bar and the computer screen lit up.

The first open window that caught his attention was a search for Saint Jude. Frey examined the page for insight into Agnes's state of mind, and possibly Jude's as well. The window behind it was her email inbox.

'I don't think we should,' Martha said, guilty over such an invasion of Agnes's privacy.

'It's for her own good,' Frey said flatly. 'The more I know about your daughter, the easier it will be to treat her.'

Martha relented and the doctor scrolled through the incoming and saved entries. Most were from school friends or social media notifications, local discounts and spam. The emails that jumped out at him, however, were from a boy: Finn Blair.

'A boyfriend?' Frey inquired. 'That's a good sign.'

'Apparently he's a new boy in school that likes her. I've encouraged it because I thought that might help take her mind off things, turn her around, but it doesn't seem to be going anywhere.'

Frey was perturbed. 'She is quite tied to her notions of idealistic love,' he commented. 'Now more than ever it seems.'

'Those two girls and that boy are to blame for all of this, God forgive me!' Martha wailed. 'It's like she's brainwashed. Possessed.'

Dr Frey leaned over and placed his hand on her shoulders as she heaved in distress. 'Such a heavy cross to bear.'

'I can't do it anymore, Dr Frey,' Martha pleaded. 'Please, please help us!'

Frey stepped back, put his hands in his pocket and paced the living room floor pensively. 'It will be difficult,' he said, 'but if you and I are on the same page, if you are willing to join

me in what is necessary for Agnes's own good, then I may be able to help her.'

'What do I need to do?'

Agnes's Elegy

*T*he bath water was milky, like her skin.

Agnes submerged her naked body in the warm liquid and held her breath.

The only thing that stayed dry was some of her wavy copper hair still floating on the surface. And her black and gold mourning ring that she had on her finger, her arm on the rim of the porcelain claw foot tub.

Once under she opened her eyes wide and stared at the ceiling through the cloudy water.

This is what it must be like to be dead.

This wasn't the first time she practised. But, it was nearer to her now. More of a realistic run-through. She wanted to know what it felt like. What he felt like when it happened, and what she would feel when it eventually, inevitably happened to her.

After a short while, it seemed as though she could

breathe under the water.

She felt heavy, but calm.

Feeling with her breath.

The ripples from a violet flower petal caught her attention. It was floating on the water above her head. She watched it float around like a tiny vessel. Vibrant.

Then, a magenta petal followed. Next, white. And then scarlet.

Agnes looked up and saw a figure sitting on the edge of the tub, above her arm, by her head. She couldn't make out who it was. But, she knew it was a guy. He was throwing the petals on to the water off a lush bouquet that he was holding.

She tried desperately to lift herself out of the water, but she couldn't. Her body was too heavy.

She mouthed the words, 'Please help me out of here,' but he couldn't hear her. He just kept showering her with petals.

Agnes wanted to grab him with her hand, the one laid on the side of the tub, but even that wouldn't move. It no longer felt part of her body. Numb.

He was so close above her, but she couldn't reach out for him, call out to him. She was trapped inside her own body.

Like a lover throwing petals on the grave of his beloved.

She started to panic. Suck in water, but it there was no water. It was air. She was only breathing.

He threw more petals until the water was covered.

Was it him?

237

Was he there to shower her with flower petals to take her to himself?

She was ready now.

Agnes could see his silhouette stand up and face her. He watched her, and then, slowly, started to take off his clothes.

First, his shirt.

Next, he peeled off his black jeans.

Finally, his boots.

He dipped one foot in the water and then the other.

She scooted over to make room for him. But, he moved her back in the middle with his foot.

She watched him. His every move. She wanted him more with each passing second. She was craving his touch.

He placed one foot near her right leg and the other on her left side.

He slowly fell to his knees.

She could feel his legs cocooning hers. Feel his thighs on hers.

As he pulled her hips closer, she could feel everything.

His face skimmed the water.

He was not him.

It was Finn.

'No!' she silently screamed.

But, there was nothing she could do.

He ran his fingers along her jawline, down her throat, then to her stomach. He felt her pelvis. Grabbed it with both hands and propped it up.

'NO!' she demanded.

'You are acting like you've never seen evil before,' he said. 'Evil is a mirror.'

She was his to have. To do whatever he wanted to do.

She could see a dark mass growing up from her feet, over her legs and up her body. Agnes noticed the hair. Sebastian's hair. Growing once again, from the strand she had kept safe in her mourning ring. It was growing over her exposed body. Protecting her nakedness. Her vulnerability.

Finn could not penetrate it. Or her.

The hair finished covering her and then wrapped itself around Finn's throat, choking him. His veins popped out of his temples. His body thrashed around, trying to break hold, but it was not use.

Agnes was safe. Silent. Under Sebastian's hair. She felt nothing.

After a few minutes, Finn stopped fighting and fell from a standing position out of the bathtub. Replaced on top of her by Sebastian.

She could speak, move and hear again. She lifted her head above the water. Born again into the world. Back to life.

'Are you really here?' she asked him.

'Where else would I be?'

'Am I really here.'

'Where else would you be?'

'I can be in two places at once.'

'You can live your life, and always be with me.'

'That is not possible.'

Then you don't think love is possible.

'That is not love.'

Suddenly, the petals from the water swirled together into an elaborate, lush headpiece and wound around her gorgeous wavy hair.

She was righteous. Glorified. Triumphant. Beautiful.

You legend.

You martyr.

Take me.

20

Not All Who Wander Are Lost

The cab rolled quietly down Henry Street, passing brownstone after brownstone, schools, shops and restaurants as midnight approached. It was a beautiful spring night, dry and clear. She was sober, very different from the last time she been here.

'Far corner,' Lucy told the cabbie, reaching into her purse.

The driver pulled to stop. 'Here you are, Miss.'

'Thank you.' She handed a twenty-dollar bill through the plexiglass partition.

The driver shook his head and cleared the meter.

She looked at his rearview mirror and saw a rosary hanging from it.

She smiled at him and stepped from the car. He waited for a moment, watching her, his lips moving, praying as she walked across the street to Precious Blood.

Lucy stopped in front of the old church and took it in. The scaffolding and mesh were gone, out of caution that the winter weather might have caused an accident. There was no need to erect them any longer since the conversion of the place was now very much in doubt. Score one for them, she thought, and for the separation of church and real estate. Thanks to the petitioners and their tireless social media campaign.

The neighbourhood people had got the attention of the press who'd got the attention of the Archdiocese and the city that had put the hold and construction and short-circuited Frey's investor group, whose names had not been revealed. It was one big notoriety circle jerk, from the bottom up.

'Lucy.'

She tightened up. Ready for anything. Unable at first to place the deep throaty voice. A burly guy stepped out of shadows. Tall, muscled, well groomed. Like a security guard. Or a bouncer.

'Tony! You came.' She ran to him and stopped, opening her arms for a hug. He stepped back, uncertainly.

'What's the matter?'

'I don't know if I feel right kissing you,' he said. 'I've kissed a few chicks in my time but nobody like you.'

'You're gonna make me cry,' she said. 'Come here.'

She grabbed him and brought her cheek to his barrel chest. He held her for a minute, dropping his head and kissing her cheek as they parted.

'Long time no see,' Tony said. 'Guess you got better things to do than club every night.'

'Things are different now, but I'm still the same.'

'I'm not so sure about that.'

They both laughed and she grabbed his hand. 'You got my message.'

'I did. What's up?'

'I need to get inside.' Lucy pointed to the chained entrance.

'No problem.' Tony slipped a long thick metal bar hidden in his trouser leg up and out of the waistband of his jeans. He looked around and ushered her up the steps. He tucked the crowbar between the door and the links and twisted it once around, shortening and tightening the length of chain.

'Look out,' he said to her.

He raised the bar and slammed it down, again and again, as if he were starting the propeller of an old airplane, until the chain snapped open. He pushed open the door, but didn't enter. 'It's all yours.'

'This could be dangerous for you. Maybe you should leave?'

'I'll be OK,' he said.

'My friends are coming in a few minutes, will you look out for them?'

He stood tall and puffed out his chest. 'I'm a doorman, ain't I?'

'Best in the city,' she said, raising her hand for a high-five.

'Damn right,' Tony replied, smacking her up top.

'Their names are—' Lucy said about to name them.

'I know who they are,' he assured her.

'I'm going inside now.'

Tony nodded.

'Don't worry, Lucy. Nothing is gonna happen to any of you,' Tony assured her, smacking the bar into the palm of his hand. 'I guarantee it.'

'Don't make promises you can't keep, Tony.'

'My word is good, Lucy.'

Lucy got up on the balls of her spiked heels and gave him a kiss. She watched him blush and stepped inside. She pulled a small penlight from her pocket and shone it around as she walked through the vestibule into the nave. The church was filled with cool silence and little else. She reached down for the holy water stoup only to find it gone. Wall plaster was cracked and bubbled, and dust rained down from above with each of her steps, almost turning the space into a giant hourglass. The air smelled of smoke.

Debris had been cleared or taken away as evidence and the pews that hadn't been burned had been removed. Votive stands

remained, minus the votives. Piles of lumber, neatly covered, sat idle. The door to the sacristy that led to the underground chapel was boarded off. The confessional was gone.

She turned her flashlight on the ceiling vaults to see gaps in the roof tarped over and then on the floor beneath her, which was dry as a bone. Puddles of rain she'd once sloshed through had evaporated, leaving behind only a gritty ashen film. There was nothing left but a faded, brownish stain in the centre aisle, barely visible in the dim light. It was where Sebastian had fallen.

She stopped, replaying those last horrible moments over and over again in her mind. Instant recall. The screams, the shouts, the smoke, the shots. Her own heart was pounding in her chest at the memory. And at her dream. She inhaled deeply and picked up the faintest scent of incense through the soot and mildew. It was calming. Lucy felt him. His presence. A living thing. Waiting for her, for them, as he had the night they met. If there was ever a place for them to launch their quest, it was here.

'Hey,' Cecilia called out as she entered the church.

Lucy raised her hand and lit CeCe's path to the front of the church. Her boot heels echoed loudly through the cavernous space.

'Hey,' Lucy said quietly.

CeCe took the penlight from Lucy's hand and shone it around as Lucy had. There was no need to speak. Lucy knew

exactly what she was thinking and feeling.

'Is Agnes coming?' Cecilia asked.

'She'll be here.'

'I kinda wish she wasn't.'

'Why?'

'You know what we're planning to do isn't going to be easy,' Cecilia said. 'I just don't want her to . . . get hurt.'

'The cards have been dealt,' Lucy said. 'You know?'

'I know,' Cecilia continued. 'But she's different from us.'

'I worry about her, too.'

'Don't,' Agnes shouted from the entrance, pushing the door closed hard behind her.

'Lucy and I can handle this,' Cecilia said.

'Not without me,' Agnes insisted.

'Agnes, you won't be letting us down,' Lucy said.

'We'll do it together,' Agnes explained. 'Each of us. All of us.'

Agnes joined Lucy and Cecilia before the altar. They stood silently as Lucy shined her light, illuminating the ruin.

'Not much left,' CeCe said sadly.

'Not for long,' Agnes said.

The intercom on his desk buzzed and Dr Frey hit the reply button.

'Your three-thirty appointment is here.'

'Show him in,' Frey answered.

The door opened and a teenage boy walked through. At first glance, he appeared fragile, shy, even afraid. He was casually but conservatively dressed, hair neatly combed. The obedient, dutiful type. Anxious to please. He averted his sunken eyes as he took a seat, clearly fidgety and uncomfortable. Shaky, like a user in need of a fix.

'Mr Blair.'

'Hello, Doctor.'

'How are you feeling?'

'Better every day, thanks to you.'

'You were a model patient,' Frey extolled. 'I understand you are back at school.'

'Yes.'

'Classes not too overwhelming?'

'No. So far so good.'

'Making any friends?'

'A few. Well, one.'

'Good,' Frey noted. 'You remember we discussed the importance of strong personal relationships in your healing and recovery.'

'I understand.'

Finn continued to fidget, anxious at the direction in which the conversation was heading.

'I know you understand, Mr Blair, but I'm interested in actions, not words.'

'She likes me.'

'Once again, irrelevant,' Frey sniffed. 'Do you have her confidence?'

'We talk about this place. About Sebastian. About you.'

'Does she trust you?'

'I'm not sure,' he said honestly.

'Without that, you won't find your way into her head, her heart or her bed.'

'She's so certain of what she believes,' Finn said.

'So am I, son.' Frey replied. 'You understand that I could change your status with the stroke of a pen.'

'Why are you threatening me?'

'You were released for one reason, Finn.'

'Yes, I know,' Finn acknowledged, his voice cracking.

Finn eyed the doctor's prescription pad anxiously.

'Then do what needs to be done,' Frey insisted, writing out opiate painkiller and sleeping pill scrips and handing them over to the teen. 'Doctor's orders.'

21

The Nirvana Fallacy

Captain Murphy swirled the lukewarm coffee around his mouth as he studied the rap sheets of the two dead men from the subway and the OD they'd fished out of the canal.

The two were repeat offenders, busted for drugs, robbery, assault, weapons possession. In and out of the system with increasing frequency and little notice. The usual. From the looks of things, their problems started at an early age. Broken homes, abuse, expelled from school. It was almost fated. The whole slippery slope argument that once seemed almost quaint – beer leads to heroin – was back with a vengeance these days. Theirs was a generation of conscienceless slackers, bent on taking rather than making a life for themselves. Lazy, short-tempered and violent. Numb. It was no surprise that they'd turned to murder and no loss that they wound up dead. It was even predictable.

The OD was a different story, but not much. Same background but a little more ambitious. He had a job. Looked good on the surface, but rumours had been building for a while that he'd been part of an elaborate organ theft ring run out of the morgue. Employed, but no Boy Scout by any stretch of the imagination.

The troubling thing, he thought, was that these guys were all Born Again residents and supposed to be on the road to recovery, examples of how the system could work even for the hardest, hopeless cases. Cecilia's words echoed in the detective's head – Dr Frey had signed off on their cases and vouched for their progress, if not their character. In any event, they were deemed safe enough to release into the community, a pretty high standard had to be met. Why would he stake his illustrious reputation, as well as the mayor's and police commissioner's?

'Captain?'

'Yes, Officer.'

'There's someone to see you,' the desk sergeant advised. 'Jesse Arens.'

The detective thought about turning him away but didn't. 'I'll see him.'

Jesse walked in, less fidgety and nervous than Murphy

remembered. He appeared to be focused. Manic almost. A man on a mission.

'Hello, Captain.'

'Mr Arens. What can I do for you?' Murphy asked snidely. 'Somebody steal your drink tickets?'

'I know we don't like each other,' Jesse began. 'But you know what I have to say is important if I'm here.'

'OK,' Murphy said, sitting up in his chair. 'Spit.'

'I came here for help,' Jesse admitted, taking a seat.

'Help with what?'

'Saving their lives.'

Frey exited the shuttle terminal at Reagan National and headed for the cabstand.

'Massachusetts Avenue,' he said. 'The Nunciature, please.'

The driver sped off, zipping past the monuments and repositories of American greatness. The Lincoln Memorial, the Treasury Department, northwest Foggy Bottom, along the edge of Georgetown and past the Naval Observatory. He'd seen it all before, but was nevertheless impressed by the sheer grandeur of it all. Unlike the borough in which he lived and worked, not a single statue of a saint or archangel in sight, no Jesus or Mary. These were icons of a different sort. Edifices to earthly power and achievement, almost pagan, one could say, if not for the 'In God We Trust' printed on the bills he turned over to the cabbie.

He paid his fare and entered the Apostolic Nunciature on Embassy Row beneath the flag of the Vatican, which flew from a large sculpted balcony overhead. An older man gamboled out to the foyer, his hand extended in greeting.

'Dr Frey,' he said.

'Cardinal DeCarlo.'

The men clasped hands, shook quickly and proceeded to DeCarlo's office.

'Nice to see you again.'

'It's been a long time,' Frey responded.

'I recall our seminary days fondly.'

'That makes one of us, Cardinal.'

'They say that former priests are worse than former smokers, Doctor.'

'As far as I'm concerned, both can ruin your life.'

'Same old Alan, I see,' DeCarlo observed. 'Good of you to come.'

'I needed to be here today anyway.'

'On business?'

'Yes, I'm moderating a psychiatric panel at Georgetown,' Frey told him.

'A cocktail party is being thrown this evening by mutual friends of ours at the White House. You are most welcome to attend as my guest.'

'Thank you, but my duties will keep me here,' DeCarlo declined. 'What is the subject of your discussion?'

252

'Possession and Exorcism: a Psychiatric Viewpoint.'

'A most interesting topic,' DeCarlo acknowledged. 'But not one for strenuous debate.'

'Oh?'

'Possession only takes place in movies these days,' Cardinal DeCarlo observed wryly. 'All you need is two hours and a bucket of popcorn to make the demon disappear.'

'Ah yes, but perhaps that is why more people believe in it then ever before, Father.'

'Then you you've got your work cut out for you, Doctor. Even the Church is on the side of science in regard to this foolishness. It's nothing a bottle of Paxil can't cure, am I right, Doctor?'

'If you say so.'

'Quite coincidental timing for your panel, given the circumstances?'

'You might even call it,' Frey paused searching for just the right word, 'providence.'

DeCarlo motioned for his secretary to leave them and the heavy wooden door snapped shut as he departed. The cardinal got down to business.

'The situation in Brooklyn is quite troubling.'

'An understatement,' Frey said. 'I can tell you first hand.'

'It reflects badly on the Church.'

'And the faithful for buying into such hysterical nonsense,' Frey added sharply.

'On this matter we will agree to disagree,' DeCarlo said. 'I'm content to say we are happy with the saints we already have.'

'As you wish, Your Eminence.'

'These claims are delicate matters for us,' he explained. 'They need to be treated with the greatest care. For political, if not ecclesiastical, reasons.'

'Fraud is fraud, Prefect,' Frey said. 'Surely, the Church does not tolerate false miracles or false prophets.'

'Strong words, Doctor.'

'Not strong enough, Cardinal. I know them. Drop-outs, runaways, teenage dreamers, psychotics. Not exactly icons of virtue. I treated Sebastian.'

'Most disturbing are the whispers of a supposed relic being secreted and worshipped.'

Frey's expression hardened as he turned the meeting from a conversation to a negotiation. 'They are not merely whispers.'

DeCarlo stood, understanding the doctor's meaning.

'We've had to deal with these sorts of uprisings throughout history,' DeCarlo advised. 'Sects of all kinds challenging the church from within and without. Yet despite it all, we have survived.'

'But this threat is different,' Frey observed.

'Are you trying to drive up your price?' DeCarlo admonished.

'I'm pointing out that the saints, as you call them, pre-date the church and some might say are largely responsible for

driving people to the church to begin with, for essentially creating the grass roots movement toward faith, which could easily happen again. Without you.'

'That's far too simplistic, Doctor.'

'Is it? Then why am I here?'

'Since we are being frank,' DeCarlo countered, 'we both have much to fear from the spread of these lies.'

'Different motivations, but a common goal,' Frey concluded.

'The relic must be destroyed.'

'For a price.'

'What do you have in mind?'

'There is a market for such things, as you know,' Frey explained. 'And a great deal of interest from many of our colleagues with less noble intentions than yours.'

'Name your price.'

'What I require is more than you or anyone can pay monetarily,' Frey stated.

'I don't understand.'

'It is not enough that the heart is destroyed, it is only a symbol. An important and powerful one, but a symbol nevertheless. The real danger is the girls. They must be discredited. Unmistakably discredited and eliminated.'

'We are not assassins, Doctor,' DeCarlo reminded. 'Besides, death would only serve their purpose, feed their legend. You saw what happened after Sebastian.'

'Whether they die as fools or live on as fools doesn't matter

to me. Only that they are rejected for the world to see. Made to recant.'

'Recant?'

DeCarlo considered his options. Such a thing would need to be done publicly, not privately. Secretly, as he was planning to dispose of the relic.

'That is my price,' Frey reiterated. 'You see it is not the money, it is the myth that concerns me, that should concern us both.'

'I've recently returned from Rome,' DeCarlo advised. 'I believe I finally have the Holy Father's attention on this matter.'

'Good. It's about time. Then you can explain my proposal.'

'There is an investigation underway. Someone will be sent shortly to supervise.'

'What is there to investigate?' Frey asked.

Frey stood and extended his hand.

'Who will be sent?'

'We do not know,' Nuncio DeCarlo explained. 'There is a process to these things. I am to travel to New York to meet with the emissary of the Holy See tomorrow.'

'I trust you will keep me informed.'

'Indeed.'

'Do we understand each other?' Frey asked.

'We do,' the Nuncio agreed. 'I will take your offer under serious consideration.'

The two men shook hands and the Cardinal escorted Frey to the door.

'As the philosopher said,' Frey concluded, 'let not the perfect be the enemy of the good.'

'This Pope is not like us, nor like some who have gone before him,' DeCarlo explained. 'Not, shall I say, practical. He will be difficult to persuade.'

'With all due respect, Your Eminence, that is your problem.'

Lucy, Cecilia and Agnes pried the boards from the Sacristy doorway. The walls and furniture were charred; signs of smoke and water damage everywhere. Lucy led them to the doorway at the back, which was open except for a few blanks leaning against it.

'Heaven or hell?' Lucy said, as she peered down the stone staircase. 'I still don't know.'

'We'll find out soon, one way or the other,' Cecilia added.

'Let's do this the right way,' Agnes said, pulling three candles from her shoulder bag.

She handed one each to Lucy and CeCe, who reached into her jeans pocket for her Zippo. She lit the candles, and the girls proceeded down the steps and into the chapel, which was empty. Sebastian's fevered scrawls on the walls had been painted over, the shattered stained-glass windows removed, the bone chandelier dismantled and carted off. To their surprise, all that remained were the statues of their namesakes

and Sebastian's, painstakingly reconstructed. They were cracked, burned and damaged. Scarred but still standing.

They moved to touch them, running their fingers along the crevices and the chips. Lucy paused to stare at the eyes of Saint Lucy, sitting on a golden plate.

'It felt like a womb when we first came down here,' Cecilia observed. 'Now I understand why. This is where we were born.'

'The search for his heart has led us here, right back where we started.'

'Just as it should be.' Lucy reached for her wrist.

'When Sebastian gave these to us, they were a gift,' Lucy said, exposing her chaplet. 'He asked us to have faith in him, just as he had in us. But we hadn't earned them yet. I think it's time we did.'

She removed it and placed on the pedestalled figure. Cecilia and Agnes did the same.

Lucy reached down for the partially melted remnants of candles from the bone chandelier that once hung in the chapel. She dug her fingernail into each one, freeing its wick. Then she placed one in Cecilia and Agnes's palms and lit them.

Lucy, Cecilia and Agnes stood in silent reflection, candles burning, hot wax dripping to their hands along their forearms, slowly coating them, turning them to human candles. The flames grew brighter, casting more light and greater shadows on the walls of the sacred chapel as the candles burned down to their flesh.

They made vow to each other and to him.

'We won't come back for them until we bring Sebastian with us,' Lucy promised.

A sudden pain in her forehead drove her to her knees. Cecilia and Agnes reached for her. She opened her eyes and they sparkled a translucent blue, the light from their candles reflected in each iris.

'I see,' she said smiling, just as she had to Sebastian on that fateful night of their ordeal.

Cecilia and Agnes let her rest for a few minutes and brought her back to consciousness.

'Are you going to be OK?' Agnes asked.

'Yes,' she answered, gazing intensely at the statue of Saint Lucy before her. 'I will be fine.'

'Let's meet at Born Again.'

She grabbed her candle and led them out of the chapel and up the stairs.

'What do you think she saw?' Agnes asked Cecilia.

'Our future.'

The Passion of Sebastian

*T*he white marble columns of the Eternal City fade in the distance. *Hooves pound the stony trail, throwing clouds of orange dust upward nearly obscuring the chariots, with archers aboard, that draw nearer and nearer.*

Fires burn, blue flames flicker upward, jumping through the thick black smoke of smouldering olive branches and disappear in the daylight.

Sebastian stands proudly, the bright Mediterranean summer sun gleaming from his armour.

'They are coming,' he warns.

The three women draw closer to him.

'We are not afraid,' one says, holding firmly to his bronze breastplate, the others each grabbing him tightly by the vambraces on his wrists. 'They will need to take us first.'

'There is a time to fight and a time to yield.'

'We choose to fight for you.'

'No, you must be my witnesses. No matter what, do not waver.'

The soldiers arrive and dismount. They rush forward, swords drawn on one of their own.

'Sebastian!'

'It is I.'

'Do you shield yourself with women?'

'No, with love. Killers, I disarm myself.'

Spatha, shield, armour and galea drop piece by piece to the ground at the accused's feet, exposing his flesh.

'Centurion, you are accused of sedition, of heresy. A traitor to Caesar. Will you make amends to the gods for your offences?'

Sacrificial incense is offered and refused.

'I am the sacrifice.'

'You have chosen your fate.'

He addresses the women.

'We are only mud. Death is life.'

The soldiers pounce. He does not resist.

The cries of defiance from the three echo across the pale plain. They struggle against the grasp of the guards to reach him, to untie him from the tree to which he is bound.

The Praetorian issues his command.

'Sagittarii!'

The archers descend from the chariots and fall in line.

'I do not fear iron or clubs or spears or arrows, Praetorian. Empty your quivers!'

'It is not me you will fear.'

The Praetorian gestures to the guards to release the women and then to the archers, who approached them, offering their bows and quivers.

'No,' they scream, refusing.

The archers fix their arrows and draw back their bows, aimed squarely on the women.

'Take them,' Sebastian asked. 'I will be the target.'

The Praetorian smiled.

The first is brought before him.

'It will not be by my hand that you die, but by theirs.'

The first is dragged before him and walked back the prescribed distance. He raises his head, proudly, naked, defenceless but ready for battle.

'Telum ponite,'* the Roman orders.

'Sing, Cecilia.'

'I have too much love on my lips to sing. My heart strangles me.'

'Bracchia reducite,'** the Roman orders.

She turns suddenly and fixes the Praetorian in her site.

'No! I can't.'

'You must.'

Her shaking hand pulls back the string to her ear.

'Save yourself,' she calls out to him. 'Break free.'

'I wish there were other ways, but there aren't.'

---

*   Place the arrow
**   Draw back the bow

'Don't!' Lucy and Agnes shout.

'Whoever wounds me most deeply loves me most.'

'Let fly!'

Her aim is true. The body shudders, the flesh is pierced, blood flows purple to the ground.

Cecilia's sad song, nearly choked back with grief, fills the air. 'From his face he illuminates my sorrow and the summer night.'

Sebastian cries out in reply, 'The melody of holy combat.'

Agnes is brought before him, inconsolable. 'What will the world be like without our love?'

Sebastian steels himself and reassures her thorugh his pain. 'The flower is cut back only to see it re-grow.'

'Hostes dirigite.'*

She whispers, 'My spirit, my flame, my love.'

'Do not tremble. Do not cry.'

The command comes. 'Iacite!'**

The second arrow flies and strikes. She drops the bow and falls to her knees, reaching out to him across the emptiness. 'Eternal love.'

The last is brought forward.

'I cannot look,' she frets.

'You must to make a good hit.'

Tears of milk and honey stain her garment and anoint the bloody ground. 'All that is beautiful the devil takes.'

---

*　　Take aim
**　　Shoot!

With heaving chest, he smiles and replies. 'Takes but cannot keep.'

Lucy's words of praise grow ouder as she draws back the bow. 'You are the star which is nailed to the living heart of the heavens.'

Sebastian's command. 'I call forth your terrible love!'

*'Ad caelum!'**

The final shaft is launched. He is struck. A pillow of iron and wood and feathers.

She beseeches, 'Tear the gates from their hinges. Rise to the heaven which is studded with your immortal wounds.'

'I suffer. I bleed. The world is red with my torment.'

Lucy shouts in exaltation, 'Imperishable stem of the most beautiful flower. Praise the name it bears.'

They cry out together. 'Sebastian!'

He gasps. 'I've found an exit.'

*'Desiste!'***

The archers depart. The women approach and free him from his bindings. They tear the garments from their bodies to staunch his bleeding, fill his wounds with their fingers.

Cecilia sings:

'You are praised
Faraway, star speaks to star
And says one name: Yours.
God crowns you

---

*   To the sky!
**   Stop!

All the night, like a drop that dissolves on your forehead, Sebastian.'

Agnes laments:

'Blood flows in the shadow that believes.'

Lucy's eyes are raised heavenward. 'You are a saint. Whoever holds you in his heart will shine with your grace. You die but to be re-born forever.'

22

I Wanna Be Adored

'I've heard it all before, Mr Arens,' Murphy said.

'You don't believe me?' Jesse asked.

'Why would I? You don't have much credibility with me or anyone else for that matter.'

'Frey is behind these deaths. Open your goddamn eyes!'

'Your girlfriend said the same thing. What evidence do you have to support your accusation, kid?'

Jesse was unsure how much to disclose. If he told Murphy about the heart, he'd probably find himself locked up in Frey's ward before he could get the words out. Still, Murphy was listening, engaged. Jesse took it as a positive sign.

'I happen to know the guy they found in the Gowanus yesterday.'

'Is that so?'

'He was a source of mine.'

'Birds of a feather.'

'What is it going to take to make you see?' Jesse pushed back. 'He's going to kill them and use his rejects at Born Again to do it.'

'Spare me your insensitivities, Mr Arens.'

'Spare me the sanctimony, Captain,' Jesse snapped. 'You let him skate once before.'

'If you had a single fact to present, I might continue this conversation. Right now, all you have is a grudge. The police don't investigate grudges and the prosecutors don't try them.'

'Not until someone is dead. Is that it?'

'Careful, son. These are the big leagues you are playing in. Another man might take that as a threat.'

'Another man might pull his head out of his ass,' Jesse shouted, banging his hand on Murphy's desk.

The captain's door opened swiftly and the desk sergeant popped his head in.

'Everything OK in here, Captain?'

Murphy nodded. He looked into Jesse's eyes and spoke calmly.

'You still haven't answered the big question. Why? Why would Dr Frey want to do that?'

'He isn't who you think he is,' Jesse said.

'Listen kids, in the grand scheme of things, these girls aren't worth risking his reputation over.'

'It's the grand scheme of things I'm talking about, Captain,' Jesse argued. 'He will risk anything. Because he knows who they are. And he's afraid.'

'Now I've heard everything.'

'No, Captain. You haven't heard the last of this. I guarantee that.'

'Would you like to like make a formal complaint, Mr Arens?' Murphy asked condescendingly. 'I can send someone over to your apartment to take a statement. And have a look around while we're at it.'

Jesse pushed back. 'How many more dead bodies need to turn up before you'll listen to me?'

'We aren't new at this,' Murphy railed. 'We have our best serial killer units out there, scouring other clinics and out patient facilities around the city.

'The problem is they are looking for a killer, not a demon.'

Murphy exhaled and tried to stay professional.

'There's nothing supernatural at work here. Whoever is doing this will reveal himself before too long.'

'Apparently not,' Jesse mumbled. 'He's even got you totally fooled.'

'When you have something other than your opinion for me to go on, come back and see me.'

'By that time, it will be too late.'

The small dingy Bushwick nightclub was nearly empty. A typical, all-ages, open mic night in the neighbourhood. A comedian, poetry slammer, a few folkies taking the stage one after another. Content to entertain each other for the most part.

The music had been lowered in preparation for the start of the show and all that anyone could hear were the waitresses calling out mixed drink orders for the customers and the clinking of cracking ice in cocktail glasses. A blaring voice from off-stage shot through the PA system and attempted to awaken the gathering.

'Welcome to the stage, Cat Walsh.'

Catherine stepped up to the postage stamp sized platform to indifferent applause and began to strum, finding her key.

'Hi,' she said shyly to the few girls seated nearest the stage.

She recognized them from Cecilia's shows. She felt both grateful and embarrassed, suspecting that the ten-dollar cover charge each had paid was mostly a pity purchase. Still, Catherine was proud to have peeled off a few of her mentor's staunchest supporters, who were genuine if nothing else. They raised their non-alcoholic brews and air clapped furiously, encouraging her.

Catherine began to sing, one song after another, originals mostly. Songs about love, about hurt, about loss, about struggle, about dreams. Everything she'd been feeling. The

crowd might have been small but she was winning them over, moving them with her tales of misplaced trust and love gone wrong. As she finished the third song of her short set, Catherine noticed a man enter the room and walk toward a table near the back, obscured by shadows. He was wearing a suit, that much she could tell from the silhouette as he moved, and a tall drink was already sitting on the table as if he'd been expected.

She was intrigued, wondering if she was the reason he'd come and why she was even wondering. Bushwick was not exactly suit and tie territory. She finished her fourth tune and by the fifth and final song, 'I Wanna Be Adored' by the Stone Roses, she could see the mystery man at the back tapping his knuckles to her beat.

I don't need to sell my soul
He's already in me
I wanna be adored
I wanna be adored

Adored

Catherine's eyes were closed when she ended the song. It was her call to action, her desperation on the surface for all to see. Raw, just like Cecilia. Cat smiled and bowed to the scattered applause as she left the stage, looking back over her shoulder toward the rear of the club.

She crossed paths with the next act, who handed her a folded piece of paper.

'From the dude in the back,' the MC whispered and shrugged. 'You never know.'

Catherine stopped in the backstage hallway and placed her guitar in its case, rubbing the note between her fingers deciding whether to open it or not. Her curiosity got the best of her and she flicked it open.

'Come see me,' it read and it was signed. 'D.L.'

'No. Shit!' she screamed, banging her hands angrily against her head. 'I'm really going to do this?'

Catherine fussed with her hair and wiped the beads of sweat from her forehead, straightened her sleeveless vest and headed over to the mystery man's table. He stood before she got to within ten feet of the table.

'You were great,' he complimented just as she was coming into earshot.

He was tall, thin, well dressed. Older. Serious.

'Thanks,' Catherine said, 'but who are you?'

'Daniel. Daniel Less.'

Catherine felt her knees wobble and her heart start to pound.

'From Tritone Records?' she stammered. '*The* Daniel Less?'

'Call me Danny,' he said, gesturing for her to join him at the table and sit down.

Getting a better look she recognized him from the features

in the music trades and interviews on the cable networks. Here he was. Head of the coolest and most cred indie label in the world. Sitting not more than eighteen inches away from her. Catherine tried to find words. 'I saw you walk in.'

'I saw you too,' he said with a smile.

'Did you come here to see me?'

'I did,' he acknowledged. 'Does that surprise you?'

'I mean, that's cool,' Catherine gushed. 'I just never imagined you'd even know who I was.'

'Word gets around.'

'Even from a black hole like this place like this?'

'Pop stars, rock stars, don't come pre-loaded with mansions, yachts and Rolls Royces,' he said. 'Everyone starts at some place like this.'

'At the bottom,' Catherine replied, flashing a knowing smile of her own.

Danny looked around the joint. 'Yes, the bottom,' he laughed.

'Well, no place to go but up, I always say.'

'If you're lucky,' Less said. 'The girls in front seem to dig it anyway.'

'Oh them, they are really fans of Cecilia Trent's.'

'Makes sense,' Less said, taking off his horn-rimmed glasses and cleaning the lenses. 'There is a lot of her in you.'

'You really think so?

'I really do.'

Less could see that Catherine was flattered.

'That's so cool because we're really good friends. That's how those girls know about me.'

'You don't say,' Less replied. 'I've been trying to track her down for a while now.'

'For?'

'A deal, possibly.'

Catherine became suddenly wary and more than a little jealous. 'Oh. Well. She's not easy to reach. I don't know how much you know about her but . . .'

Danny interrupted. The no nonsense record executive in him breaking through the niceties. 'But you know how to reach her, correct?'

'I'm not her agent,' Catherine snapped, the street-smart performer in her emerging. 'I have a career of my own to look after.'

The two stared at each other across the table for a tense moment.

'I like you,' the executive said. 'Bring me to Cecilia and let's see if we can't work something out. For both of you.'

Cecilia spent the afternoon preparing her things and herself. Getting her affairs, few though they were, in order. She cleaned, wrapped and boxed the only things that were most important to her and dropped individually written and addressed notes inside. The same independent streak that led her to New York,

to the stage, would not permit her to turn her personal history over to anyone else. Into a box with a spare set of keys, cheques for rent and utilities she dropped an envelope that read 'Landlord'. Into another filled with souvenirs, press reviews, fan mail and personal photos, she dropped an envelope that read 'Mom & Dad'. Into the final open carton, filled with CDs and memory sticks of her demos, song notebook and laptop she placed an envelope that read 'Catherine'.

There was one other box left. Not one she'd packed but one she still hadn't opened. Cecilia walked over and stood over it, still not sure if she really wanted to deal with the contents, but she forced herself. She peeled back the layer of masking tape from the carton revealing a hand-bound book titled, *Our Lady*. She opened the book and began reading. It was her story. She told Bill to write it all down, and, he did just that. It was a beauty take on her life. All on the record. For her. She was speechless, her tears began to flow. She set the book aside and dug deeper through the sheets of crumbled newspaper he used as padding. But not just any editions. These were pages of reports of the events at Precious Blood and what followed, of Sebastian's death, of the investigation, all of it. The good, the bad, the ugly. A scrapbook of her sorrow and fame used to pad a bubble-wrapped gift lying at the bottom of the box.

Cecilia removed the item and untied the twine fastening revealing a coiled metallic strip with an elaborately engraved handle. There was a card from Bill with a handwritten description of the gift and its history as he knew it. It was an urumi, a curling blade from India, the note explained. For her protection. She turned the card over and received his final words, an instruction, more like. 'Keep fighting' it read simply.

She grasped the handle of the urumi and felt it unspool, clanging to the floor like some kind of killer slinky. The only thing that had ever felt more comfortable in her hand was her guitar. Cecilia instinctively began to whip the sword, slowly, cautiously at first and then with increasing confidence and speed until she lost control. The air crackled all around her.

'Oh shit,' she gasped, as the blade sliced through a thrift shop candelabra and some corner deli flowers she had next to her window seat at the back of her loft.

She ran to the spot, stamped out the burgeoning flames that had fallen to the floor and examined the cuts the urumi had made in the wax stalks. Clean, precise cuts.

She whirled the blade around again and again, striking the columns, brick walls and wide plank flooring over and over, sending a tornado of chips of plaster, wood and stone flying everywhere. Time passed but she barely noticed, working her stroke until she was exhausted and sweating.

'Practice makes perfect,' she said, placing the urumi on the floor.

She had never loved Bill more, and knew he was with her in head and heart, just like a father would be. He believed she was destined for greatness, and she believed him.

After a while, she reached for her guitar, the only personal possession of hers in the apartment still unwrapped and slung it around her shoulder. She kneeled to the knotty wide plank floor, littered with debris and took the simple urn containing Bill's ashes. She placed the canister before her, lit a few candles and a cigarette and began to sing, to serenade him, holding her own private memorial service just for him. Fragments of lullabies, hymns, ballads and blues – whatever came to her – were played in his honour, played in gratitude. A sonic puzzle of words and music, which she felt, Bill would have appreciated.

Once her tribute concluded, she wound the urumi around her chest like a beauty queen's sash, grabbed the urn and headed up to the roof. She pushed open the unsecured security door and ran out into the breezy dusk, walked to the edge of the roof and stepped up on the ledge, closed her eyes, popped open the urn and reached in, grabbing a handful of ashes. The dust trailed from between her fingers down to her feet, coating her. Cecilia reached her long arm out and released the handful of dust on to the wind.

Again and again, she reached in and released, spreading Bill far and wide as the sun set, over the rooftops and empty lots, the abandoned factories and the dusty windows, mixing him, almost unnoticeably, with the grit and grime of the streets they both loved. Stretching her arm upon the wind for the final time, she noticed the tattoo of Sebastian on her wrist. She'd made him a part of her, but it was only appropriate, she felt, that she shared Bill with the city, his faithful mistress.

Cecilia stood on the roof for a long while waiting for all traces of Bill to completely vanish along with the sun. As the first stars began to twinkle over the city skyline, she felt a buzz in her back pocket and reach for her cell. A text from Catherine: *Coming tonight?*

Yes, Cecilia typed and sent.

She left the roof, grabbed the guitar from her apartment and headed off into the starry night.

23

The Heathen

Agnes sat on the bench in her garden for a long while, the blank sheet of stationery staring back at her from her lap, dogwoods blossoming all around. She'd only been able to get two words down. The salutation:

Dear Mom,

Only two, but the two most important. Saying goodbye was harder than she thought. She'd skipped that step with the whole wrist thing. It wasn't until she'd arrived at the ER that she even thought about dying.

How could she explain to someone else, even someone so close, what she could barely comprehend herself? The easy explanation was also the most sanctimonious. Duty calls. I'm off to do something bigger than me. Some quote or legend they could carve into your memorial. The truth was harder to articulate. How do you explain a need? A desire, so deep, that you are entirely without choice. A love, so strong, that you willingly choose against your own self-interest, against your own instinct of self-preservation itself. But then, what would life be if she chose otherwise?

Agnes went back into her room and opened her locked box. She pulled out the page from the Legenda that she'd taken from the underground chapel. Not so much to educate herself as to remind herself. Of what suffering meant. What it was really all about. What she was really all about. A victim soul.

She put the pad down and bowed her head.

'Why me?' she began to sob and to ask and to pray. 'Why us?'

She'd cried such self-pitying tears before. Over guys. Over her dad. Her mom. But never over herself. In the past, the very act of crying seemed to alleviate the problem. Getting it out made her feel better. Now, the sobs that poured from her were born of a pain that could never be eased or provided answers for the kind of suffering she was not just facing, but seeking. Courting.

Dr Frey told her mother it was just some manifestation of guilt. Granted, she, Cecilia and Lucy had plenty to be guilty about. Frey, she thought, understood the power of shame.

But not the power of love.

Agnes picked up her Victorian tear catcher, caught a few more of her tears, sealed it up tight, and left with it.

'C'mon, pick up,' Lucy said impatiently.

'You've reached the office of Byte. Please listen carefully because the options have changed.'

'What office?' she said out loud to herself, waiting for the menu.

'For Editorial, press one. For Advertising, press two. For Tips, press three. For Complaints and Retractions, press star, go fuck yourself.'

Lucy pressed three. It was the box he checked most often.

'Jesse, it's me,' Lucy said. 'If you're there, pick up. Jesse?'

The frustration in her voice gave way to solemnity.

'We're going to Born Again.'

She paused.

'It's time.'

Again a long thoughtful pause and a deep breath.

'If anything happens to us, or we don't come back it's up to you to tell the story.'

Then, a sweetness she rarely used with anyone, and never with him.

'I know I can count on you Jesse. I . . . always could. Thank you. For everything.'

She ended the call and grabbed her coat.

* * *

Cecilia carried her guitar case to Catherine's gig and an odd feeling came over her. For the first time in a long time, she didn't feel she was being followed. She walked up to the backstage door and knocked. The bouncer opened it a crack, saw who it was, and let her pass.

Tonight's performance was unannounced officially but Catherine had got out quickly nevertheless and filled the place even on such short notice. It was the biggest crowd Catherine had ever seen, which the local promoter was happy about. Like comics who go back to the small clubs to work out new material, Cecilia had some things she wanted to work out as well.

'How does it feel to be a very special guest?' Catherine said, hugging Cecilia.

'Feels good,' Cecilia admitted.

'What are we gonna do?'

Cecilia handed over a scrap of paper with a title and chord progression.

'Know it?' Cecilia asked.

'Perfect,' Catherine said. 'Wanna rehearse?'

'No,' Cecilia said smiling, 'I know it will be fine.'

'Thanks,' Catherine said. 'That means a lot.'

'If you are uncomfortable with me being here, you can say so,' Cecilia said sincerely. 'I know it can get dangerous around me.'

'That's what I like about you,' Catherine said unflinchingly.

Cecilia reached into her bag and pulled out a set of keys.

'I want you to have these just in case,' Cecilia said.

'Just in case what?' Catherine queried.

'In case you ever need to get into my apartment.'

'The keys to the kingdom,' Catherine shouted, raising her arms with faux evangelical fervour. 'Praise be!'

'And pass the ammunition,' Cecilia laughed, motioning for her guitar.

'Sure you don't have time for more than one song?' Catherine asked. 'The crowd is really here for you.'

'They're here for us.'

'No pressure.'

'Listen, Catherine, there is something I need to do tonight and I might not see you for a while.'

'Anything I can do to help?' Catherine offered.

Cecilia fumbled for words. 'No, but I want you to know two things: One, I'm proud of you.'

Catherine was moved by her kindness and also ashamed that she was so jealous of her when she talked to Less.

'And two, I'm glad you didn't take my advice about leaving Brooklyn. You belong here.'

'Thank you.'

'Don't give up. Ever.'

They sat in the dressing room, in the wall-to-wall, over lit make-up mirror tuning their guitars, warming up their voices, letting the crowd and anticipation build. CeCe was preoccupied

with thoughts of Lucy and Agnes. About Jesse. About Bill. About Sebastian. She stood and removed her black ostrich feather coat she'd been wearing, almost ready for the stage.

'That's amazing,' Catherine said, pointing to the jewelled metal belt Cecilia was sporting around her waist. 'Vintage?'

'It was a gift from Bill. From India. Said he got it outside the shrine of Saint Alphonsa.'

'Make sense, it looks like a talisman or something.'

'It's for protection his note said.'

'Protection from what? Bad reviews? Horny guys?'

'Not exactly,' Cecilia explained. 'It's an urumi. An ancient weapon.'

Cecilia reached for the leather grip that she'd inserted into her back pocket and whipped the belt from her waist, decimating the hospitality tray and spring water bottles on the vanity into a volcanic spray of Swiss, cheddar and crackers.

'Right,' Catherine said nervously. 'That kind of protection.'

'Yeah, that kind of protection.'

Cecilia coiled the urumi back around her.

The knock from the stage manager came and she placed the guitar strap over her head. They walked down the narrow hallway to the stage steps.

Catherine took the stage first. The crowd warmed to her quickly, but it was obviously Cecilia they were waiting for. A few songs into her set, Catherine stopped and pointed stage right. The rafters of the old club shook as fans stomped their

feet in the balcony in anticipation.

There was no introduction. None was necessary. She walked out on to the stage and the crowd exploded. She smiled and spread her arms wide, as if offering herself up to them.

'This is for the one I love. And, for me. And for all of you.'

White light flooded the stage, bathing them in brightness, obscuring them Catherine turned the small vintage drum machine sitting next to her and turned a few knobs, programming the beat. The cold, mechanical snares snapped out a rhythm and Cecilia began the slow sombre hypnotic riff of The Cure song, 'Faith'. Catherine joined in the vocals, weaving in and out of the verses like a ghost. The crowd began to sway from the orchestra to the balcony. The whole building was moving, like a joyless revival.

> Catch me if I fall
> I'm losing hold
> I can't just carry on this way

Cecilia sang soulfully, but softly, almost swallowing the words.

> And every time
> I turn away
> Lose another blind game
> The idea of perfection holds me
> Suddenly I see you change

Everything at once
The same
But the mountain never moves

Each verse more intense than the next. Hitting her strings a little hard, her voice growing softer. Tears were falling from both their eyes and soon from the audience. Blood and water dripped from Cecilia down the neck and body of her guitar on to her outfit, and to the floor.

Christened in blood
Painted like an unknown saint
There's nothing left but hope
Your voice is dead
And old
And always empty
Trust in me through closing years
Perfect moments wait
If only we could stay

The communion between Cecilia and the crowd reached a zenith. This, she thought, was what Sebastian had sought them for. Was their real power and what Frey feared the most. The joining together of minds, hearts and souls in an unforgettable moment that would be shouted, broadcast, tweeted and posted from the mountaintops.

Slowly, imperceptibly at first, Cecilia began to rise from the stage. The audience gasped and even the crew shot looks at each other, curious about some special effect CeCe had planned without telling them. She levitated a few inches at first and then higher, a few feet from the floorboards. Some were astonished, some confused, others frightened, but nobody moved. They were transfixed. Cecilia rose, playing and singing and the spotlight followed her up, bathing her in a full body yellow-white halo, like a human exclamation point.

'A miracle,' some apostles shouted. The more sceptical in the venue craned their necks, looking for wires. Catherine fell to her knees and many in the crowd followed her lead. Cecilia remained suspended there and opened her arms to her apostles. They cheered and roared their approval. Their acceptance. Their understanding.

> I went away alone
> With nothing left
> But faith.

Cecilia descended gradually to the stage as the song ended. The crowd was hers to do with whatever she wished with them, like a puppeteer. But, she did nothing.

She was done.

24

Hail

It was dark inside Born Again. No lights shining in the upper story windows. It was late and the residents had a curfew. At least they were supposed to have a curfew, Jesse was thinking as he approached the building. He turned his head up toward the streetlamp and noted that the video camera had yet to be connected. Whatever was about to go down would not be recorded or monitored by Murphy's pals at central command.

Jesse walked up the recently restored steps to the large wooden double doors. If he didn't know better, he might have assumed he was calling on one of the doctors, lawyers or Wall Street brokers that populated these neighbourhoods. He reached into his pocket for a pick and slid it inside the keyhole hole. It was a skill he'd become expert at years ago while breaking curfew in his parents' home. His dad used to joke that he could have a great career as a cat burglar. Jesse always assumed what his dad was telling him was that he was a sneaky bastard, so his transition to a blog gossip king made perfect sense.

As he brought his ear closer to the metal plate and listened for the sound of the lock popping open, he quietly twisted the doorknob, only to find it already unlocked. Jesse pushed on it and felt the door give way. He didn't call inside for permission. He just stepped into the blackened foyer, the flashlight app on his cell blazing. A first glance there was nothing unusual. Just a small desk and a phone in the foyer, which doubled as a visitor's lobby. Flocked floral wallpaper and refinished vintage furniture captured the period feel of the building and added some charm and a lived-in vibe. It looked more to him like a shabby chic Maine bed and breakfast than a halfway house.

'Our tax dollars at work,' Jesse mumbled.

He felt for the blackjack in his pocket and lit the way upstairs to the first landing. All these houses were the same, he thought. He could have found his way around blindfolded. There were two doors at either end of the narrow hall. Piled next to that door were construction tools, folded tarps and paint cans. He turned the knob on the one closest to him. It was empty except for the dry and dusty new paint smell that wafted toward him. He turned and walked to the other end of the hallway and was startled by a loud thud, as if someone had fallen from the floor above. Or jumped.

Jesse brought his phone up to see which and just as quickly felt a powerful smack against his forearm, knocking the phone out of his hand and him off balance. He tumbled to the wide plank pine floor. Hard.

'I wasn't expecting you.'

'Sorry, the door was open,' Jesse said, wiping at his lip.

'Visiting hours are over.'

'I'm not here to visit anyone,' Jesse said, removing the blackjack from his pocket. 'I'm working. Cleaning up.' He crouched. Ready.

'Cleaning up is woman's work,' the attacker growled.

'Where is it?'

'Where are the girls?'

'They're planning your funeral, douchebag,' Jesse cracked.

The vandal rushed him, but Jesse sidestepped him and brought the blackjack down swiftly on the back of his head. Jesse wasn't a tough guy but the rush he got at fighting back, at cracking this animal's skull, at defending Lucy, Cecilia and Agnes was more satisfying then anything he'd ever felt. Jesse pounced. He slammed his weapon over and over into the vandal's body, drawing blood and shattering teeth.

'Say hello to Dr Frey,' Jesse said.

A single desperate blow knocked Jesse off of him and against the railing. He was dizzy and hurting. Jesse rose but his opponent rose faster, kicking him in the stomach and punching him squarely in the jaw. Jesse felt his cheeks swelling and his mouth fill with blood. His gasps for breath released a gooey torrent of red down his shirt and trousers. A final kick to the head did him in and he fell, nearly unconscious to the floor.

The vandal limped over to him and grabbed Jesse by the shirt and sat him up against the plaster wall.

'Next time, you should knock first.'

He stretched over to the doorway and grabbed the nail gun and tugged at the hose that connected it to the portable air compressor.

'I've never seen people seek out suffering like your crew.'

He flipped the switch on the compressor with his foot and lifted Jesse up against the wall, his feet dangling a few inches above it. Jesse was limp. Unable to resist.

'Let's try this the Roman way,' the prep taunted, spitting out a few last bits of incisor in Jesse's battered face. 'This will only hurt for a second. I think.'

He held Jessed against the wall, his hand to his chest, and placed the head of the nail gun into the palm of Jesse's left hand. He pressed it against the wall and raised his arm to shoulder height. The pop of the compressor and the snap of the nail gun was almost instantaneous, like flashbulbs going off at an A-list soiree. The flathead nail was through Jesse's hand

and into the wall stud before he could feel it. Jesse cried out as his entire body shivered in agony.

The vandal raised his other arm to equal height and fired again, sending a spike through Jesse's right palm. Muscle, bone and blood vessels were shredded as the second nail affixed him firmly to the wall. Hung like a painting. The pain was so intense it returned him fully to consciousness. He stared, wide-eyed at his assailant, the weight of his body, pulling downward and making it harder and harder to breathe.

He reached down to the floor and picked up Jesse's phone. He opened the camera app, turned on the flash and took a picture.

'There's an exclusive for you,' he mocked, tucking the phone in Jesse's breast pocket. 'Make it your homepage.'

Jesse moaned and tried unsuccessfully to pull his arms free. The vandal dipped his fingernail in Jesse's blood and drew a halo on the wall above his head.

'By the way, what you're looking for? It ain't here. You should have just asked,' he smiled. 'It was those girls I was waiting on. But you'll do for now.'

Jesse was fading.

'You know, the thing about crucifixion is you don't actually die from the nails,' the man said, reaching for his jacket and slipping it on. 'You die from suffocation.'

Jesse continued to gasp, and to bleed.

'It takes a while but, you'll die,' he said indifferently, walking down the stairs. 'Eventually.'

The motorcade transporting Cardinal DeCarlo approached the Archbishop's residence on Madison Avenue. He'd spent a restless night and all of the short flight from D.C. pondering Dr Frey's offer, not so much whether to take it, but how he could persuade the emissary and the Pope to see the wisdom of it. Alternatively, he plotted to bypass them completely, if necessary.

'Your Eminence,' the young priest greeted, kissing the Cardinal's ring.

'Has the appointee arrived?

'Not yet.'

'Good. There is still much to be done.'

He was escorted to a visiting dignitary's suite complete with chapel, office, dining and bedroom. The door to the office was closed and the Cardinal took a seat at a large desk beneath a recreation of Michelangelo's The Creation of Adam. He placed the leather satchel he was carrying on the floor beside his chair.

'Here are the files you requested, Father.'

The priest handed the Cardinal three files, which DeCarlo placed down on the desk. The tab on each carried a different name, written in black marker.

Cecilia Trent.

Lucy Ambrose.

Agnes Fremont.

'These are the testimonials?' DeCarlo asked.

'Yes, Father.'

'Thank you. You are excused.'

Alone, the Cardinal opened the files one by one and reviewed each thoroughly. Police reports. Eyewitness statements. Media coverage. Medical files. Personal histories. Every aspect of the events preceding and following Sebastian's death. The evidence was powerful as were their recollections of Sebastian and Precious Blood. The ecstasies they experienced and agonies they endured within the chapels underground walls rang with authenticity. He'd heard it, read it, seen it before, in others canonized by the Church with much lesser proof.

The processes to confirm or dispute claims of sainthood were lengthy and thorough and the Cardinal, as Fidei Defensor, Defender Of Faith, was in a unique position to influence any Vatican investigation. He had seen many such claims, most unworthy of the time spent, but this was different. There was an authenticity to these girls, a reliability that, in an age of media fuelled celebrity, also presented a great danger to the status quo. A challenge most directly to their authority.

The Pope had a much softer spot for such claims and no doubt his handpicked investigator would as well. The boy's death, the protests at Precious Blood and the cult developing around these girls had drawn much unwanted attention. It had

to stop. Once and for all.

'This blasphemy,' DeCarlo said out loud to himself. He pressed the button for his intercom. 'Can you please call Dr Alan Frey?'

25

Sorrowful Mysteries

The doorbell rang at the Fremonts'.

Ever since the police station, Martha had been in the habit of answering herself. She peeked through the peephole. Even through the distorting fish eye lens, she could see the boy on the other side was very good-looking. She opened the door and greeted him. 'Hello, Finn. How nice to see you.'

'Nice to see you too, Mrs Fremont.'

'I didn't realize you two had plans,' Martha said, a surprised and hopeful tone in her voice.

'Me neither,' he said. 'She just called a little while ago.'

'Just a minute, I'll let her know you're here.'

Martha walked back to Agnes's room with a sly smile on her

face and knocked on her door.

'Agnes, your boyfriend is here.'

Agnes rolled her eyes. 'He's not my boyfriend.'

'Whatever you say, dear. Inviting him over when you know I'm on my way out. Sneaky.'

'We're just going to talk.'

'I don't blame you, he is very cute,' she mused. 'If I were just a little younger.'

Agnes puked in her mouth a little, and just exhaled in frustration. The whole cougar pose was getting so old. At first she thought Martha was just trying to shock her out of the 'doldrums' as her mom called it, but now it seemed more like wishful thinking. And gross.

'How many times do I have to tell you, Mother? It's not what I want.'

Agnes followed Martha back down the hall to the living room where Finn was fidgeting. Agnes greeted him with a slight wave and he smiled back. Martha acknowledged the obvious connection with a coy smile thrown at Agnes. Martha reached for her coat and then for the door. 'Have fun, you kids,' she said, almost gloating.

Agnes looked at Finn. Embarrassed. 'Sorry,' she said sheepishly.

Finn shrugged. 'What's up? Sounded urgent.'

'Come with me.' Agnes led Finn back to her room. A place where she felt safe and comfortable enough to confide her

deepest secrets. He waited for her to invite him into her most personal space and entered.

'Are you going to tell me what's up?'

'There is something that I have to do. Something that could be dangerous.'

'You're scaring me, Agnes.'

'Can I trust you, Finn?' she said, sitting at the edge of her bed.

'You know you can,' he said, sitting beside her. 'Is it about what everyone says about you?'

Agnes thought about how to put it without getting into the arcane and unbelievable details. 'I don't know why I'm telling you this . . .'

'Seems like you need to tell someone.'

'Yeah, exactly,' she agreed, her eyes lighting up. 'And Hazel would never understand. She'd go right to my mom and tell her. I'm going to leave here tonight to meet my friends.'

'The other two girls?'

'Yes. And . . .'

'And what?'

'I don't know if I'll be coming back.'

'You're not thinking about running away are you?' he said, his hand unobtrusively taking hold of hers.

'No, I mean never coming back.'

He looked deeply into her eyes.

'Agnes, don't talk like that.'

'I'm sorry to put such a burden on you,' she apologized. 'But just in case, I needed for someone to know.'

'What's going on?' he said sincerely, moving his hand up to her shoulder, gently tossing her hair behind her. 'You can tell me.'

'I can't explain. Something that belongs to us has been taken. And we need to get it back.'

'Maybe I can help?'

'No,' she said, tearing up. 'We have to do it ourselves.'

He dried the tear falling down her cheek and she smiled. It was a most vulnerable moment.

'Agnes, you know how I feel about you.'

She nodded. 'I know. But . . .'

'But you love someone else.'

'I do.'

He leaned in. 'Can a dead guy do this?' Finn whispered, bringing his lips close to hers.

Agnes slid back. Warily. 'Finn, please. Don't. That's not why I asked you to come over.'

She felt a violent tug at her long mane and everything change in the room and in Finn's demeanour. Even his voice deepened.

'Isn't it?' he said angrily, grabbing a fistful of hair in a drug-fuelled attack.

He pulled her back down to the bed and manoeuvred

himself on top of her, grinding his pelvis into hers, ripping her shirt open.

'Stop it, Finn,' she shouted at him. 'I said STOP!'

She smacked his face and he recoiled. The kindness she'd seen in his eyes disappeared, replaced by a manic, determined and conscienceless expression. One, he imagined, Dr Frey would approve of.

'Invite a guy over. Into your bedroom. I know exactly what you are,' he said, reaching for the button on her jeans. 'You're no saint. You're a teaser, bitch.'

'Don't . . .' she started to say, scratching at his face.

'You won't be a virgin when I'm done with you.'

'Don't make me hurt you.' She reached for a fountain pen on her night table, the one she used to write her childhood journals, and brought the point to his throat, his carotid artery and pushed inward. He felt the sharp metal edge cut through the top layer of his skin, and poised to sever the vessel, a drop of blood begin to run down his neck. He stopped and moved back. She moved forward, the opener still pressed against him, until he was off her and had backed away. 'I was an idiot to trust you.'

'You were,' he said.

She picked up her phone.

'Get your sorry ass out of here now or I'll call the police, if I don't kill you first.'

26

Mercy Corps

'Ready?' Lucy asked.

'Yeah,' Cecilia answered bravely.

'Where's Agnes?'

'I don't know but we can't wait.' Cecilia said. 'She'll be here.'

They approached Born Again cautiously, ready for the battle of their lives. For their lives. Cecilia turned the knob and found the door open. Her palms were burning. A bad sign, she thought.

It was quiet and dark without a sign of life inside, only a barely audible moan coming from somewhere upstairs.

Cecilia brought her finger to her lips before Lucy could speak and led her to the staircase. They walked up quietly.

CeCe stopping at the first door and Lucy signalling she would check the second. Lucy moved slowly down the hallway, leaning against the wall for support and guidance through the darkened space until her progress was impeded by something. She gasped, but didn't cry out. It felt like a statue, it was definitely life-size but immobile. Nothing to be concerned about, she figured. She reached for her phone and swiped it on.

The dim blue glow illuminated a horror.

'Oh God. Jesse!' Lucy's shrieks drew Cecilia out into the hallway. He was pale, paler even than the cool white beam that Lucy shone to illuminate him and cool to the touch. Cecilia saw the bigger picture as she approached, his arms outstretched, hair matted with sweat, blood trailing down the wall from either hand. She spied a pair of pliers along with other tools piled up nearby.

'Lucy, hold him under his arms,' CeCe ordered.

'Is he dead?' Lucy sobbed uncontrollably. 'Please don't let him be dead.'

'Hold him!' CeCe grasped the nail head in his left hand with the pliers and pulled with all her might.

'Don't hurt him,' Lucy begged, as if any further damage could possibly be done.

Cecilia freed one hand, and then the other and Jesse's body fell into Lucy's arm, the weight of his body and her sorrow carrying them to the bloody floor. A shallow, raspy rattle came

from his throat and she saw him try to swallow.

'He's alive!'

'Just barely,' Cecilia said. 'I'm calling an ambulance.'

Lucy wiped at his face, fussing over him, her warm tears replacing the beads of cold sweat that had formed. Cecilia ripped pieces of her vest and wrapped his wrists with them. Jesse struggled to open his eyes. 'Lucy,' he gasped.

'You're going to be OK,' she assured him. 'Try not to talk.'

'It's not here,' he said, falling into unconsciousness. 'Frey has it.'

Agnes ran up to the swarm of ambulances, emergency vehicles and police cars that had descended on the halfway house. She arrived just as Captain Murphy pulled up in an unmarked sedan and Jesse was being loaded into the EMT van. 'Lucy,' she shouted, spotting her friend. 'What happened?'

Cecilia grabbed hold of her. 'It's Jesse,' she said. 'We found him here.'

'Is he gonna be all right?'

'I don't know. He lost a lot of blood.'

'Why Jesse?' Agnes asked, tearily.

'He felt guilty about leading Frey to Perpetua's. He came looking for the heart.'

Lucy walked over. Still in shock. 'They are taking him to the hospital. I'm going to go and be with him.'

'Was he able to tell you anything?' Agnes asked.

'Only that the heart's not here,' Cecilia said.

'They were waiting for us, not him,' Lucy surmised grimly. 'This is all a game for Frey and he's still one step ahead.'

'He knows we're coming for it,' Cecilia added. 'But how could he have known when?'

Agnes began to tremble. 'It's my fault,' Agnes admitted. 'The guy I met at school. He seemed so vulnerable. I confided in him. He must have told Dr Frey. He tried, he tried to . . .' Agnes couldn't bring herself to speak the words and didn't need to. Lucy took her hand.

'Don't you see? This is it. This is our suffering. Always doubted. Mocked. Hounded. Never knowing who to trust. Never knowing which of the ones you love will be put in danger. Never knowing if someone wants to kiss you, or kill you.'

'Or rape you,' Cecilia spat.

Lucy nodded. 'And it's just the beginning.'

'Did you tell the police?' Cecilia asked.

'No, I just left a note for my mom in case he tried to call or come back.'

'OK, good. After we take care of Jesse, we'll pay Finn a visit.'

A gruff, angry voice interrupted. 'Take care of who?' Captain Murphy barked.

'Jesse,' Lucy answered, changing the subject.

'I told you this would happen.' Murphy was steaming mad and barely listening.

'Will he be OK?' Agnes asked softly.

'Did he look OK?' Murphy chided. 'What the hell was he doing in there?'

There was no response from any of them.

'What were you doing there for that matter?' Murphy asked them.

'Can we go or are you charging us?

The detective's frustration was plain to see. 'Not yet, but your blogger buddy is looking at breaking and entering,' Murphy fumed. 'If he survives.'

As he trudged back to his car, he turned and walked back to them. Calmer and more collected, he issued a warning. 'Your problems are bigger than just me now. We're hearing that the Vatican is sending an investigator. The advance team, including a cardinal, is already here. They are looking to rip the skin off this fantasy you three have going. Don't say I didn't warn you.'

'Captain,' Lucy said, as he walked away, 'thank you.'

'Don't thank me. I can protect you from a lot of things, if you let me,' he said. 'But I can't protect you from yourselves.'

Murphy trudged off.

'The Vatican?' Agnes shuddered.

'The Vatican is looking for us,' Cecilia said, lost in thought. 'That's the answer. We need to bring Sebastian to them.'

Lucy sat in the chair beside Jesse in the Perpetual Help ER,

watching the blood and antibiotic trickle into him. She'd never seen him so still or so quiet. Her mind raced, she wondered if he got her phone message, if she could have stopped it, if only they'd got there first. She chastised herself for a million different reasons. None of which, she realized, mattered at all right then.

A nurse entered to check Jesse's vitals. Lucy recognized her from her stay in the ER. And the nurse recognized her.

'No offence, but I want him moved to another hospital,' Lucy all but demanded. 'He's not safe here.'

'No offence likewise, haven't you caused enough trouble?' the nurse shot back, as she recorded blood pressure, respiratory rate and urine volume. 'There is a cop at the desk and you have no authority. We've contacted his family. They can make decisions on his behalf. Besides, this hospital was good enough for you.'

Under her breath Lucy grumbled loud enough for the testy RN to hear.

'Is this the only hospital in Brooklyn?'

'No,' the nurse said tersely, adjusting Jesse's IV drip before leaving. 'Just the best. The EMT's don't take requests about where to bring a dying man. It's not a limo service.'

Lucy stroked his forearm, letting him know that someone, that she, was there, hoping to reach through the coma to comfort him. colour was returning with each drop of fluid, but not consciousness.

She'd persuaded the intake staff to place him in a more private bay, which they did, away from the prying eyes that followed her everywhere. Her notoriety had been good for something at least.

She recalled her night there not so long ago. A fateful one. But for all the changes she, Cecilia and Agnes had undergone, perhaps Jesse was the one who'd changed the most. Lucy had mocked him in the church for being jealous and spiteful and weak, but he was brave. And decent. And loyal. All these qualities inside of him, waiting for the chance to surface. If such a transformation was possible for him, it might be for anybody, she thought. Lucy placed her hand in his and held on to it tight.

'Come on, Jesse.'

A sudden rush of hospital techs and equipment brushed by the curtain and began their hourly examination of the critically ill guy. They unlocked the wheels of his hospital bed and prepared him to be transported,

'Where are you taking him?' Lucy asked.

'For an MRI.'

'Is he bleeding internally or something?'

'An MRI of the brain.'

Lucy felt a fast moving panic grip her. A more reasonable voice then the one inside her head spoke.

'Glad to see you looking so well, Ms Ambrose.'

'Dr Moss?'

'I'm surprised you remember,' the ER chief said. 'Considering the state you were in.'

'How could I forget?' Lucy said, extending her hand. 'Coming here that night saved me.'

Moss circled the patient, taking a look at him and the chart.

'Sometimes, with massive bleeding, there can be some brain damage,' Dr Moss, the ER resident, explained, and checking Jesse's pupils. 'Memory loss. Paralysis. We need to check.'

The techs finished their preparations and waited on the doctor's order.

'OK, ladies and gentleman,' Moss said. 'Let's take him upstairs.'

'Upstairs?' Lucy asked.

'To Psych. It's where the scanners are.'

'Dr Frey's floor?'

'Yes, do you know him?'

Lucy paused. 'Yes. I know him.'

'He'll be in good hands up there,' Moss comforted.

She watched the orderlies wheel him out carefully and stop Doctor Moss for one final question. 'Will he be OK? Will he ever wake up?'

Dr Moss considered his words carefully as he offered his prognosis.

'In my professional medical opinion, Miss Ambrose, it will take a miracle.'

27

Bleach Black

Cardinal DeCarlo's calls and emails to the Vatican were unreturned. It was unusual for there to be any sort of radio silence with regard to him, considering the importance of his position and his closeness, both personally and clerically, to the Pontiff. But then, this was a most unusual matter. Ordinarily, he would be able to activate a network of associates in the curia for advance notice of even the most consequential decisions, but not this time. Whoever the Pope appointed for this duty would remain a mystery to him for now.

The lack of information was problematic, but not insurmountable. Instead of working his like-minded Vatican sources, he focused on speed rather than stealth. The threat presented by Lucy, Cecilia and Agnes, by the relic, had to be extinguished and fast. There wasn't time to persuade the Pope and his allies if it was not clear to them already. All an investigation would produce would be delay, the thing he could least afford.

The recantation suggested by Frey at first seemed oddly retro, even to a man charged with upholding a two-thousand-year-old faith. On the other hand, it was a reaction certainly in keeping with a long history of challenges to the Church's authority. Witches, Satanists, apostates, heretics of all stripes had been brought to judgment effectively in the past, so why not now, he considered? What were these girls, other than reprobates daring to dress themselves in the all-forgiving finery of sanctity. There were rules in place, standards established. DeCarlo was not at all willing to see these teenage upstarts pass themselves off as saints. Debunking them, have them refute themselves, would be major news. After all, they were primarily a media creation in the first place.

In this, he and Frey absolutely had different motivation but the same goal. From the moment he received the doctor's letter he sensed that he was communing with a kindred spirit, though the doctor might scoff at the description. Others called them Ciphers, evil puppet masters bent on world domination, but that really overstated the case. Like their brethren in the military, politics, law enforcement, media and business, they were simply power brokers with agendas.

And their primary agenda was the status quo.

Grassroots movements, he reasoned, created fragmentation and were necessarily adversarial to centralized authority. Sebastian's faith could not be contained in a pew or confined to Sunday mornings and therefore could not be controlled. It was unpredictable. Better a thousand sheep, then a single wolf. Ironic, DeCarlo thought, that he – a man of the cloth – and Frey – a man of science – perceived the same danger in the spread of Sebastian's message and the appeal of these girls and now had reached the same conclusion. It was time to act. One in the name of progress, the other for the sake of tradition.

'Cardinal, your call,' the deacon announced urgently on the office intercom.

'Thank you,' DeCarlo replied reaching for his desk phone. 'Dr Frey?'

'Yes Cardinal?'

'I have considered your offer,' DeCarlo said. 'I accept.'

'You've been able to bring your superior to your point of view?'

'As you said, that is my problem and no concern of yours,' DeCarlo advised. 'I will meet your price.'

'How shall we make the transaction?'

'Time is short. The envoy will be arriving within hours. I need you to arrange a meeting with these girls here at the Archbishop's residence.'

'It can be arranged.'

'Good. I'm staying at the Archbishop's residence. We can be assured our privacy here.'

'Very good. I know where I can find at least one. When would you like to meet?'

'Immediately.'

'Oh, and Dr,' DeCarlo added. 'I'd like you to attend. With your keepsake.'

Lucy exited Perpetual Help, satisfied that Jesse had been returned to his room safely. Her biggest worry was that Frey would find an excuse to keep him up there. She turned the corner and saw an orderly smoking. She stopped and asked to bum a cigarette. The orderly held out his pack of cigarettes and pushed one forward at her with his fingers. Lucy bent to grab it between her teeth when she was suddenly grabbed from behind. She felt a wet cloth against her face and noxious fumes filled her nostrils. A flash of anger, at herself, for letting her guard down sped through her brain and then nothing. The last thing she remembered before blacking out was being pushed into the back seat of a car.

She came to finally, her hands bound. The room was large, the ceiling high. Paintings and frescoes, religious scenes, lined the walls. A figure in a long red robe walked toward her.

'So nice to meet you, Miss Ambrose. Not even your photos do justice to your beauty.'

'Where am I?' she asked.

'Does it matter? You are here.'

'Who are you?'

'I am Cardinal DeCarlo, Prefect for the Congregation for the Doctrine of the Faith.'

Her head was clearing from the brain fog, but she still couldn't make sense of any of it.

'Are you the investigator that has been sent?'

'No, that would be a representative from the Congregation for the Causes of Saints.'

'Then what do you want with me?'

'This is not the time for a lesson in Church history or operations of the Curia, but I'm concerned the investigator might find himself over his head in the case of you three. They are used to pursuing these matters posthumously.'

Lucy strained to see. To get a fix on her situation. From the looks of things, she could have been in a museum, but as her vision cleared, she could visualize signs that the space was active, used, lived in. A desk. A table with a gold water pitcher, a teapot and porcelain cups. Expensive-looking. Antique. The large grandfather clock showed just past twelve. Through the windows she could see it was night, but lights from apartment windows were clearly visible. She couldn't be far from where she was taken. Still in the city. Her purse was at her feet, so whatever this was, it wasn't a robbery.

He stepped closer to her, just inches from her face, and

looked directly into her eyes.

'Quite beautiful, indeed,' he noted. 'Like a painting.' He walked around her. 'We take in so much information through our eyes, don't we, Lucy? May I call you Lucy?'

'Why am I here?'

'You are here to answer questions.'

'What questions?'

'The Church's questions,' he declared.

'You mean your questions, don't you?'

The Cardinal retreated to the desk and chose a file, the one marked Lucy. He picked up his bag and placed it on a small table in front of her.

'Let's just say for our purposes here, I am the Church.'

'What do you want from me?'

'I am charged with a great responsibility. You see, my congratio was known at one time as the Holy Office of the Inquisition.'

Lucy didn't fully grasp his meaning. The whole ludicrous farce, being hunted, attacked, kidnapped. Inquisitors and mad scientists. It was all too surreal.

'So you've come to excommunicate me?' she asked incredulously. 'Or exorcise me?'

'An exorcist's job is to extract demons.

'But you have come to extract a confession, isn't that right?' she presumed.

The Cardinal opened his bag and removed several vintage

implements and placed them on the table. Lucy eyed each of the ancient instruments of torture, sensing their purpose.

'I have come to find out the truth.'

Cecilia and Agnes met at Perpetual Help to visit Jesse and to check on Lucy.

'It's past visiting hours. Only family are permitted,' the nurse advised.

'We are family,' Agnes said.

The nurse looked over at Dr Moss, who saw Cecilia and Agnes and nodded affirmatively to let them in. The girls smiled at the nurse and the doctor and walked toward the back of the ER. It was grim and busy as ever. Buzzing with life support machinery, smelling vaguely of drying blood, warm vomit and disinfectant. They stepped in the curtained space and saw Jesse, but not Lucy. He was motionless, several pints of blood and an IV tethered to him, gauzed and bandaged, wrapped tightly in sheets and blankets to keep him warm.

'He looks bad,' Agnes whispered, tears in her eyes.

'But he's alive,' Cecilia said hopefully. 'Let's not mourn him yet.'

Agnes sat next to him and spoke. Encouraging him. Thanking him. Praying for him. Fussed over him. Cecilia checked his chart and his meds, the names of his doctors and the frequency of his examinations. They behaved like advocates. Caretakers. Roles they had no experience with, but seemed to

come naturally, almost instinctively, now.

Time was passing and Lucy had not shown up as expected.

'Where do you think she is?' Cecilia asked, rubbing her hand.

'I don't know. I'll text her.'

'I need a cigarette.'

'I'll come with you,' Agnes said.

They headed down the hall for the exit, smiling at the desk nurse who'd let them through.

'Have you seen anyone else in the room this evening?'

'We were supposed to meet our friend here.'

Once again, Dr Moss intervened. 'Lucy Ambrose was here a little while ago.'

'She stepped outside and that was the last I saw of her,' the nurse added.

'Thanks,' Cecilia said, taking Agnes by the arm and walking toward the lobby. 'I don't like this.' Just as the words were tumbling from Cecilia's mouth, Agnes face filled with surprised. She pulled CeCe toward the wall, out of sight.

'It's Frey,' Agnes said.

The doctor was wearing his coat and carrying his oversized satchel, obviously leaving for the night.

'Where do you think he's going?' Cecilia wondered. 'And what's with the bag?'

'We're going to find out,' Agnes said.

* * *

Sister Dorothea was awoken by a sharp knock at her door. 'Sister!'

The nun rose, put on her robe and rushed to answer the urgent rapping at her door. She checked her clock and noticed it was long past midnight. 'What is it?'

'A call from a neighbour of Jude's foster family. They need you to come right away.'

'Did they say what was the matter?'

'No,' the novitiate informed. 'I took the liberty of calling the car service for you.'

'Thank you,' Sister Dorothea said. 'I'll be down in just a moment.'

The nun dressed and arrived in the foyer of the convent just as her car pulled up. She got in and gave the driver an address in Carroll Gardens, not very far away. Even in the few minutes it took to get there, the street was already filled with police and emergency vehicles and an ambulance from Perpetual Help. Sister Dorothea feared the worst. She exited the vehicle and ran quickly down the block as fast as her legs would take her.

The closer she got to the modest home the more worried she became; the only two sounds reaching her were sirens and a distinct high-pitched squeal, one she recognized as Jude's. Police barricades and tape had already been erected. Neighbours' homes were being hastily evacuated. Local news trucks were on the scene, beginning to raise their satellite dishes and unload their correspondents. It was officially a

crime scene. Sister Dorothea pressed forward, getting as close as she could before running into a wall of blue.

'That's as far as you go, Sister.'

'What's happened here officer?'

'Gas leak. Took out almost the whole family. Shame.'

Sister Dorothea was in shock. 'Almost?'

'There's a kid in there screaming. He's off the rails. We're trying to get him under control but he's got a knife.'

'Jude,' Sister Dorothea said.

The block was cordoned off and NYPD officers were crouched behind their vehicles, guns drawn.

'I know the boy, Officer. I can help you.'

'I'm sorry, Sister, but this is an active crime scene. Leave this to the professionals.'

An unmarked car pulled up and Captain Murphy jumped out, taking charge.

'What do we got?' he barked.

'Gas leak. Suspicious. Three dead. Carbon monoxide poisoning. Young boy inside. Armed. Resisting.'

'He's not resisting. He's scared. He's mute, Captain. Autistic,' Dorothea advised intruding on the conversation.

'You know the boy?'

'Yes, I've taught him,' she advised. 'He will listen to me.'

'All right, come with me.' Murphy took the nun gently by the arm and escorted her slowly to the front door, where several more armed officers were positioned. She stepped

through the front door and Jude let out a horrible wail. She'd heard it before. On playgrounds when noisy garbage trucks rolled through or when the jackhammer pistons of Con Ed workers tore up the street, or when someone unexpectedly sneezed. When Jude was overloaded he was impossible to reason with, in total fight or flight mode. At school, it might just warrant a trip to the nurse's office, now it could well mean a trip to the morgue.

'Jude,' she called out.

The only response she got was the reflective glint of the overhead kitchen from the blade of his knife, which we he was brandishing menacingly.

'Jude, it's Sister Dorothea,' she said. 'Please come out. The police won't hurt you.'

Still nothing from the boy.

'Sister, we're out of time. This whole place could blow.'

Murphy motioned for his men to come closer.

'Jude,' she called out desperately a third time.

The boy stepped into view, shaking and unsteady. Overwhelmed by his raw emotion and the odourless gas, which still permeated the home.

'It's OK. It's OK, Jude.'

Murphy signalled for his men to stand down temporarily. Sister Dorothea got down on her knees and opened her arms to the boy, who inched forward still holding the knife. She could see tears running down his cheek. He stepped closer and

the officers raised their Tasers, ready to fire.

Jude dropped the knife and ran into Sister Dorothea's arms.

'Thank God,' she cried.

She began to sob, relieved that the danger to the boy was over and for his family that was lost. She brushed the hair from his face and the tears from his eyes, and after a moment stood and turned to face Captain Murphy.

'I'll take him back to the convent with me, at least for tonight.'

'No, Sister, you won't.'

'This boy is traumatized. Surely you aren't going to arrest him? He can't answer any of your questions. '

'We ran a background check on the family and the kid. He's in the city system. Under psychiatric care at Perpetual Help.'

'But, Captain—'

'I'm sorry. I don't have the authority to release him to you or anyone.'

'Who does have the authority?'

'Says on his paperwork he is a patient of . . . Alan Frey,' Murphy informed her, surprised that Frey would be listed in the child's file as physician of record. 'I'm sure they'll send him up there after the ER checks him out. You can speak to him in the morning.'

At the mention of Frey's name, Jude became agitated once again and began to run. Two officers blocked his path and grabbed him, carrying him to the ambulance sent from

Perpetual Help. The boy was placed on a stretcher and restrained as Sister Dorothea called out to him reassuringly. The whole scene was violent. Tears welled up at the sight of him fighting to be let go. Jude knew what was waiting for him. Mercilessly he cried, like a lamb to the slaughter, as Sister stood there helplessly. The rear door was slammed shut on the emergency vehicle and it peeled away, siren blasting, drowning out Jude's last desperate wails.

Murphy ordered his men and the crew from the Medical Examiner's office into the house to go about their dismal duties of collecting bodies and collecting evidence.

'You don't know what you're doing,' Sister pleaded. 'Please, let me help?'

'There is one way you can help.' Murphy answered.

'I'll do anything.'

'Say your prayers.'

28

Riot and Ritual

The cardinal studied closely the dishevelled girl before him. She was unkempt but unbowed, sitting bolt upright, defiant, unafraid, not a tear in her eyes. Lucy was undeniably attractive, and appealing, more so in person, he thought. Even a man of his advanced age, having taken a vow of chastity long ago, could not help but be moved by her. Her inner fortitude and outward beauty were a compelling and powerful mix. He understood almost instantly why she'd been so successful in transmitting her message. She had chosen her career wisely and Sebastian too had chosen wisely. Lucy was not one to wither in the limelight.

'Tell me about Sebastian,' the Prefect asked.

'What do you want to know?'

'A question is not an answer to a question.'

'He was a beautiful, kind and wonderful guy,' Lucy said. 'A saint.'

'A saint?' DeCarlo recoiled. 'He was accused of kidnapping and murder.'

'Lies,' Lucy spat. 'Those files aren't worth the paper they're printed on.'

'You acknowledge he was confined in the hospital,' DeCarlo continued. 'Under a psychiatrist's care?'

'A psychiatrist?' Lucy mocked.

'Do you doubt Dr Frey's credentials?'

'His degree as a psychiatrist or his past as a priest? I dispute them both.'

DeCarlo seemed surprised that Lucy would have possessed this knowledge.

'You are not in a position to dispute anything,' DeCarlo explained ominously.

Lucy struggled with the bindings and roared at the Prefect.

'Sebastian wasn't crazy, if that's what you mean.'

'We no longer use such terminology, my dear. The official diagnosis I see here was schizophrenia and bi-polar disorder.'

'You can't trust any of it.'

'False claims are made all the time, sins committed, particularly the sins of pride and vanity, Miss Ambrose. And it is upon me, to expose them and root them out. For the good

of the faithful, you understand.'

Lucy was beginning to understand. DeCarlo was not sent to investigate her and the others. He was there to indict them. 'I don't claim anything.'

'Yes, well the problem is that others do,' he countered. 'Those who follow you, those whose modesty is not as evident or evolved as yours. They seek an answer to the troubles but they are looking in the wrong place.'

'They find something to relate to in us as we found in Sebastian. Something they aren't getting elsewhere in their lives. Is that so wrong?'

'Something to relate to?' he pondered, reviewing her file. 'You are a vain, drunken, self-serving egomaniac, a profiteer and a profligate, with delusions of sainthood. The very definition of a blasphemer.'

'I am me. Nothing more, nothing less.'

'One man with a new idea and twelve followers from a tiny town in Judea brought down an empire and changed the world for all time. It is not you that concerns me. It is the idea of you.'

'Don't blame me because so many have lost faith in you.'

'On the contrary, Miss Ambrose,' DeCarlo explained coldly. 'I'm happy to trade the unpredictable, the disaffected, the disillusioned for the docile, the obedient.'

'You are as bad as Dr Frey,' Lucy shouted. 'I thought you would protect us, that you would understand.'

'You will have the chance to compare and contrast soon enough,' the Cardinal informed.

A buzzing in Lucy's purse interrupted the question and answer session. He reached into her purse and removed her phone. On the screen a signal text. From Cecilia: *Where the hell r u?*

The cardinal replied, typing in a Madison Avenue address as Lucy struggled to free herself of the bindings on her wrist.

'The doctor is on his way. And now, so are your friends.'

'Follow that car,' CeCe told the gypsy cab driver.

Frey's sedan was already halfway to Atlantic Avenue and Agnes and Cecilia's only prayer of keeping up was the fact that it was late and traffic was light. As both cars crossed the Manhattan Bridge into the lower east side and headed up the Bowery, Cecilia received a reply to her text.

'What does it say?' Agnes asked.

'It says "Come Quickly" and there's an uptown Madison Avenue address.'

Agnes punched the address into her mobile phone search engine. She was stunned at the result. It was the direction in which they were already headed.

'It's the Archbishop's residence,' Agnes said. 'What would she be doing there?'

'That's what I wanna know,' CeCe said. 'And, what's he going there for?'

Cecilia grabbed Agnes's hand and they sped along toward what they felt was their destiny.

'It's a trap,' Agnes mused.

'Probably, but it doesn't matter,' Cecilia agreed. 'Does it? Lucy needs us.'

They were silent for the remainder of the ride. Watching Frey's car bounce along the potholed avenue, eventually arriving at its destination. They weren't following so much as they were being led.

'Stop here,' Cecilia said to the driver, as they approached a half a block from the residence.

They waited until Frey got out of his car and was met by two men. They all entered the building. Agnes and Cecilia got out of their cab and walked guardedly towards the front doors. They were unlocked.

'Just like Precious Blood and Born Again,' Cecilia said. 'We're expected.'

Lucy could sense the cardinal becoming increasingly impatient with her. He got closer and began to run his fingers lovingly along the instruments he'd removed from his bag. He picked up a bottle of holy water and sprinkled her with it. Lucy blinked as the droplets dripped from her forehead and ran down her face like a stream of tears.

'Did you expect me to catch fire?' she said.

'No, I expected you to be forgiven,' DeCarlo said. 'Even a

heretic deserves as much.'

'I expect no forgiveness from you and I ask for none,' Lucy rebuffed. 'I'll leave it to a higher authority.'

DeCarlo was irritated by the challenge to his priestly power. 'Do you know the story of Saint Lucy?' DeCarlo asked sternly. 'The virgin martyr whose legend you dare to claim? Whose legacy you stain with your every breath?'

'I do,' she said, fearlessly. 'Do you?'

'You seek to wrap yourself in a legacy without any of the sacrifice.'

'And you wrap yourself in the mantle of respectability of holiness. Which of us is the bigger hypocrite?'

'The martyrs did not march off into the sunset, as in some glorious Hollywood finale,' DeCarlo explained. 'They suffered!'

'For what they believed in,' Lucy answered.

'Stop this foolishness,' DeCarlo shouted. 'Save yourself.'

Lucy laughed quietly to herself at the cardinal's admonition.

The door flew open suddenly and Dr Frey walked through. He greeted them both casually, as if nothing extraordinary was happening.

'Cardinal,' he said. 'Miss Ambrose. I hope I'm not interrupting anything.'

Lucy stared daggers at him.

'Any news of the investigator?'

'Our time is short,' DeCarlo assured him.

He opened his satchel and removed a canister from the bag.

It contained Sebastian's heart. He held it up, taunting her.

'Is this what you've been looking for?'

Lucy was overwhelmed but kept her cool.

The cardinal pointed to a large sack on the floor at Lucy's feet and Frey reached for it. He held it up, getting a sense of its weight and placed it in his satchel, into the space the heart had occupied.

'These funds will be put to good use,' Frey noted. 'We are planning a new Born Again facility in the city.'

'More soldiers for your psycho army,' Lucy snapped. 'You call yourself a doctor.'

'Don't be so judgmental,' Frey responded snidely. 'It's just brand extension, dear, surely you can appreciate that.'

'You're a disgrace,' Lucy shot back.

Cardinal DeCarlo interrupted. 'Saint Lucy's eyes were torn from her, by her own hand, rather than deny her faith and her virtue. She took her most attractive trait to men out of her head with her own fingers,' DeCarlo said. 'From her empty sockets fell tears of milk and honey. Her's was a brutal and painful death for her beliefs.'

'I'm not afraid to die.'

'That very well may be, blinded to reality by this folly you and the others are engaged in,' Frey said. 'In fact, I'm sure you want to die to fulfill your mission, otherwise you're just punch lines, failures.'

Lucy was silent.

'Whether you live or die, what is important to me is that you fail,' Frey continued. 'That you are repudiated by the one institution that can verify you and abandoned by those who follow you.'

Frey placed the canister down on the table in front of her and loosened the shackles that held her.

'If you move, I will destroy it.'

He extended a stand and mounted his phone on to it, turning on the video function to capture events for later use. To humiliate her, to rebuke her, publicly.

'You're friend Jesse might be interested in this footage,' Frey said. 'If he lives.'

'A hostage video, Doctor?' Lucy said, eyeing the canister and the tools spread out before her.

'Think of it as an infomercial,' he said snidely. 'You are familiar with those, I'm sure.'

'I have nothing to sell,' she said.

'Except yourself, isn't that right? Who you believe yourself to be?'

'I make no claims so I have nothing to deny.'

'You are stubborn, Lucy, strong willed,' Frey opined. 'In my profession, we call it oppositional defiance.'

'I don't need a diagnosis, Doctor.'

'No, that's true. I'm afraid you and your friends are past help.'

'I have all the help I'll ever need.'

'Well, I will leave it to you and the good Cardinal here to resolve this disagreement,' Frey said. 'I trust you will be in touch, Your Eminence.'

The cardinal nodded and Frey departed as stealthily as he'd come. He resumed his interrogation, in his best fire and brimstone voice.

'Who are you?' DeCarlo demanded. 'Tell me!'

'You already know,' she said bravely, 'or I wouldn't be here.'

Cecilia and Agnes waited in the shadows as Frey departed.

'That was quick,' Agnes noted.

'Whatever is happening in there,' Cecilia said, 'he doesn't want to get his hands dirty.'

They peeked in the doorway and quickly pulled away, out of sight, backs to the wall.

'We're outnumbered,' Agnes observed sombrely.

'I'm used to it by now.'

The guards had a hungry look in their eyes. Agnes swallowed hard and smiled nervously.

'Seriously, Cecilia, the two of us aren't going to be able to take them.'

'You're right,' Cecilia said. 'I'll handle them, you get to Lucy.'

'How?'

'What you did in the subway. Can you do it again?'

Agnes paused uncertainly. 'I don't know.'

Cecilia took Agnes firmly by the shoulders.

'Lucy is in there. The heart is in there. We need to get inside that room.'

'But, what about you?'

'I'll keep them busy.'

'That's suicide, Cecilia!'

Agnes reached for her friend and held her tight. Cecilia brushed Agnes's hair away gently.

'Lucy needs us.'

Agnes nodded. 'I'll see you inside.'

CeCe started toward the heavily guarded door and called back to Agnes. 'Do your thing.'

29

Spiritus Sanctus

The brown four-door sedan swerved around potholes as it rolled up and Captain Murphy stepped out.

A uniformed officer in charge of the scene walked quickly towards him.

'What do you got?' Murphy asked.

'Teenage male. Deceased.'

The officer pointed toward an alleyway between the coffin factory and the hot dog stand.

To Murphy's ears it sounded like a hundred other deaths. Death by misadventure, it was mostly called. Unintentional. Death by stupidity is what Murphy called it. Young people, with everything to live for, pissing away their most valuable possession. Their lives. Drinking, drugs, gang murder and every kind of foolishness. For some reason his mind travelled instantly to Lucy, Cecilia and Agnes, each of whom, he believed, was putting herself in great danger unnecessarily.

'And you needed me here because?' the captain queried, as he spied the flashes of the crime scene photographer's camera flickering like a nightclub strobe light.

'I thought you should see this.'

Murphy saw a young man, dangling from fire escape, a jumper cable twisted several times around his neck. His body swung easily in the light breeze, his back to the crowd of law enforcement gathering just beneath it.

'Suicide?' Murphy groused. 'I've got to escort a diplomat arriving at JFK in an hour and you drag me down here for a suicide?'

'No, I dragged you down here for this.' The officer grabbed the stiffening legs of the victim by the ankles and spun him slowly around.

Murphy looked up and saw the pale and bluing face of the teen. He was young and handsome, but that wasn't the thing that troubled him so deeply. What troubled him most was the long blade sticking out of his chest.

'Not a suicide,' Murphy mumbled, looking at the officer. 'Do we have an ID?'

'We found a wallet lying on the ground. Right here,' the officer pointed to a spot directly below the hanging corpse.

Murphy opened the black leather holder and pulled out a high school identification card. He recognized it as the school attended by Agnes Freemont.

'Finn Blair.'

He exhaled and handed the wallet back. 'Let me know what you find out,' Captain Murphy ordered. 'Take him down!'

'Yes, Captain.'

Finn's body was lifted down gently on to a stretcher.

'Oh and Sergeant, send a car over to the Freemont house in Park Slope,' Murphy ordered.

'Any particular reason?'

'Just check in. Make sure the girl and her mother are OK.'

'I'll call it in now.'

Murphy walked back toward his car.

'Captain!' the sergeant called to him.

Murphy turned and walked back to the officer hovering over Finn's body.

'Look at this.'

The sergeant ordered the Medical Examiner's office evidence collector to lift the lapel of Finn's jacket, where the blade had pierced his heart. There was a piece of paper about the size of a large post-it note affixed to Finn's bloody shirt pocket by the blade. The sergeant shined a small flashlight on the paper on which was written a single word.

'Sinner.'

'Cancel the squad car,' Murphy said. 'I'll go myself.'

Agnes could feel the cold brick and mortar cutting into her shoulder blades as she leaned against the exterior wall of the Archbishop's residence for support. She crouched down, let her neck relax and her head hang forward to her knees.

Her hair fell to the ground, enshrouding her.

She tried to relax, despite the stakes, and get to that place. The place where heart and soul, mind and body, come together, so that they could come apart. A place only Sebastian had been able to take her. Agnes pictured his eyes, his mouth, his hair. She imagined his voice, his touch. She let herself . . . dream.

She felt herself disappear, break down, transform, like paraffin melting into liquid, dripping, looking for a new place to re-form and solidify. She separated from herself and departed, her mind, her senses were intact. In an instant she found herself in a quiet, wood-panelled antechamber between two sets of doors. She heard the noises of battle, grunts and screams.

She pressed her ear against the heavy mahogany barrier before her and listened. Agnes heard the forceful threats of an older man as well as Lucy's defiant protests coming from the next room.

'Repent!' Cardinal DeCarlo admonished. 'Confess your sin.'

'Confess my sins to a sinner?' Lucy shouted back.

The tension in their voices was clearly rising. Agnes turned the large golden knob slowly and opened the door just a crack.

It was unguarded. As ominous as the sounds of the dispute were, what Agnes saw was even more mind-boggling. Lucy was seated in a large uncomfortable chair, a tall but hunched figure lording over her, the bottom of his red cardinal robe bouncing along the floor with each frustrated gesture. On the table in front of her, a collection of instruments, none of which Agnes recognized but all of which looked medieval and deadly.

'You have made your choice and left me with none,' DeCarlo admonished. 'In pain will you find truth and redemption?'

DeCarlo approached the table and raised the iron implement, part scoop, part claw, like a cat's paw, and waved it slowly in front of her face as he prayed.

Lucy closed her eyes as DeCarlo brought the torture instrument closer.

'Deny Sebastian. Deny this blasphemy.'

'Never!' she screamed.

'No! Stop!' Agnes screamed, running toward them, feeling herself suddenly torn away.

Cecilia approached the doors of the cardinal's quarters guarded by a small group of men who'd escorted Dr Frey inside. She approached the thuggish human wall slowly, counting heads.

Three men in priest's robes stood guard at the entrance to the Archbishop's office. The tattoos showing above their collars and holsters bulging under their garments at their hips indicated that these were the most aggressive men of the

cloth she'd ever encountered.

'Waiting for an audience with the Archbishop?' CeCe snarked. 'I hear he's away for a few days.'

'Can I help you?' one asked.

'I've come for my friend.'

'She's inside,' another said coldly, daring her to pass, each flashing a black hardwood baton.

'Let me tell you something about myself,' Cecilia began.

The men started laughing condescendingly. 'These are your last words. You can say whatever you want.'

Cecilia took a few steps back reached for her belt and unfastened it. The guards tensed up. Ready for an attack.

'You know,' she mused, 'when I was little, my father would warn me that I was about to get punished by taking off his belt and hanging it from the chair of the kitchen table.'

'Maybe that's why you have a thing for older guys.'

Cecilia heard the dis and recognized the voice of the man who'd murdered Bill. What had started as a rescue had suddenly become even more intensely personal. The chance to kill two birds with one stone. She continued, emotionless, on the outside at least.

'That if I pushed him just one tiny bit further, I was gonna get it,' she continued, stepping closer. 'I knew that he meant business, knew what was in store for me, but somehow I just couldn't stop myself.'

'Come to Daddy, naughty girl,' one said, wagging his fingers.

Cecilia smiled. 'Time for a spanking.'

'Are we going to fight or fuck?' the guard said, laughing.

'Are you going to whip us for being bad?' the other mocked, licking his lips.

Cecilia let the urumi unspool, two thin metal straps hitting the floor with a springy metallic crack.

'Whip you?' she said flatly. 'No . . . I would never whip you.' She paused. 'I'm going to cut the tips of your fingers off, then I'm going to slice off your ears, then your balls, before cutting you into little pieces. That's what I do to bad boys.'

The guards rushed Cecilia.

She whirled the belt sword around her like a helicopter blade, and struck, slicing up the first attacker. His legs were cut off at the knees and he dropped to his bloody stumps crying out in agony. 'Change of plans,' she said. 'It's a killer accessory. Don't you think?'

'So's this,' another shouted, he and his partner drawing their guns.

Before they could squeeze off their first shots, Cecilia levitated straight up from the floor, and the spray of bullets flew by beneath her. The attackers were momentarily stunned by the sight of Cecilia's lithe body floating above them.

She put her head down and the bullets raced to her head as if she were magnetized, forming a golden headpiece still smoking from friction. She raised her head. They raised their guns. Aiming higher for a second shot but Cecilia was faster,

snapping the metallic whip, removing the guns and their hands with them in a single, swirling strike. A second angular stroke, as she descended, across both of their thighs cut through their trousers and through their femoral arteries. Both men writhed in pain, immobilized, torrents of blood spewing from terminal wounds.

'Bleed for me, boys,' CeCe said, standing over them, not a hint of remorse or satisfaction in her eyes. She watched them grow paler and colder as the puddles of ooze quickly expanded and thickened.

'Like the good book says, do unto others, before they do unto you,' she sermonized. 'I'm paraphrasing of course.'

Her headpiece fell to the ground and the bullets scattered everywhere, like rain.

She approached the first attacker who was still squirming on the floor. He tried to raise himself. She kicked him hard and sent him sprawling, a smear of his own blood trailing him.

'You're no better than us,' he spat.

'Maybe,' she admitted, surveying the carnage she'd wrought.

'Who made you judge and jury?'

'This isn't a trial,' she replied.

He struggled to right himself, cursing her name.

'You want to get up?' she asked. 'Let me help you.'

She grabbed him by the hair and pulled until he was balanced on his bloody stumps, upright. His screams echoed through the grand foyer. Cecilia dragged the urumi from side to side through his blood pooling beneath him.

'Some people think Jesus went to India to preach,' Cecilia said, circling him like a lion tamer.

'Tell someone who gives a shit,' he snapped, still grabbing for her.

Cecilia ignored the slight. 'You know who also went to India? My friend Bill. Remember him?'

'No,' the legless killer laughed gurgling blood. 'Does anyone?'

'I do,' Cecilia answered solemnly. 'He got this sword there.'

Cecilia knelt before the killer and wrapped her urumi around his neck three times then stood holding the handle. He was helpless to stop her, and gasping for breath.

'If there's a hell below . . .' the man sang maniacally through cracked and blood-soaked teeth.

She knew the song. Cecilia sang the chorus back to him, tapping her foot. Marking time. His.

'I said don't worry,' she sang softly in a gospel-blues cadence, raising her hand in faux spiritual praise.

CeCe looked directly into his eyes and he looked back at her, heavy lidded, fading fast but croaking the song louder with his last watery breath.

'I said if there's a hell below, we're all going to gooooo.'

'You first,' she rasped, pulling the handle on the whip.

Cecilia briefly surveyed the carnage around her, blood, bone and guts smearing the Archbishop's home. A sudden

scream from inside, which she recognized immediately as Agnes's, and a commotion outside, cars approaching the residence, engines and headlights blazing startled her all at once. She ran to the entrance to wake Agnes entranced body. Cecilia grabbed Agnes by the shoulders and shook her gently at first and then harder, calling her name.

'Agnes!'

Agnes murmured 'No' urgently over and over again as she came to.

Cecilia held her head steady to focus her.

'What's happening?'

'We have to get in there. Now!'

Sister Dorothea arrived at Perpetual Help hospital searching for some word of Jude. She approached the triage desk in the emergency room and gave his name. The nurse checked the computer for him and frowned.

'He's already been transferred,' she informed.

'So quickly?'

'He was unmanageable when he arrived,' she said perfunctorily.

'Where is he?'

'Upstairs,' she said. 'In Psych.'

The nun walked straight to the row of lifts and pressed up. The nurse nodded to the watchman to let her pass. Sister Dorothea stepped on to the penthouse floor. She'd been there

before with Jude on one of his many visits, but she'd never been there to see him.

'May I help you?' the night nurse asked.

'Yes, I'm looking for a boy, Jude, who was admitted earlier.'

'Are you next of kin?' the nurse asked, checking her sheet.

'There is no next of kin,' the nun replied.

'I'm sorry but I'm not permitted to give out any information on our patients.'

She'd hoped that Jude might be released to her but perhaps under the circumstances that was too much to ask for. The best she could hope for was to find a new home for him and get his city assigned case workers to cut a few corners and get him out of there.

'Can you just tell me if he's here? If he's all right?'

Before the question escaped her lips, Sister Dorothea saw the boy escorted from a room at the end of the hall, dressed only in a smock.

'Jude!' she screamed.

Her dulled cries just barely reached the boy and he turned. The look of terror on his face was undeniable and one she'd seen many times before on the playground. He reached out his hands for her, straining against the grasp of the orderly holding him. The nun reached for the doorknob, pulling at it, twisting it, and pounding on the shatterproof glass to no avail. Within sections, the night watchman from the desk downstairs appeared as the lift opened.

'Sister!' the guard shouted, reaching for her shoulders to calm her. 'You need to leave here. Now.'

Reluctantly, the nun stepped away from the door and gathered herself.

'When will he be released?'

'There is no plan to discharge now,' the nurse advised. 'You'll have to talk to Dr Frey about that and any other questions you have.'

A cold chill ran through Sister Dorothea at the mention of Frey's name.

'I'll be sure to do that,' Sister said, trembling and stepping toward the lift.

'Don't worry,' the nurse called to her. 'We'll keep a close watch on him.'

Martha rushed for the door hoping it might be Agnes. She pulled the lace curtain aside and looked out the window to make sure it wasn't any of the 'weirdos' that hung around outside. All she could see was a car double-parked, emergency flashes blinking. She opened the door a crack.

'Good evening, Mrs Fremont.'

'Oh, Captain Murphy,' she said anxiously.

'You seem disappointed,' he offered. 'Are you expecting someone at this hour?'

'No, well, I was hoping.'

'Hoping?'

'That it was Agnes at the door.'

Martha could see the concern in his eyes and held the door open signalling Murphy to enter. She wanted to talk.

'Isn't she here?' Murphy asked. 'I was just coming over to check in on you both.'

'No.'

'When was the last time you saw her?'

'Earlier this evening. I left her with her boyfriend.'

'Boyfriend?' I didn't know she had a boyfriend?'

'Well, no, not a boyfriend, you know, a boy who's a friend, from school . . .'

'What is his name?'

'Finn. Finn Blair,' she said.

'Did you say Finn Blair?'

'Yes.'

Murphy did his best not to let his expression give him away.

'I left them alone thinking they might get to know each other better,' Martha laughed. 'How often do you hear a mother say that in this day and age?'

'I understand,' Murphy said. 'You trust her.'

Martha was clearly on the verge of breaking down. 'That's just it. I don't. I don't trust her judgment at all anymore. I just want all this nonsense to stop. These people outside to go away. Some normalcy.'

'Are they harassing you or Agnes?' he asked sympathetically. 'I can send a car to disperse them.'

'It's not them. They're just looking for something. I can see that.'

Murphy nodded, still wondering what, if anything, he should say about Finn. The thought of worrying Martha unnecessarily was a high priority, but so too was finding Agnes if she might be in danger or worse.

'Do you think she left with Finn?'

'No,' Mrs Fremont replied, reaching into her pocket.

'Are you sure?'

She produced a note, handwritten on Agnes's stationery. It mentioned Finn. The attack on her. Not to respond to him if he tried to get in touch. A moot point now, Murphy thought.

'Why didn't you call us?' Murphy asked, perplexed.

'It says she didn't want anyone to know.'

'You understand that's not a good reason?' Murphy answered, the tension in his voice prompting a more detailed explanation from the woman.

'You want to know what I did when I read this note? I called Dr Frey.'

'Frey?'

'Because he treated Agnes and he treated Finn,' Martha continued. 'I thought it would be good that they had that in common. Open her up a little.'

'I didn't know that.'

Martha went quiet and began to shudder, like a pregnant volcano about to blow or a listing ship about to sink.

'Do you know what it's like living with a child that's different?' Martha challenged, the frustration inside her turning to anger.

'No, ma'am.' Murphy admitted.

'I don't know whether anything she says or thinks is true anymore,' Martha admitted. 'I'm worried sick for her, but also embarrassed for her and for myself. Do you know how guilty that makes me feel?'

'I can't imagine.'

Mrs Fremont approached the captain, her fist and teeth clenched tight.

'No, you can't. I have a daughter with a death wish. Who actually believes that she might be some kind of reincarnated saint. And there are twenty people out there all hours of the day and night praying to her. How do you fight that?'

'I promise I'll do everything I can.'

Martha dropped her head and threw up here hands, convulsing in tears.

'I don't want promises, Captain.' Martha wept. 'I want our life back. I want my daughter back.'

Cecilia and Agnes burst into the room. Lucy stiffened and shuddered as her eyes widened and began to sparkle. Her head flew back. A blinding light spread throughout the room from the canister containing Sebastian's heart. In the beams of light, he appeared. Like a vision. Cardinal DeCarlo recoiled, dropping

the torture implement on the table. It was clear to Agnes that this was more than just her imagination.

He saw Sebastian, too.

Lucy stopped. He smiled gently at her. Cecilia approached, urumi in hand, ready to pounce on DeCarlo. Sebastian shook his head no.

Arms open wide, Sebastian beckoned her. A sense of calm fell over her. And determination.

'Save yourself,' she whispered.

'Lucy, no,' Agnes screamed.

Lucy turned to Agnes, then Cecilia.

'This is why,' Lucy said.

'Please, don't,' Cecilia begged.

'I love you, both,' she said, peacefully. Lucy reached down to the table and grabbed the rusty implement, brought it to her brow. She took one last look at Cecilia and Agnes and then looked in the way of Sebastian. He smiled at her and their lips moved in unison, as his image faded from their view.

'There is a time to fight and a time to yield.'

She turned toward the video camera and spoke, quoting again from her vision in the chapel.

'I am the sacrifice.'

As she did, she plunged the implement into her right eye, and then, to her left, gouging them out. She trembled and cried out in agony, reaching again for the table, for the canister. She raised it and held it tight to her chest as blood filled her eye

sockets, staining her dress and pooling on the floor beneath her.

'You . . . you were so . . . beautiful!' DeCarlo mumbled in shock and disbelief.

'Now, I am only beautiful to him,' Lucy said, crimson tears running down her porcelain face.

'She's blinded herself,' Cecilia called out.

'No, it is now that I can actually see,' Lucy said with a smile wiping across her face.

Lucy collapsed.

Cecilia and Agnes raced to her aide to staunch her bleeding. DeCarlo stood back.

'She's dying!' Agnes screamed.

Cecilia reached for the phone but the line was dead.

Suddenly, a loud commotion outside of car tyres screeching accompanied by sirens blaring descended on the scene. It was a diplomatic motorcade and police escort. The lights from the vehicles were blinding, shining through the front door and the foyer all the way into the archbishop's office. A large entourage exited the string of vehicles and assembled as they walked through the front door and toward them.

'It must be the Vatican investigator,' Agnes cried.

Robed men, nearly a dozen, approached; Agnes and Cecilia could all at once see more clearly who had arrived.

'Yes,' Cecilia said in amazement.

30

The Gruesome and the Glory

The cardinal looked at the figure approaching him and backed away from the girl.

'Holy Father,' he said, bowing his head before the appearance of the Pope himself. 'Where is the investigator you promised?'

'I am the investigator,' he replied.

Lucy, blinded and mutilated, turned on wobbly legs to face the Pope. She began to walk uncertainly toward the sound of his voice.

'I have the files!' DeCarlo shouted in desperation. 'They are blasphemers!'

'Silence,' the Holy Father ordered. 'I will see for myself.'

'Lucy!' Cecilia screamed, running to her with Agnes close behind.

She felt her friend's hands on her and let the momentary comfort they brought sweep over her.

'Let us help you walk,' Agnes said. As Agnes placed her hand on Lucy, Lucy felt immediately at peace, with less pain.

'You both are my eyes now,' Lucy responded weakly, to both Agnes and Cecilia.

'Come to me, my child,' the Pope requested.

Cecilia and Agnes stepped aside and Lucy continued a few steps further before falling to her knees. Cecilia's and Agnes's wailing filled the room and the cardinals in the Pope's entourage blessed themselves and bowed their heads.

Lucy crawled the last few yards to the Pope, who removed his mitre and knelt down before her, to receive her and her gift. She handed the canister to him.

'Forgive me,' she said.

'It is we who should request forgiveness of you,' the Pope said, placing his hand on her head and blessing her and offering her absolution. '*Ego te absolvo a peccatis tuis in nomine Patris, et Filii, et Spritius Sancti. Amen.*'

'Holy Father, do not be fooled!' DeCarlo shouted.

'I am not fooled, Cardinal DeCarlo.'

The Pontiff placed his finger near Lucy's cheek, took her tear of blood, and brought it to his lips. The sweetest taste filled his mouth and lingered on his tongue.

'Her tears of blood, turned to milk and honey,' his holiness said. 'Santa Lucia,' he declared, raising his eyes upward. 'Pray for us.'

DeCarlo made a final plea for the Pope's good graces as the police descended on him. 'The heart has power to influence, to deceive the faithful. It has already brought death and despair.'

'No,' the Pope declared. 'The power of the heart is love.'

He called Cecilia and Agnes over to them to comfort to their dying friend. They cradled her in their arms, weeping, as Lucy took her last breaths.

'Only love.'

With her last breath, Lucy smiled and reached her arms upward, as if to welcome the grasp of someone picking her up. Carrying her home. Just like he promised he would.

The motorcade processed through the streets of Brooklyn, thousands lining the sidewalks, not just to see the Pope, whose surprise visit had been revealed, but Cecilia and Agnes, who sat beside him, and the hearse carrying Lucy to her funeral mass. Even the hastily made arrangements could not dampen the outpouring of emotion for her.

The news reports of her death galvanized the city and the rededication of Precious Blood was now a foregone conclusion. The media turned up in droves, cameras flashing, bloggers posting, bystanders tweeting. Some carried signs with messages of reconciliation and respect. 'All is forgiven', read one.

Another: 'Lucy, pray for us'. Others blasted their horns both in anger at the pomp and the inconvenience it was causing.

'I'm tryinta make a living here!' a cabbie groused out of his driver-side window.

Lucy would have loved it, the ruckus she was causing, Agnes thought. All of it.

Inside, Precious Blood was packed with political and religious dignitaries from the city and the Vatican, sitting side by side with local parishioners. Temporary pews and a simple altar had been hastily built. Loudspeakers were affixed to the exterior of the church to pump out the service to those unable to gain entrance.

A reverent silence fell as the Pope entered, carrying Sebastian's remains, with Lucy's glass casket behind him. Cecilia and Agnes followed, like bridesmaids, carrying his heart. Lucy was dressed in white and adorned with a headpiece of lush roses.

Glorified.

Agnes looked down at her hand, the one holding his heart, and noticed that Sebastian's hair inside was growing once again. The Pope stopped. He bowed his head at the spot where Sebastian was killed, said a prayer, and continued to the altar. The church was still a ruin, without electricity, shattered stained glass and rubble still strewn about the aisles. The Pope had insisted the church not be cleaned up for his visit, but that it be left exactly as it was following the storm and the fire and the murder. Nevertheless, it felt totally transformed from crime

scene to cathedral.

Lit only by rows of votives, the darkened space filled with the heavy smoke of incense, exuded a raw and ancient majesty befitting the ceremony that was about to begin. To Cecilia and Agnes it felt as the earliest Christian ceremonies must have, taking place in secret, in caves, in cellars and in underground aqueducts of the Roman Empire.

But there was much more than smoke in the air. There was heart. There was soul. There was magic. For Cecilia it was the kind of magic she'd only felt at the best shows she'd given. The congregation signing in unison with the choir, a lead vocal strong enough to raise the roof and reach the ears of Heaven itself. Agnes took CeCe's hand in hers and CeCe squeezed it tightly as Lucy's bier was placed in the sanctuary of the church, feet facing the altar as was customary. She was incensed and sprinkled with holy water as the faithful watched and waited in reflective silence.

'She is so beautiful,' Agnes marvelled, tearfully.

'She always will be,' Cecilia replied.

The funeral mass began, the Pope speaking the Requiem in Latin and following the traditional Roman funeral rite.

'*Réquiem ætérnam dona eis, Dómine; et lux perpétua lúceat eis.*'*

The gathering responded. 'Amen.'

---

*   Eternal rest give to them, O Lord; and let perpetual light shine
       upon them.

Agnes and Cecilia stood, sat and kneeled at the appropriate times along with the congregation in honour of their fallen sister. The mass progressed and the Pope began to chant the Deis Irae, a medieval hymn reserved for the Mass of the Dead that describes the Day of Judgment.

'Deis Irae! Dies illa
Solvet saeclum in favilla.'

Agnes whispered her translation simultaneously, as if reading it from some supernatural teleprompter.

'Day of wrath and doom impending
Heaven and earth in ashes ending.'

And so it continued, line by line, verse by verse, with increasing urgency and solemnity.

'Confutatis maledictis
Flammis acribus addictis:
Voca me cum benedictis'

'While the wicked are confounded,
Doomed to flames of woe unbounded
Call me with thy saints surrounded'

'Lacrimosa dies illa
Qua resurget ex favilla
Ludicandus homo reus'

'The day of tears and mourning
From the dust of earth returning
Man for judgment must repair him'

Agnes spoke the final line with him.
'*Dona eis requiem. Amen.*'

In line for communion, Agnes spotted a middle-aged man, weeping inconsolably as he approached the bier and altar, begging forgiveness under his breath at first, and then so loudly, he overwhelmed even the choir. He collapsed at her coffin, heaving with sorrow.

Cecilia recognized him as Lucy's dad from news clips, as did many others in the church, who looked upon with little sympathy. Cecilia stepped out into the aisle with Agnes before the ushers could reach him and have him removed.

'Mr Ambrose,' Cecilia kneeled and whispered.

'It's too late,' he moaned, over and over.

Cecilia lifted him up to his feet and Agnes cradled his face in her hands, comforting him. 'It's never too late.'

Agnes and Cecilia accompanied Lucy's dad to the Holy Father who administered communion to him.

'Thank you,' he said softly, and headed silently for the exit.

The mass was ended and the Pope said a final few words before he dismissed the congregation.

'The renewal of faith, of hope, of love is at work before your

very eyes if only you choose to see it,' he advised. 'Go in peace.'

After a long while, the church emptied.

The Pope accompanied Cecilia and Agnes downstairs to the chapel where Sebastian's heart was placed in a gold and glass case. Lucy's funeral bier was placed beside them. He gestured for the papal retinue to leave them.

Agnes took her Victorian tear catcher from around her neck, and emptied all of the tears she'd cried for Sebastian over his heart.

The Pope stood back and watched. As did Cecilia.

The Pope then walked over to the table where the three had left their chaplets and chose one – Lucy's. He lifted the glass coffin lid and gently slipped the bracelet over her wrist.

Restored.

He took the other two in his hands and prayed over them. 'I believe these belong to you,' he said, offering one to each of them.

Agnes and CeCe slipped them on.

'The world owes the three of you a great debt. By your deeds, your sacrifice and your example, there will be more good. The path is prepared stone by stone until the road is complete.'

'One at a time,' Cecilia whispered.

The Pope gave a final blessing to Lucy, to the relics and to Cecilia and Agnes. The girls approached Lucy's casket, placed

their hands on it gently and kissed the glass.

'Our guide,' Cecilia whispered through her tears. 'You showed us the way.'

'A light in the darkness for us to follow,' Agnes added.

The two girls turned to face the Pope, seeking comfort, seeking answers. Agnes found herself suddenly overcome with emotion. 'Are they in heaven?'

'I believe they both will find immediate favour with the Lord.'

Agnes reached for his hand, to kiss his ring in the traditional act of homage, but the Pope pulled it back. He opened his arms broadly and leaned in for an embrace and to kiss her on the cheek. He did likewise with Cecilia.

'Why us?' Agnes asked. 'If anyone knows it must be you.'

'For a short time here in this world, I am Pope,' the pontiff responded. 'That is God's decision.'

'Why now?' Cecilia pressed.

'The time has come,' he said. 'God needs you.'

Silence filled the room. They each meditated on what was just said. The importance of it.

'Your work is not yet done,' the Pope said, breaking the silence, with sadness in his eyes. 'The path you tread is a thorny one.'

'We know,' Agnes replied.

'Your enemies are legion and ever vigilant,' the Pope reminded. 'Near at hand.'

'We're ready,' Cecilia added.

'Even I won't be able to help you,' he informed regrettably. 'It is in the hands of the Almighty.'

'And ours,' Cecilia added.

Agnes turned toward the gold casing holding Sebastian's heart and read the Latin inscription out loud.

'*Noli timere.*'

'What does that mean?' Cecilia asked the Holy Father.

'Do not be afraid.'

Jesse's parents lingered over their son's motionless body tearfully, waiting for the doctor.

Moss arrived, grim-faced.

'How is he, Doctor? his mom asked.

'Will he ever wake up?' his dad enquired.

'The honest truth is, we just don't know. His vital signs are stable. We've done all we can do medically and we will continue to do all we can.'

'What happens now, Doctor?' his Dad continued.

'He'll be sent upstairs to Psych for continued observation and whatever treatment is necessary. It's a waiting game.'

'Is there anything else we can do, Doctor?' Jesse's mom asked urgently.

'Pray,' the doctor said.

The onetime couple, long estranged, lingered over their son like the first day he was born. Stroking his hands and face,

whispering sweet nothings to him. Telling him how much they loved him. How proud they were of him. His mom noticed he was warm and brought a glycerin stick to his dried lips to moisten them while his father opened a window. Mr Arens escorted his ex-wife out and headed for the chapel at Perpetual Help.

The buzzing and pinging of machines, and rustling of hospital staff through the halls continued apace, the sick were admitted, the healthy discharged. The patient lying there, oblivious to all of it, alive but not present. The night was dry and cool and a light breeze blew into the hospital room. It brushed across his body, passed through him.

Jesse opened his eyes.

He whispered softly, 'Lucy.'

Epilogue

D r Frey stood at his office window high above the streets of Brooklyn looking downward at the city sanitation crew cleaning up after Lucy's procession. He resembled nothing so much as a gargoyle keeping watch from the toppled bell tower of Precious Blood, directly across the skyline from him. The doctor checked his watch and noticed it was time for him to begin his rounds.

He walked down the hall to the patient rooms, stopping at Jude's room along the route. He peeked into the window of the reinforced door and spied the child sitting on the edge of his bed, looking blankly at the wall. After a while, the boy turned and stared at the doctor observing him. Their eyes locked and wills struggled, neither wanting to blink first. Eventually, Jude retrained his gaze on the white wall in front of him. Frey smiled and moved along to check in on

another patient of particular interest.

The doctor checked Jesse's chart. His vitals, Frey considered, were surprisingly stable considering the trauma he'd endured. CAT scan and MRI were normal but these were not determinative. The patient remained in a semi-coma, experiencing only intermittent consciousness. Frey performed an examination of his own, lingering over Jesse, to personally assess his condition and reassure himself of the prognosis. It was impossible to tell how functional he was or would be. One thing was certain: Jesse would be with him for a while.

Frey's examination was interrupted by a call coming through on his cell phone. He stepped out of the room and answered.

'Call from a Sister Dorothea?'

'I'll take it.'

The nurse bridged the call.

'Alan Frey speaking.'

'I'm calling about Jude,' she said sternly. 'I haven't been able to get any information.'

'Well, that is understandable, Sister. Patient confidentiality being what it is.'

She felt she was being brushed off.

'All I want to know is when he will be released.'

Frey paused.

'Oh, I couldn't say, Sister. Jude was quite traumatized by the events at his foster home.'

'I was there, Doctor. I want to be sure even more damage

isn't done by keeping him in your facility.'

'He is perfectly safe here,' Frey assured her.

'The boy needs to be in school. With friends.'

'You needn't worry, Sister. That is exactly where he is,' Frey said.

'With friends.'

Catherine and Cecilia headed for a meeting with Daniel Less at the open mic club where Catherine had first met him. He'd been pressing, especially after all the attention Cecilia had got in recent days. They walked and talked.

'I'm so sorry about Lucy,' Catherine sympathized sincerely.

'Me too,' Cecilia said.

'Nothing is going to happen to you is it?'

'Not with you to protect me,' Cecilia smiled.

The girls walked along Myrtle Avenue and down Wilson Avenue into the Bushwick section of Brooklyn. The L train rolled by overhead, pausing their conversation for a just a moment, when Cecilia spied an enormous edifice with two bell towers visible in the distance. They strolled up to the church and Cecilia looked up to admire the century old building, a towering baroque structure with white marble and yellow brick façade.

'Saint Barbara's,' Catherine said. 'She was a martyr too. I mean a saint. I mean . . .'

CeCe took Catherine's hand in hers, calming her.

'It's beautiful,' CeCe noted. 'I want to go inside for a second, OK?'

'Sure, if it's open.'

'It's open,' Cecilia said confidentially, stamping out her cigarette and grabbing the front door handle.

They entered and stood in awe at the statuary along the columns in the nave, the shrines to Jesus and Mary, the elaborate pulpit, gloriously painted ceiling vault and dome above the altar. Cecilia walked to the votive stand, dropped some change in the poor box and lit two candles. The coins struck the bottom of the metal container and echoed through the cavernous space like a vesper bell. She allowed herself a moment of reflection as the candle flames danced joyfully in the glass votive cups.

'Praying for a good deal?' Catherine said.

'No, just praying,' Cecilia replied.

'It's a real neighbourhood landmark,' Catherine explained. 'Named for Saint Barbara but also the daughter of the family who donated the land for the church. She was Barbara too.

'Just a normal little girl?' Cecilia asked.

'Yep.'

'I love it,' Cecilia said, as they exited the church.

They walked a few blocks further to the club and went inside. It was still afternoon and the place was empty except for the guy at the back table, working his smartphone. He stood and dropped it in the breast pocket of his suit jacket as

Catherine and Cecilia approached.

Catherine led the way.

'Daniel Less, I'd like to introduce you to—'

'Cecilia Trent,' he greeted, extending his hand.

Cecilia grabbed it and shook firmly, her own hand wrapped in loose gauze, to absorb any random droplets of blood. It had become almost her trademark. Besides, she knew it looked cool and made a strong first impression.

'Do they hurt?' he asked.

'Only when I feel taken advantage of,' she said with a sly smile.

He returned the gesture with a toothy boardroom grin of his own.

'Please sit,' he requested. 'So, I'm sure Catherine has told you, I've been following you for a while now.'

'Coming from you that's very flattering.'

'I've watched your following grow along with your creativity. You've done it the old-fashioned way.'

'One at a time,' Cecilia said. 'That's my mantra.'

'I like to think of my label as an artist-friendly company. A place where we can help you express who you are as a songwriter and performer.'

'That's good,' CeCe responded, 'because I really don't need some jerk-off junior A & R guy telling me how to sell myself or what to do.'

'If it comforts you, the only jerk-off you'll need to deal with

is me,' he said. 'Besides, I think you've got that part of it down. The music and the marketing.'

Cecilia paused for a moment.

'The only reason I want to do this is because I know it's the only way to reach the greatest number of people and get my message out.'

'Then we agree.'

'As long as it's on my own terms.'

Less reached into his briefcase and pulled out an eight-and-a-half inch document.

'I took the liberty of bringing a contract along, forgive my arrogance.'

'You're forgiven,' CeCe joked. 'Got a pen?'

Catherine was smiling ear to ear, celebrating not only the sealing of Cecilia's deal but also the prospects of her own.

'It's a seven-year deal, sure you don't want to read it?'

'Not necessary,' Cecilia answered.

Less offered a pen, holding it directly above the paperwork.

'Then all that is left is for you to sign on the line which is dotted.'

She was momentarily distracted by the load noise of sirens blaring just outside and the sound of cars screeching to a halt.

'Another afternoon in Brooklyn,' Catherine fretted, shaking her head.

Cecilia took the pen and moved her hand toward the document. She looked down as she was about to sign and

noticed a ruby red droplet on the signature line. Then another and another. It wasn't ink. She looked at the bandage on her hand and noticed it was soaked through with fresh blood and dripping.

An army of officers burst in the club entrance, guns drawn. Her first reaction was confusion, then relief. Perhaps the cops were sent over by Murphy to protect her, she surmised. Since Lucy's death, they must have been on high alert, investigating every threat to her and to Agnes. Whatever it was, it must be serious to send armed guards after her.

But then a second thought occurred. Perhaps these weren't guards at all, but vandals sent by Frey's minions in the police force to finish the job. Wolves in blue uniforms.

'Cecilia!' Catherine screamed, jumping in front of her and standing tall like a human shield.

Less also bounced up, in shock and anger.

'What's going on here?' he said arrogantly. 'You're interrupting a business meeting.'

'Shut up and stand back,' the lead officer ordered.

'You too kid,' another insisted.

Daniel and Catherine stepped aside and the officers formed a wall directly in front of Cecilia.

'Cecilia Trent?' another asked.

'You know damn well who I am.'

'Hands over your head.'

CeCe complied as Catherine watched in disbelief.

Two officers approached, each took an arm and brought it behind her back. Firmly. One fastened her wrists with a plastic tie and spun her around.

'You're under arrest.'

'For what?'

'You have the right to remain silent,' the officer dutifully recited the Miranda warnings. 'Anything you say can and will be used against you.'

'I said for what?'

'The murder of Finn Blair.'

He continued reading her rights as Cecilia was dragged out of the club and escorted into waiting a squad car. A few apostles that had texted her whereabouts to each other, fretted tearfully as she was loaded in, ungraciously, to the back seat. She smiled back reassuringly at them and Catherine through the dirty car window and mouthed 'Don't worry' which did little to console them. The squad car sped away.

'We have the suspect. En route to the station.'

A voice crackled through the car radio with orders for a detour that sent shivers up Cecilia's spine.

'Re-route. Re-route. Deliver suspect to Perpetual Help hospital. Psych ward. Do you copy?'

'Ten-four.'

Agnes and Martha walked along the Park Slope side streets. Agnes was talking about the weather but thinking about Lucy.

'Spring is finally here,' Martha said cheerfully, hoping to bring a rare smile to her daughter's face.

'I guess,' Agnes replied. 'Hard for me to appreciate it right now.'

'I understand, honey,' Martha said sympathetically. 'Maybe you should talk to someone.'

'Oh please, Mother. Not again.'

Turning the corner on to their street, Agnes could see some commotion going on down the block, very near their home. Agnes felt her mom's grip tighten on her arm as they continued to walk. It was an ambulance with lights flashing but siren off. A crowd of Agnes's followers surrounding it.

'What's going on here?' Agnes asked.

'Agnes Fremont?' an officer inquired.

'Yes.'

'Please come with us,' he said reaching for her arm.

'No,' she screamed pulling away. 'Mother, what is going on here?'

Instead of intervening on her behalf, Martha released Agnes arm and all but pushed her into the EMT's arms.

'I'm sorry, Agnes!' Martha wailed.

'What's happening?' she screamed, struggling against the men who'd come to pick her up. 'How could you do this to me, Mother?'

'I saw the suicide note you left. I just can't take any chances, Agnes. You are sick.'

'You are having me committed?'

'Dr Frey said it would be best. To save you.'

'You believe him and not your own eyes? Not me?'

'You saw what just happened! It's all true!' Agnes shouted.

'I don't care if Jesus stepped off the cross and told me to believe it. You are my daughter and I will not let that happen to you.'

Her followers rushed to her aide but were driven back as NYPD officers pulled their guns.

'Stop,' Agnes shouted, putting the safety of the others first, resigning herself to her fate. 'I'll go.'

She gave herself over. Her hands were cuffed and she was placed in the ambulance, humiliated and imprisoned.

'Sebastian was right. It is those close to you that must be feared the most.'

The rear doors slammed closed and the ambulance pulled quickly away.

Martha looked on at the small crowd dropping to their knees in tears with anger and disgust. She watched the ambulance fade away into the distance and quietly whispered.

'God, help her.'

The Word According to Lucy

For those who see things differently,
The ones who think they know,
For those who want more to be,
Then all that was for show.

Craving excess more and more
The drug of the trend
Pain and suffering left empty
Pray broken hearts to mend.

Speaking in tongues of whispers
Worry what they say.
It's the way you see it,
There is no other way.

Removed the shadows from my sight,
This I pray to thee,
Once I was blind,
But now I am Me.

Lucy, ora pro nobis

ACKNOWLEDGEMENTS

I would like to thank my UK editor extraordinaire Naomi Pottesman for believing in this story. And to UK designer Michelle Brackenborough and the rest of the team at Hodder Children's Books.

Special thanks to Tracy Hurley Martin, Michael Pagnotta, Oscar Martin and Vincent Martin. This book would not have been possible without you.